D0232087

THE POCKET BOOK OF
SCOTTISH QUOTATIONS

THE POCKET BOOK OF SCOTTISH QUOTATIONS

Compiled and Edited by

David Ross

BIRLINN

This edition published in 2012 by
Birlinn Limited
West Newington House
10 Newington Road
Edinburgh
EH9 1QS

www.birlinn.co.uk

Copyright © David Ross 2000 and 2012

The moral right of David Ross to be identified
as the author of this work has been asserted by
them in accordance with the Copyright,
Designs and Patents Act 1988.

All rights reserved. No part of this publication may be
reproduced, stored or transmitted in any form without
the express written permission of the publisher.

ISBN 978 1 78027 087 6

British Library Cataloguing-in-Publication Data
A catalogue record for this book is available
from the British Library.

Typeset by Brinnoven, Livingston
Printed and bound by Clays Ltd, St Ives plc

Contents

Introductory Note

Apart from its other uses, a compendium of quotations, ranging widely over topic and time, is perhaps the best way of exploring that many-faceted, multi-dimensional, semi-abstract organ, the Scottish mind. While the main purpose is to provide a broad selection of interesting, entertaining, revealing and informative quotations from the writings and sayings of Scots, on every topic under the sun, it also includes many comments made by non-Scots on Scots and Scotland.

Advice, Aphorisms and Epithets

Don't quote your proverb until you bring your ship into port.
  Gaelic Proverb

Three things come without seeking – jealousy, terror and love.
  Traditional saying, from Gaelic

Ye'll be a man before your mither yet.
  Anonymous, from Rob Roy MacGregor, *or* Auld Lang Syne, *a musical show of 1819*

The wee man's gotten his parritch at last.
  Anonymous, from Rob Roy MacGregor, *or* Auld Lang Syne, *on the death of Rashleigh*

Gae seek your succour where ye paid blackmail.
  Anonymous, Jamie Telfer in the Fair Dodhead

This Way is That Way. That Way is This Way.
  Double signpost seen in a Scottish garden

Times daily change and we likewise in them;
Things out of sight do straight forgotten die.
  Sir William Alexander (c.1567–1640), Aurora

'Tis not too late tomorrow to be brave.
  John Armstrong (c.1709–1779), The Art of Preserving Health

a door never fully recovers from being opened with a boot.
  Neal Ascherson (1932–), Stone Voices

You have been warned against letting the golden hours slip by. Yes, but some of them are golden only because we let them slip.
  Sir J.M. Barrie (1860–1937), Rectorial Address, St Andrews University

Concentrate though your coat-tails be on fire.
  Sir J.M. Barrie, Tommy and Grizel

We can pay our debts to the past by putting the future in debt
to ourselves.

> *John Buchan (1875–1940), Coronation address to the people of
> Canada,* 1937

A fool and his money are soon parted.

> *Attributed to George Buchanan (c.1506–1582)*

Nae man can tether time nor tide.

> *Robert Burns (1759–1796),* Tam O'Shanter

The rank is but the guinea's stamp,
The Man's the gowd for a' that.

> *Robert Burns,* A Man's a Man for a' That

For a' that, and a' that,
It's comin yet for a' that,
That Man to Man, the world o'er,
Shall brothers be, for a' that.

> *Robert Burns,* A Man's a Man for a' That

Heaven can boil the pot
Tho' the Deil piss in the fire

> *Robert Burns,* The Dean of Faculty

Facts are chiels that winna ding
And daurna be disputed

> *Robert Burns,* A Dream

Ne'er mind how Fortune waft and warp;
She's but a bitch.

> *Robert Burns,* Second Epistle to J. Lapraik

I dare not speak for mankind
I know so little of myself

> *John Burnside (1955–),* Landscapes

Winning isn't everything. There should be no conceit in victory
and no despair in defeat.

> *Sir Matt Busby (1909–1994)*

When one has been threatened with a great injustice, one accepts a
smaller as a favour.

> *Jane Welsh Carlyle (1801–1866),* Diary, November 1855

He that has a secret should not only hide it, but hide that he has something to hide.
    Thomas Carlyle (1795–1881), The French Revolution

Happy the people whose annals are blank in history.
    Thomas Carlyle, Frederick the Great

To a shower of gold, most things are penetrable.
    Thomas Carlyle

Organise, organise, organise.
    Thomas Chalmers (1780–1847), speech in Edinburgh, 1842, in anticipation of the Disruption of the Church of Scotland

Timid souls are always in a hurry.
    John Davidson (1857–1909), Godfrida

And do to me as ye would be done to.
    Gavin Douglas (1475–1522), Prologue to The Aeneid

It takes a wise man to handle a lie. A fool had better remain honest.
    Norman Douglas (1868–1952)

Mediocrity knows nothing higher than itself; but talent instantly recognises genius.
    Sir Arthur Conan Doyle (1859–1930)

Unless a man undertakes more than he can possibly do, he will never do all he can do.
    Henry Drummond (1851–1897)

The man who is intent on making the most of his opportunities is too busy to bother about luck.
    Bertie Charles Forbes (1890–1954), Forbes Epigrams

You have no idea how big the other fellow's troubles are.
    Bertie Charles Forbes, Forbes Epigrams

The truth doesn't hurt unless it ought to.
    Bertie Charles Forbes, Forbes Epigrams

The Trick is to Keep Breathing
    Janice Galloway (1955–), book title

In Scotland, talking about yourself is considered the eighth deadly sin.
Janice Galloway, at the Edinburgh International Book Festival, 2011

By creating we think, by living we learn.
Sir Patrick Geddes (1854–1932), sociologist. Conference paper, 1924

Think locally, act globally.
Attributed to Sir Patrick Geddes

It needs smeddum to be either right coarse or right kind.
Lewis Grassic Gibbon (James Leslie Mitchell, 1901–1935), Smeddum

They loved this state; it kept them warm; it saved them trouble; and they enshrined their tastes in their sayings – 'the mair dirt the less hurt', 'the clartier the cosier' . . . Another saying was 'Muck makes luck'.
H. Grey Graham, The Social Life of Scotland in the Eighteenth Century *(1899)*

A real leader of men is someone who is afraid to go anywhere by himself.
Cliff Hanley (1922–1999)

Who has enough, of no more has he need.
Robert Henryson (c.1425–1500), The Town Mouse and the Country Mouse

That action is best, which procures the greatest happiness for the greatest numbers.
Francis Hutcheson (1694–1746), An Inquiry into the Original of Our Ideas of Beauty and Virtue

If folk think I'm mean, they'll no' expect too much.
Sir Harry Lauder (1870–1950), quoted in Albert Mackie, The Scotch Comedians

Men are immortal till their work is done.
David Livingstone (1813–1873), Letters

Experience teaches that it doesn't.
Norman MacCaig (1910–1996), Bruce and That Spider – the Truth

Beauty and sadness always go together.
    George Macdonald (1852–1905), Within and Without

There is hope in honest error; none in icy perfection.
    Charles Rennie Mackintosh (1868–1928)

Men are never so good or so bad as their opinions.
    Sir James Mackintosh (1765–1832), Ethical Philosophy

No man is wiser than another –
And none knoweth much.
    Fiona MacLeod (William Sharp, 1855–1905), From the
    Hills of Dream

Truth will stand when a' thin's failin'
    Lady Nairne (1766–1845), Caller Herrin'

Fate's book, but my italics.
    Don Paterson (1963–)

We are all in the stars,
but some of us are
looking at the gutter.
    Walter Perrie (1949–), Proverb

Sorrows remembered sweeten present joy.
    Robert Pollok (1798–1827), The Course of Time

Behave yoursel' before folk;
What'er ye do, when out o' view,
Be cautious aye before folk.
    Alexander Rodger (1784–1846), Behave Yoursel' Before Folk

I always say appearance is only sin deep.
    Saki (H.H. Munro, 1870–1916)

It's the early Christian that gets the fattest lion.
    Saki, Reginald's Choir Treat

A little inaccuracy sometimes saves tons of explanation.
    Saki, The Square Egg

Scandal is merely the compassionate allowance which the gay make to the humdrum. Think how many blameless lives are brightened by the indiscretions of other people.
   Saki

Bluid is thicker than water.
   Sir Walter Scott (1771–1832), Guy Mannering

As cross as two sticks.
   Sir Walter Scott, Journal

A place for everything, and everything in its place.
   Samuel Smiles (1812–1904), Thrift

Hope is like the sun, which, as we journey towards it, casts the shadow of our burden behind us.
   Samuel Smiles, Self-Help

Some folks are wise, and some are otherwise.
   Tobias Smollett (1721–1771), The Adventures of Roderick Random

'Dark glasses hide dark thoughts.' I said.
'Is that a saying?'
'Not that I've heard. But it is one now.'
   Muriel Spark (1918–2006), The Dark Glasses

Whoever you pretend to be, you must face yourself eventually.
   Al Stewart (1945–) Scottish-born US lyricist and musician

No worker of what are called good works can be sure that in the long run he does more good than harm.
   James Thomson (1834–1882), The Sayings of Sigvat

Better to love in the lowliest cot
Than pine in a palace alone.
   George Whyte-Melville (1821–1878), Chastelar

The Animal Kingdom

Ayont the dike, adist the thorn,
I heard an auld man blaw his horn,
His beard was flesh, his neb was horn,
And sic a beast was never born.
Traditional Kirkcudbrightshire riddle for a cockerel

A goloch is an awesome beast,
Souple an' scaly,
Wi' a horny heid an' a hantle o' feet,
An' a forky tailie.
Traditional

Said the whitrick to the stoat,
'I see ye've on your winter coat;
I dinna see the sense ava!
Ye're shairly no expectin' snaw?'
J.K. Annand (1908–1993), Fur Coats

She had the fiercie and the fleuk,
The wheezloch and the wanton yeuk;
On ilka knee she had a breuk –
What ail'd the beast to dee?
Patrick Birnie (fl. 1660s), The Auld Man's Mear's Dead

I turned a grey stone over: a hundred forky-tails seethed from under
it like thoughts out of an evil mind.
George Mackay Brown (1921–1996), Five Green Waves

Wee sleeket, cow'rin, tim'rous beastie,
O, what a panic's in thy breastie!
Thou needna start awa sae hasty
Wi' bickerin' brattle!
I wad be laith to rin and chase thee,
Wi' murderin' pattle!
Robert Burns (1759–1796), To a Mouse

He was a gash and faithfu' tyke
As ever lap a sheugh or dyke.
    Robert Burns, The Twa Dogs

Ye ugly, creepin, blasted wonner,
Detested, shunn'd by saint and sinner,
How daur ye set your fit upon her –
Sae fine a lady?
Gae somewhere else, and seek your dinner
On some poor body.
    Robert Burns, To a Louse

puddocks is nae fat they eesed tae be.
    J.M. Caie (1878–1949), The Puddock

A cat is the ideal literary companion. A wife, I am sure, cannot
compare except to her disadvantage. A dog is out of the question
. . . Its function is that of a familiar. It is at once decorative
– contemplative – philosophical, and it begets in me great calm and
contentment.
    William Y. Darling (1885–1962), 'Memoirs of a Bankrupt Bookseller',
    quoted in Hamish Whyte, The Scottish Cat (1987)

A stag of warrant, a stag, a stag,
A runnable stag, a kingly crop,
Brow, bay and tray and three on top,
A stag, a runnable stag.
    John Davidson (1857–1909), A Runnable Stag

O lovely O most charming pug
Thy gracefull air and heavenly mug
The beauties of his mind do shine
And every bit is shaped so fine
Your very tail is most devine . . .
His noses cast is of the roman
He is a very pretty weomen
I could not get a rhyme for roman
And was oblidged to call it weoman.
    Marjory Fleming (1803–1811)

I recall the now almost classical story of the aircraft (this was in the earlier days of flying) travelling at approximately ninety miles an hour, which was overtaken by a golden eagle flying on the same course. The pilot saw the eagle eye the aircraft with calm indifference before it slowly drew ahead of him.

Seton Gordon (1886–1977), A Highland Year

I have never yet met anyone who really believed in a pterodactyl; but every honest person believes in dragons.

Kenneth Grahame (1859–1932), Introduction to 100 Fables of Aesop

I'm a cat, I'm a cat, I'm a Glesga cat and my name is Sam the Skull, I've got claws in my paws like a crocodile's jaws and a heid like a fermer's bull.

Harry Hagan, Sam the Skull, *from Ewen McVicar, gallusglasgowsongs website*

When three hens go a-walking, they
Observe this order and array:
The first hen walks in front, and then
Behind her walks the second hen,
While, move they slow or move they fast,
You find the third hen walking last.

Henry Johnstone (1844–1931), When Three Hens Go Walking

There was a snake that dwelt in Skye
Over the misty sea, oh;
He lived on nothing but gooseberry pie,
For breakfast, dinner and tea, oh!

Henry Johnstone, The Fastidious Serpent

She flowed through fences like a piece of black wind

Norman MacCaig (1910–1996), Praise of a Collie

The collie underneath the table
Slumps with a world-rejecting sigh.

Norman MacCaig, Crofter's Kitchen, Evening

Above all, I love them because,
Pursued in water, they never
panic so much that they fail
to make stylish triangles
with their ballet dancer's
legs.
   Norman MacCaig, Frogs

And shambles-ward nae cattle-beast e'er passes
But I mind hoo the saft e'en o' the kine
Lichted Christ's cradle wi' their canny shine.
   Hugh MacDiarmid (C.M. Grieve, 1892–1978), Gairmscoile

A bird knows nothing of gladness,
Is only a song-machine.
   George Macdonald (1824–1905), A Book of Dreams

And houseless slugs, white, black and red –
Snails too lazy to build a shed.
   George Macdonald, Little Boy Blue

The myriad gnats that dance like a wall
   George Macdonald, Lessons for a Child

Holy, Holy, Holy,
A wee brown bird am I:
But my breast is ruddy
For I saw Christ die.
   Fiona MacLeod (William Sharp, 1855–1905), The Bird of Christ

At sunrise here, in proud disdain
The eagle scans his vast domain.
   Fiona MacLeod, The Eagle

The four-legged brain of a walk-ecstatic dog
   Harold Monro (1879–1932), Dog

. . . the cat is grown small and thin with desire,
Transformed to a creeping lust for milk.
   Harold Monro, Milk for the Cat

Though frail as dust it meet thine eye,
He form'd this gnat who built the sky.
   James Montgomery (1771–1854), The Gnat

'The Congo's no' to be compared wi' the West o' Scotland when ye come to insects,' said Para Handy. 'There's places here that's chust deplorable whenever the weather's the least bit warm. Look at Tighnabruaich! – they're that bad there, they'll bite their way through corrugated iron roofs to get at ye!'

> *Neil Munro (1864–1930)*, The Vital Spark

'What kind of a canary is it?' asked the Brodick man, jealously. 'Is it a Norwich?'

Para Handy put up his hand as usual to scratch his ear, and checked the act half-way. 'No, nor a Sandwich; it's chust a plain yellow wan.'

> *Neil Munro*, The Vital Spark

Up frae the rashes, heich abune the trees,
Intil the lift wi eldrich skraich an cletter,
In thair ticht squadrons tovin,
the wild geese I watch in joy
wing frae the braid lown watter.

> *William Neill (1922–2010)*, On Loch Ken Side

. . . those poor souls who claim
to own a cat, who long to recognise
in bland and narrowing eyes a look like love,
are bound to suffer.

> *Alastair Reid (1926–)*, Propinquity

. . . a bird
In song outside made evening suddenly splendid.
. . . I listened
Without a wound, accepting the song I was given,
Content to accept it as song, the years gone over
When sight of a seagull's swoop upon grey water
Or petals fluttering butterfly-bright from flowers
Could solve at a stroke the puzzle of all existence.

> *Alexander Scott (1926–1989)*, Evensong

My ewie wi' the crookit horn!
A' that kend her would hae sworn
Sic a ewie ne'er was born
Hereabouts nor far awa'.

> *John Skinner (1721–1807)*, The Ewie wi' the Crookit Horn

The friendly cow, all red and white,
I love with all my heart;
She gives me cream with all her might,
To eat with apple-tart.
    Robert Louis Stevenson (1850–1894), The Cow

. . . a diminutive she-ass, not much bigger than a dog, the colour
of a mouse, with a kindly eye and determined under-jaw. There
was something neat and high-bred, a quakerish elegance, about the
rogue that hit my fancy on the spot.
    Robert Louis Stevenson, Travels with a Donkey

Who's that ringing at our door-bell?
'I'm a little black cat and I'm not very well.'
Then rub your little nose with a little mutton fat,
And that's the best cure for a little black cat.
    Sir D'Arcy Wentworth Thompson (1860–1948), The Little Black Cat

. . . does it make for death to be
Oneself a living armoury?
    Andrew Young (1885–1971), The Dead Crab

There are all sorts of cute puppy dogs, but it doesn't stop people
from going out and buying Dobermans.
    Angus Young (1959–)

Art and Architecture

It's grand, and you cannot expect to be baith grand and comfortable.
 Sir J.M. Barrie (1860–1937), The Little Minister

. . . a jewel of great price: St Magnus Cathedral . . . Unmoving still, it voyages on, the great ark of the people of Orkney, into unknown centuries.
 George Mackay Brown (1921–1996), An Orkney Tapestry

This mony a year I've stood the flood an' tide:
And tho' wi' crazy eild I'm sair forfairn,
I'll be a brig when ye're a shapeless cairn.
 Robert Burns (1759–1796), The Brigs of Ayr

At times it's very good, at times it's bloody awful. It's a lesser school with a few high points . . . They didn't influence anybody.
 Timothy Clifford (1946–), quoted in Scotland on Sunday, *January 1994, on Scottish art*

They gazed with blanched faces at the House with the Green Shutters, sitting there dark and terrible, beneath the radiant arch of dawn.
 George Douglas (George Douglas Brown, 1869–1902), The House with the Green Shutters

It is not the bulk of a fabric, the richness and quality of the materials, the multiplicity of lines, nor the gaudiness of the finishing that give the grace or beauty or grandeur to a building: but the proportion of the parts to one another and to the whole, whether entirely plain or enriched with a few ornaments properly disposed.
 James Gibbs (1682–1754), A Book of Architecture

I might not know what art is but I'll milk it for all it's worth.
 Glasgow civic leader, paraphrased by James Kelman in a lecture at Glasgow School of Art, 1996

Mr Knoxe did with our glorious Churches of Abbacies and
Monasteries (which were the greatest beauties of the Kingdome)
knocking all down to desolation; leaving naught to be seen of
admirable edifices, but like to the ruins of Troy, Tyrus, and Theba.
  William Lithgow (c.1585–1645), Comments Upon Scotland

Bungalows . . . the ceilings are so low, all you can have for tea
is kippers.
  Anonymous, quoted in Charles McKean, Thirties Scotland

All great and living architecture has been the direct expression of
the needs and beliefs of man at the time of its creation, and now, if
we would have good architecture created, this should still be so . . .
It is absurd to think it is the duty of the modern architect to make
believe he is living four, five, six hundred, or even one thousand
years before.
  Charles Rennie Mackintosh (1868–1928), Lectures and Notes

There are many decorative features in Scottish architecture which
might well be replaced by others of antiquity, but because we are
Scottish and not Greek or Roman, we reject . . . I think we should
be a little less cosmopolitan and rather more national in our
architecture.
  Charles Rennie Mackintosh, Lectures and Notes

The power which the artist possesses of representing objects to
himself explains the hallucinating character of his work – the poetry
which pervades them – and their tendency towards symbolism – but
the creative imagination is far more important. The artist cannot
attain to mastery in his art unless he is endowed in the highest
degree with the faculty of invention.
  Charles Rennie Mackintosh, in Robert Macleod, Charles Rennie
  Mackintosh *(1968)*

Abbotsford is a very strange house . . . that it should ever have been
lived in is the most astonishing, staggering, saddening thing of all.
It is surely the strangest and saddest monument that Scott's genius
created.
  Edwin Muir (1887–1959), Scottish Journey

A hoose is but a puppet-box
To keep life's images frae knocks,
But mannikins scrieve oot their sauls
Upon its craw-steps and its walls:
Whaur hae they writ them mair sublime
Than on yon gable-ends o' time?
  Lewis Spence (1874–1955), The Prows o' Reekie

A Celtic-Catalan cocktail to blow both minds and budgets.
  Catherine Slessor, Architectural Review, *on the Holyrood Parliament building, 2004*

Day by day, one new villa, one new object of offence, is added to another; all around Newington and Morningside, the dismalest structures keep springing up like mushrooms; the pleasant hills are loaded with them, each impudently squatted in its garden . . . They belong to no style of art, only to a form of business.
  Robert Louis Stevenson (1850–1894), Picturesque Notes on Edinburgh

A statement of sparkling excellence
  Judges of the Stirling Prize, on the Holyrood Parliament building, 2004

No art that is not intellectual can be worthy of Scotland. Bleak as are her mountains, and homely as are her people, they have yet in their habits and occupations a characteristic acuteness and feeling.
  Sir David Wilkie (1785–1841), from a speech made in Rome, 1827

Boasts, Vaunts and Challenges

I never will turn: do you think I will fly?
But here will I ficht, and here I will die.
> *Anonymous*, The Baron of Brackley

My hands are tied, but my tongue is free
> *Anonymous*, Kinmont Willie

I can drink and nae be drunk,
I can fecht and nae be slain;
I can lie wi another man's lass
And aye be welcome tae my ain.
> *Traditional*, The Barnyards o' Delgaty

Whaur's yer Wullie Shakespeare noo?
> *Over-excited theatre-goer at the first night of John Home's play*
> Douglas, *December 1756*

Here's tae us – Wha's like us?
Damn few – and they're a' deid.
> *Traditional*

I have often heard the soldiers discussing round the camp-fires as
to who was the bravest man in the Grand Army. Some said Murat,
and some said Lassalle, and some Ney; but for my own part, when
they asked me, I merely shrugged my shoulders and smiled. It would
have seemed mere conceit if I had answered that there was no man
braver than Brigadier Gerard. At the same time, facts are facts, and
a man knows best what his own feelings are.
> *Sir Arthur Conan Doyle (1859–1930)*, The Exploits of Brigadier
> Gerard

The Scottish Parliament adjourned on the 25th day of March 1707
is hereby reconvened.
> *Winnie Ewing (1933–), Acting President of the Scottish Parliament, 1*
> *July 1999*

I on the other hand would sacrifice a million people any day for one immortal lyric. I am a scientific socialist.

Hugh MacDiarmid (C.M. Grieve, 1892–1978), Scottish Scene

Och hey! for the splendour of tartans!
And hey for the dirk and the targe!
The race that was hard as the Spartans
Shall return again to the charge.

Pittendrigh MacGillivray (1856–1930), The Return

He either fears his fate too much,
Or his deserts are small,
That puts it not unto the touch,
To win, or lose, it all.

Marquis of Montrose (1612–1650), To His Mistress

'Behold the Tiber!' the vain Roman cried,
Viewing the ample Tay from Baiglie's side;
But where's the Scot that would the vaunt repay,
And hail the puny Tiber for the Tay?

Sir Walter Scott (1771–1832), The Fair Maid of Perth

Sound, sound the trumpet, sound the fife,
Loud the glorious truth proclaim:
One crowded hour of glorious life
Is worth an age without a name

Sir Walter Scott

'And oh, man,' he cried in a kind of ecstasy, 'am I no a bonny fighter?'

Robert Louis Stevenson (1850–1894), Kidnapped

I have taken a firm resolution to conquer or to die and stand my ground as long as I have a man remaining with me.

Prince Charles Edward Stuart (1720–1788), letter to his father, 1745

Wha would shun the field of danger?
Wha to fame would be a stranger?
Now, when Freedom bids avenge her,
Wha would shun her ca', lassie?

Robert Tannahill (1774–1810), Loudon's Bonnie Woods and Braes

The Minister said it wald dee,
the cypress buss I plantit.
But the buss grew til a tree,
naething dauntit.
It's growan, stark and heich,
derk and straucht and sinister,
kirkyairdie-like and dreich.
But whaur's the Minister?

    Douglas Young (1913–1973), Last Lauch

Robert Burns

What an antithetical mind! – tenderness, roughness – delicacy,
coarseness, – sentiment, sensuality – soaring and grovelling, dirt
and deity – all mixed up in that one compound of inspired clay.
> *Lord Byron (1788–1824)*, Journal, *1813*

Whose lines are mottoes of the heart,
Whose truths electrify the sage.
> *Thomas Campbell (1777–1834)*, On Robert Burns

A Burns is infinitely better educated than a Byron.
> *Thomas Carlyle (1795–1881)*, Note Book

In a life-long crucifixion Burns summed up what the common poor
man feels in widely-severed moments of exaltation, insight and
desperation.
> *Catherine Carswell (1879–1946)*, The Life of Robert Burns

A drunk, misogynist, racist philanderer
> *Michael Fry, quoted in* The Scotsman, *4 January 2009*

Someone said, if you had shaken hands with him, his hand would
have burnt you.
> *William Hazlitt (1778–1830)*, Lectures on the English Poets

We praise him, not for gifts divine, –
His Muse was born of woman, –
His manhood breathes in every line, –
Was ever heart more human?
> *Oliver Wendell Holmes (1809–1894)*, For the Burns Centennial
> Celebration

You don't know Burns unless you hate the Lockharts and all the
estimable bourgeois and upper classes as he really did – the narrow-
gutted pigeons . . . Oh, why doesn't Burns come to life again, and
really salt them!
> *D.H.Lawrence (1885–1930), Letter to Donald Carswell, 1927*

No' wan in fifty kens a wurd Burns wrote,
But misapplied is a'body's property . . .

> *Hugh MacDiarmid (C.M. Grieve 1892–1978)*, A Drunk Man Looks
> at the Thistle

. . . the greatest peasant – next perhaps to King David of the Jews, a
peasant, a poet, a patriot and a king – whom any age had produced.

> *Charles Mackay (1814–1889)*, Forty Years' Recollections of Life,
> Literature, and Public Affairs

. . . he was always with me, for I had him by heart . . . Wherever a
Scotsman goes, there goes Burns. His grand, whole, catholic soul
squares with the good of all; therefore we find him in everything
everywhere.

> *John Muir (1838–1914)*, 'Thoughts on the Birthday of Robert Burns',
> *from L.M. Wolfe*, John of the Mountains: The Unpublished
> Journals of John Muir

He has the power of making any Scotsman, whether generous
or canny, sentimental or prosaic, religious or profane, more
wholeheartedly himself than he could have been without assistance;
and in that way perhaps more human.

> *Edwin Muir (1887–1959)*, Essays on Literature and Society

Burns of all poets is the most a Man.

> *Dante Gabriel Rossetti (1828–1882)*, On Burns

I mourned with thousands, but as one
More deeply grieved, for he was gone
Whose light I hailed when first it shone,
And showed my youth
How verse may build a princely throne
On humble truth.

> *William Wordsworth (1770–1850)*, At the Grave of Burns

Childhood and Children

Oh, will ye never learn?
Ne'er, ne'er was sic a bairn.
Breakin' my heart, ye fidgety, fidgety,
Breakin' my heart, ye fidgety bairn.
Anonymous, Ye Fidgety Bairn

Smile na sae sweet, my bonny babes,
An' ye smile sae sweet, ye'll smile me dead.
And O, bonny babes, if ye suck sair,
Ye'll never suck by my side mair.
Anonymous, The Cruel Mother

An earthly nourrice sits and sings,
And aye she sings, 'Ba, lily wean!
Little ken I my bairn's father,
Far less the land that he staps in.'
Anonymous, The Great Silkie of Sule Skerrie

Sleep an' let me to my wark –
a' thae claes to airn –
Jenny wi' the airn teeth,
Come and tak' the bairn!
Alexander Anderson ('Surfaceman', 1845–1900), Jenny Wi' the Airn
Teeth

They never heed a word I speak;
I try to gie a froon,
But aye I hap them up an' cry,
'O, bairnies, cuddle doon.'
Alexander Anderson, Cuddle Doon

Th' expectant wee things, toddlin', stacher through
To meet their dad
Robert Burns (1759–1796), The Cottar's Saturday Night

Lo! at the couch where infant beauty sleeps,
Her silent watch the mournful mother keeps.
> *Thomas Campbell (1777–1844)*, The Pleasures of Hope

Stir the fire till it lowes, let the bairnie sit,
Auld Daddy Darkness is no wantit yet.
> *James Ferguson (fl. 19th century)*, Auld Daddy Darkness

Aye maun the childer, wi'a fastin' mou',
Grumble and greet, and mak an unco mane.
> *Robert Fergusson (1750–1774)*, The Farmer's Ingle

You only need to spend an afternoon with a child to realise that
most of them, without even trying, are poets.
> *Janice Galloway (1955–), interview with Kirstin Innes*, The List, 4
> September 2008

These children are happy.
It is easier for them.
They are English.
> *Alasdair Gray (1934–)*, The Fall of Kelvin Walker

Where the pools are bright and deep,
Where the grey trout lies asleep,
Up the river and over the lea,
That's the way for Billy and me.
> *James Hogg (1770–1835)*, A Boy's Song

Because if it ever came to the choice between living and dying then
christ almighty he would lay down his life and glad to do it. They
were great wee weans. Great wee weans. Even if they were horrible
wee weans and selfish and spoilt brats he would still have done it.
> *James Kelman (1946–)*, A Disaffection

From the moment of birth, when the Stone Age baby confronts the
twentieth-century mother, the baby is subjected to these forces of
violence, called love, as its father and mother and their parents and
their parents before them, have been.
> *R.D. Laing (1927–1989)* The Politics of Experience

We are children, but some day
We'll be big, and strong, and say
None shall slave and none shall slay –
Comrades all together.
> *Socialist Sunday School hymn, from Jennie Lee (1904–1988),*
> Tomorrow is a New Day

Where did you come from, baby dear?
Out of the everywhere into the here.
> *George Macdonald (1824–1905),* At the Back of the North Wind

God thought about me, and so I grew.
> *George Macdonald,* At the Back of the North Wind

Gin they wad leave me alane!
> *Alastair Mackie (1925–1995),* Adolescence

Wee Willie Winkie rins through the toun,
Upstairs and doun stairs in his nicht-gown,
Tirling at the window, crying at the lock:
Are a' the bairnies in their bed, it's past ten o'clock?
> *William Miller (1810–1872),* Wee Willie Winkie

'Ah, but you canna be sure o' them at that age,' said the Captain.
'My brother Cherlie was merrit on a low-country woman, and the
twuns used to sit up at night and greet in the two languages, Gaalic
and Gleska, till he had to put plugs in them.'
> *Neil Munro (1864–1930),* The Vital Spark

All my life I have loved a womanly woman and admired a manly
man, but I never could stand a boily boy.
> *Lord Rosebery (1847–1929)*

Just at the age 'twixt boy and youth,
When thought is speech, and speech is truth.
> *Sir Walter Scott (1771–1832),* Marmion

O hush thee, my babie, thy sire was a knight,
Thy mother a lady both lovely and bright;
The woods and the glens, from the towers which we see,
They all are belonging, dear babie, to thee.
> *Sir Walter Scott,* Lullaby of an Infant Chief

The tear down childhood's cheek that flows
Is like the dew-drop on the rose;
When next the summer breeze comes by
And waves the bush, the flower is dry.
    Sir Walter Scott, Rokeby

The world is such a happy place,
That children, whether big or small,
Should always have a smiling face,
And never, never, sulk at all.
    Gabriel Setoun (Thomas Nicoll Hepburn 1861–1930), The World's
    Music

Aince upon a day my mither said to me:
Dinna cleip and dinna rype
And dinna tell a lee.
    William Soutar (1898–1943), Aince Upon a Day

One's prime is elusive. You little girls, when you grow up, must be
on the alert to recognise your prime, at whatever time of life it may
occur.
    Muriel Spark (1918–2006) The Prime of Miss Jean Brodie

. . . all my pupils are the crème de la crème.
    Muriel Spark, The Prime of Miss Jean Brodie

Parents learn a lot from their children about coping with life. It is
possible for parents to be corrupted or improved by their children.
    Muriel Spark, The Comforters

The funniest thing about him is the way he likes to grow –
Not at all like proper children, which is always very slow;
For he sometimes shoots up taller, like an india-rubber ball,
And he sometimes gets so little that there's none of him at all.
    Robert Louis Stevenson (1850–1894), My Shadow

Cruel children, crying babies,
All grow up as geese and gabies,
Hated, as their age increases,
By their nephews and their nieces.
    Robert Louis Stevenson, Good and Bad Children

A child should always say what's true,
And speak when he is spoken to,
And behave mannerly at table;
At least as far as he is able.

    Robert Louis Stevenson, The Whole Duty of Children

as a child, I won prizes at school and my mother's reaction was invariably: 'Very good, but don't tell folk – they'll think you're boasting.'

    Alex Wood, headteacher, in Times Educational Supplement (Scotland), *1 December 2006*

Costume

O laith, laith were our gude Scots lords
To wat their cork-heeled shoon,
But lang ere a' the play was play'd
They wat their hats aboon.
  Anonymous, Sir Patrick Spens

The kilt, being a practical outdoor garment, failed him only once,
and that occurred during a short-lived interest in bee-keeping.
  J.M. Bannerman (1901–1969), Bannerman: The Memoirs of Lord
  Bannerman of Kildonan

When I looked at myself in the glass last night in my Corsican
dress, I could not help thinking your opinion of yourself might
be yet more upraised: 'She has secured the constant affection and
admiration of so fine a fellow.'
  James Boswell (1740–1795), letter to Margaret Montgomerie

Her cutty sark, o' Paisley harn,
That while a lassie she had worn,
In longitude tho' sorely scanty,
It was her best, and she was vauntie.
  Robert Burns (1759–1796), Tam O' Shanter

This dress is called the quelt, and for the most part, they wear
the petticoat so very short that in a windy day, going up a hill, or
stooping, the indecency of it is plainly discovered.
  Edmund Burt (c.1695–1752), Letters from a Gentleman in the
  North of Scotland

Friends! Trust not the heart of that man for whom Old Clothes are
not venerable.
  Thomas Carlyle (1795–1881), Sartor Resartus

Braid claith lends fowk an unco heese,
Makes many kail-worms butter-flees
　　Robert Fergusson (1750–1774), Braid Claith

The tartan tred wad gar ye lauch;
nae problem is owre teuch.
Your surname needna end in -*och*;
they'll cleik ye up the cleuch.
A puckle dollar bills will aye
preive Hiram Teufelsdrockh
A septary of Clan McKay.
　　Robert Garioch (Robert Garioch Sutherland, 1909–1981), Embro to
　　the Ploy

. . . getting down on the floors to scrub would be an ill-like ploy,
she would warrant, for the brave silk knickers that Mrs Colquhoun
wore. For the Sourock's wife had never forgiven the minister's wife
her bit under-things, and the way she voted at the General Election.
　　Lewis Grassic Gibbon (James Leslie Mitchell, 1901–1935), Cloud Howe

Do I like women's clothes more than their bodies? Oh, no, but I
prefer their clothes to their minds. Their minds keep telling me, no
thank you, don't touch, go away. Their clothes say, look at me, want
me, I am exciting.
　　Alasdair Gray (1934–), 1982 Janine

'Whit will I wear under it?' I asked. Few of us in Lomond Street
wore underpants. 'Soldiers don't wear anything under their kilts.'
I wondered how she knew. But even if it was true, soldiers just had
Boers shooting at them, they didn't have Jock Dempster or Rab
McIntyre come whooping out of a close to snatch up their kilts and
show their bums to lassies.
　　Robin Jenkins (1912–1992), Fergus Lamont

Sick and sore I am, worn and weary,
walking no more since my limbs are confined.
Cursed be the king who stretched our stockings,
down in the dust may his face be found.
　　John MacCodrum (c.1693–1779), 'Oran Mu'n Eideadh Ghaidhealach'
　　(Song to the Highland Dress)

My kilt and tartan stockings I was wearing,
My claymore and my dirk and skian-dhu,
And when I sallied forth with manly bearing
I heard admiring whispers not a few –
'He's the best-dressed Highlander,
The best-dressed Highlander,
The best-dressed Highlander at his own expense.'
    D.M. McKay, The Best-Dressed Highlander

Wi' shanks like that ye'd better hae stuck to breeks.
    Charles Murray (1864–1941), Ay, Fegs

It was hard to believe a lady had to jump into her crinoline.
    Neil Paterson (1915–1995), Behold Thy Daughter

Her coats were kiltit, and did sweetly shaw
Her straight bare legs that whiter were than snaw;
Her cockernony snooded up fou' sleek,
Her haffet-locks hung waving on her cheek
    Allan Ramsay (1686–1758), The Gentle Shepherd

His socks compelled one's attention without losing one's respect.
    Saki (H.H. Munro, 1870–1916), The Chronicles of Clovis

Two long and bony arms were terminated at the elbow by triple
blond ruffles, and being folded saltire-ways in front of her person,
and decorated with long gloves a bright vermillion colour, presented
no bad resemblance to a pair of gigantic lobsters.
    Sir Walter Scott (1771–1832), The Antiquary

Let others boast of philibeg,
Of kilt and tartan plaid,
Whilst we the ancient trews will wear,
In which our fathers bled.
    Sir John Sinclair (1754–1835), March for the Rothesay and
    Caithness Fencibles

The kilt is . . . I don't know how to put this . . . it's an aphrodisiac. I
can't tell you why, but it works . . . hap your hurdies with the passion
pleats and it doesn't seem to matter what kind of women they are
– rich, poor, old, young, black, white and yellow – they just melt, go
shoogly in the legs, and, well, submit . . . Unconditional surrender.
    W. Gordon Smith (1928–1996), Mr Jock (1987)

There was an old man of the Cape
Who made himself garments of crape.
When asked. 'Do they tear?'
He replied, 'Here and there;
But they're perfectly splendid for shape.'

Robert Louis Stevenson (1850–1894), quoted in W. S. Baring-Gould,
The Lure of the Limerick *(1968)*

Loveliness
Needs not the foreign aid of ornament,
But is, when unadorned, adorned the most.

James Thomson (1700–1748), The Seasons

Death

Remember man, as thou goes by,
As thou art now, so once was I;
As I am now so thou shalt be,
Remember man that thou must die.

> *Inscription once mounted at the entrance to Greyfriars Churchyard,
> Edinburgh*

I am washing the shrouds of the fair men
Who are going out but shall never come in;
The death-dirge of the ready-handed men
Who shall go out, seek peril, and fall.

> *Song of the River Sprite Nigheag, from Gaelic*

This ae nighte, this ae nighte
Every nighte and alle,
Fire and fleet and candle-light;
And Christe receive thye saule.

> *Anonymous*, A Lyke-Wake Dirge

Mony an ane for him maks mane
But nane sall ken where he is gane;
Ower his white banes when they are bare,
The wind sall blaw for evermair.

> *Anonymous*, The Twa Corbies

I hae been to the wild wood, mother; mak my bed soon,
For I'm weary wi' huntin', and fain wad lie doon.

> *Anonymous*, Lord Randal

Ye Hielands and ye Lawlands,
O, whaur hae ye been?
They hae slain the Earl o' Moray,
And hae laid him on the green.

> *Anonymous*, The Bonnie Earl o' Moray

She sought him east, she sought him west,
She sought him braid and narrow,
Syne in the cleaving of a craig
She found him droon'd in Yarrow.
    Anonymous, Willie Drowned in Yarrow

Death is the port where all may refuge find,
The end of labour, entry into rest.
    Sir William Alexander (c.1567–1640), The Tragedy of Darius

Beyond the ever and the never,
I shall be soon.
    Horatius Bonar (1808–1889), Beyond the Smiling and the Weeping

Now, God be with you, my children: I have breakfasted with you
and shall sup with my Lord Jesus Christ this night.
    Robert Bruce of Kinnaird (1554–1631), on his death-bed

The wan moon is setting behind the white wave,
And Time is setting with me, O!
    Robert Burns (1759–1796), The Wan Moon is Setting Behind the
White Wave

O Death! the poor man's dearest friend –
    Robert Burns, Man Was made to Mourn

Don't let the awkward squad fire over my grave.
    Robert Burns, quoted on his deathbed

He died, seated, with a bowl of milk on his knee, of which his
ceasing to live did not spill a drop, a departure which it seemed,
after the event happened, might have been foretold of this
attenuated philosophical gentleman.
    Henry Thomas Cockburn (1779–1854), Memorials, *on the death of
Joseph Black*

To die young, is to do that soon, and in some fewer Days, which
once thou must do; it is but the giving over of a Game, that after
never so many Hazards must be lost.
    William Drummond (1585–1649), A Cypresse Grove

To live in hearts we leave behind
Is not to die.

> *Thomas Campbell (1777–1844)*, Hallowed Ground

God forbid that I should go to any heaven where there are no horses.

> *R.B. Cunninghame Graham (1852–1936), letter to President Theodore Roosevelt*

I that in heill was and in gladnes
Am trublit now with great seiknes,
And feblit with infirmitie
Timor mortis conturbat me.

> *William Dunbar (c.1460–c.1520)*, Lament for the Deth of the Makkaris

Sen for the deid remeid is none,
Best is that we for deth dispone,
Eftir our deth that leif may we:
Timor mortis conturbat me.

> *William Dunbar*, Lament for the Deth of the Makkaris

Death is a grim creditor, and a doctor but brittle bail when the hour o'reckoning's at han'!

> *John Galt (1779–1839)*, Annals of the Parish

What a pity it is, mother, that you're now dead, for here's the minister come to see you.

> *John Galt*, Annals of the Parish

No, I'll inherit
No keening in my mountain head or sea
Nor fret for few who die before I do.

> *W.S. Graham (1918–1986)*, Many without Elegy

Of kindelie death nane suld affraied be
But sich as hope for na felicitie.

> *Alexander Hume (c.1560–1609)*, To His Sorrofull Saull, Consolatioun

I am dying as fast as my enemies, if I have any, could wish, and as easily and cheerfully as my best friends could desire.

> *David Hume (1711–1776), recorded in William Smellie*, Literary and Characteristical Lives *(1800)*

If suicide be supposed a crime, it is only cowardice can impel us to it. If it be no crime, both prudence and courage should engage us to rid ourselves at once of existence when it becomes a burden. It is the only way we can then be useful to society
David Hume, Essays

I'd always joked about my drinking and smoking that I would hate to die with a heart attack and have a good liver, kidneys and brain. When I die I want everything to be knackered.
Hamish Imlach (1940–1996), song-writer and singer

Says she, 'Guidmen I've kistit twa,
But a change o' deils is lichtsome, lass!'
Violet Jacob (1863–1946), A Change o' Deils

Vain are all things when death comes to your door.
Murdo Mackenzie (fl. 1650s), Diomhanas nan Diomhanas *(Vanity of Vanities), translated by William Neill*

Here it was arranged the customary funeral dinner should be held, and the entertainment was somewhat prolonged. At last notice was given for the funeral party to move; but when the procession had proceeded more than a mile on the road, the undertaker came galloping up, calling, 'Gentlemen, halt, for we have forgotten the hearse.'
Joseph Mitchell (1803–1883), Reminiscences of My Life in the Highlands

Unfriendly friendly universe,
I pack your stars into my purse,
And bid you, bid you so farewell.
Edwin Muir (1887–1959), The Child Dying

Let children walk with nature, let them see the beautiful blending and communion of death and life, their joyous inseparable unity, as taught in woods and meadows, plains and mountains and streams of our blessed star, and they will learn that death is stingless indeed, and as beautiful as life, and that the grave has no victory, for it never fights. All is divine harmony.
John Muir (1838–1914)

There's nae sorrow, there John,
There's neither cauld nor care, John,
The day is aye fair,
In the land o' the leal.
　　Lady Nairne (1766–1845), The Land o' the Leal

Nae stroke o' fortune cloured wi' bloody claa,
Nor glow'ring daith wi' sudden tempest mocked,
But in his wee thatched croft he wore awa'
E'en as a cruisie flickers oot unslockt.
　　Robert Rendall (1898–1967), The Fisherman

And, at the very idea of the general grief which must have attended his death, the good-natured monarch cried heartily himself.
　　Sir Walter Scott (1771–1832), The Fortunes of Nigel

Like the dew on the mountain,
Like the foam on the river,
Like the bubble on the fountain,
Thou art gone, and forever.
　　Sir Walter Scott, The Lady of the Lake

There is a certain frame of mind to which a cemetery is, if not an antidote, at least an alleviation. If you are in a fit of the blues, go nowhere else.
　　Robert Louis Stevenson (1850–1894), Immortelles

Under the wide and starry sky
Dig the grave, and let me lie.
Glad did I live and gladly die,
And I laid me down with a will.
　　Robert Louis Stevenson, Requiem

Cruel as death, and hungry as the grave
　　James Thomson (1700–1748), Winter

This little life is all we must endure,
The grave's most holy peace is ever sure,
We fall asleep and never wake again.
　　James Thomson (1834–1882), The City of Dreadful Night

Though the Garden of thy Life be wholly waste, the sweet flowers withered, the fruit-trees barren, over its wall hangs ever the rich dark clusters of the Vine of Death, within easy reach of thy hand, which may pluck of them when it will.

James Thomson, The City of Dreadful Night

The restful rapture of the inviolate grave.

James Thomson, To Our Ladies of Death

Economics and Commerce

You are being paid as if you are superhuman, but you are not.
> *Shareholder to Royal Bank of Scotland directors at its annual meeting, quoted in* The Guardian, *24 April 2008*

We will never return to the old boom and bust.
> *Gordon Brown (1951–), Budget speech, March 2007*

Failure should not be rewarded.
> *Gordon Brown, quoted in* The Scotsman, *26 February 2009*

We cam na here to view your warks,
In hopes to be mair wise,
But only, lest we gang to hell,
It may be no surprise.
> *Robert Burns (1759–1796),* Impromptu on Carron Ironworks

Pioneering does not pay.
> *Andrew Carnegie (1835–1918), quoted in Hendrick's* Life of Carnegie.

Put all your eggs in one basket, and then watch the basket.
> *Andrew Carnegie, quoted in Hendrick's* Life of Carnegie

In every commercial state, notwithstanding any pretension to equal rights, the exaltation of a few must depress the many.
> *Adam Ferguson (1723–1816),* Essay on the History of Civil Society

MacDougall Brown, the postmaster, came down to the Square and preached on stealing, right godly-like, and you'd never have thought that him and his wife stayed up of a night sanding the sugar and watering the paraffin – or so folk said, but they tell such lies.
> *Lewis Grassic Gibbon (James Leslie Mitchell, 1901–1935),* Cloud Howe

I hope you can understand my rationale for declining your request to voluntarily reduce my pension entitlement.
> *Sir Fred Goodwin, letter to Lord Myners, quoted in* The Scotsman, *26 February 2009*

When the historian knew of happenings calculated to cast odium
on our landed gentry, he carefully excised the records, and where
he did not know, he was careful to assume, and lead others to
assume, that the period of which he was ignorant were periods of
intense social happiness, wherein a glad and thankful populace
spent their days and their nights in devising Hallelujahs in honour
of the neighbouring nobleman. And that is why the history of Scots
mining is wrapped in darkness.

   Tom Johnston (1881–1965), Our Scots Noble Families

All you folks are off your head
I'm getting rich from your sea bed
I'll go home when I see fit
All I'll leave is a heap of shit

   John McGrath (1935–2002), The Cheviot, the Stag and the Black,
   Black Oil

I cannot sit still, James, and hear you abuse the shopocracy.

   Christopher North (John Wilson, 1785–1854), Noctes Ambrosianae

Historians will be puzzled by the Oil Phenomenon: how an
intelligent, well-educated nation in a developed country became the
only people ever to discover oil and become poorer.

   Jim Sillars (1937–)

It is not from the benevolence of the butcher, the brewer, or the
baker, that we expect our dinner, but from their regard to their
own interest. We address ourselves, not to their humanity but to
their self-love, and never talk to them of our necessities but of their
advantages.

   Adam Smith (1723–1790), The Wealth Of Nations

It is not by augmenting the capital of the country, but by rendering
a greater part of that capital active and productive than would
otherwise be so, that the most judicious operations of banking can
increase the industry of the country.

   Adam Smith, The Wealth Of Nations

It is the highest impertinence and presumption . . . in kings and ministers, to pretend to watch over the economy of private people, and to restrain their expense . . . They are themselves always, and without any exception, the greatest spendthrifts in the society. Let them look well after their own expense, and they may safely trust private people with theirs. If their own extravagance does not ruin the state, that of their subjects never will.

Adam Smith, The Wealth Of Nations

Man is an animal that makes bargains: no other animal does this – no dog exchanges bones with another.

Adam Smith, The Wealth of Nations

To found a great empire for the sole purpose of raising up a people of customers, may at first sight appear a project fit only for a nation of shopkeepers

Adam Smith, The Wealth Of Nations

All money is a matter of belief.

Adam Smith

Everyone lives by selling something.

Robert Louis Stevenson (1850–1894), Beggars

Education and Schools

Mr Rhind is very kind,
He goes to kirk on Sunday.
He prays to God to give him strength
To skelp the bairns on Monday.
  Old Children's Rhyme

He would not allow Scotland to derive any credit from Lord
Mansfield; for he was educated in England. 'Much', said he, 'may be
made of a Scotchman, if he be caught young.'
  James Boswell (1740–1795), Life of Johnson

The schoolmaster is abroad, and I trust to him, armed with his
primer, more than I do the soldier in full military array, for
upholding and extending the liberties of the country . . . Education
makes a people easy to lead, but difficult to drive; easy to govern but
impossible to enslave.
  Lord Brougham (1778–1868) speech to the House of Commons, 1828

Experience is the best of schoolmasters, only the school-fees are
heavy.
  Thomas Carlyle (1795–1881), Miscellaneous Essays

When we make laws which compel our children to go to school we
assume collectively an awesome responsibility. For a period of ten
years . . . our children are conscripts; and their youth does nothing
to alter the seriousness of this fact.
  Margaret C. Donaldson (1926–), Children's Minds

One of my greatest hopes from a Scottish parliament is the
advancement of education to the point at which my Scottish
students would speak to me.
  Douglas Dunn (1942–), quoted in Neal Ascherson, Stone Voices

Afore his cless he staunds and talks
or scrieves awa wi colour'd chalks
  Robert Garioch (Robert Garioch Sutherland, 1909–1981), Garioch's
  Response Til George Buchanan

. . . monie a skelp
of triple-tonguit tawse
has gien a hyst-up and a help
towards Doctorates of Laws
   Robert Garioch, Embro to the Ploy

A single excursion under sympathetic and intelligent guidance to an
instructive quarry, river-ravine, or sea-shore, is worth many books
and a long course of systematic lectures.
   Sir Archibald Geikie (1835–1924), My First Geological Excursion

Perhaps all teachers should pour fine stuff into children's ears
and leave their memories to resurrect it when they find their own
thoughts inadequate.
   Alasdair Gray (1934–), 1982 Janine

The dawn of legibility in his handwriting has revealed his utter
inability to spell.
   Attributed to Ian Hay (John Hay Beith, 1876–1952)

Their learning is like bread in a besieged town: every man gets a
little, but no man gets a full meal.
   Samuel Johnson (1709–1784), *quoted in Boswell's* Life of Johnson

. . . the schools are not on our side. They are the agencies of the
rulers. They bring us up to do what we are told, and not to speak
back, to learn our lessons and pass the examinations. Above all, not
to ask questions.
   R.F. Mackenzie (1910–1987), A Search for Scotland

Sweet time – sad time! twa bairns at scule –
Twa bairns and but ae heart.
   William Motherwell (1797–1835), Jeanie Morrison

There is never a problem child; there is only a problem parent.
   A.S. Neill (1883–1973), The Problem Parent

A good teacher does not draw out: he gives out, and what he gives
out is love.
   A.S. Neill, The Problem Teacher

As the rough diamond from the mine,
In breakings only shews its light,
Till polishing has made it shine;
Thus learning makes the genius bright.
  Allan Ramsay (1686–1758), The Gentle Shepherd

Good gracious, you've got to educate him first. You can't expect a
boy to be vicious until he's been to a really good school.
  Saki (H.H. Munro, 1870–1916)

The discipline of colleges and universities is in general contrived,
not for the benefit of the students, but for the interest, or more
properly speaking, for the ease of the masters.
  Adam Smith (1723–1790), The Wealth Of Nations

Give me a girl at an impressionable age, and she is mine for life.
  Muriel Spark (1918–2006), The Prime of Miss Jean Brodie

The round-shot of a Latin grammar had been, I believe, tied to our
legs, to prevent our intellectually straying.
  Sir D'Arcy Wentworth Thompson (1860–1948), Daydreams of a
  Schoolmaster

Delightful task! To rear the tender thought,
To teach the young idea how to shoot.
  James Thomson (1700–1748), The Seasons

Epitaphs

Mightier was the verse of Iain,
Hearts to nerve, to kindle eyes,
Than the claymore of the valiant,
Than the counsel of the wise.

> *Epitaph on the Bard Iain Lòm, from Gaelic*

Dry up your tears and weep no more
I am not dead but gone before
Remember me, and bear in mind
You have not long to stay behind.

> *Anonymous*

John Carnegie lies here,
Descended from Adam and Eve
If any can boast of a pedigree higher
He will willingly give them leave.

> *Anonymous*

Content he was with portion small
Keeped shop in Wigtown, and that's all

> *Wigtown epitaph, from Stephen Bone*, Albion: An Artist's Britain
> *(1937)*

Scotland bore me, England adopted me, France taught me,
Germany holds me.

> *From the Latin epitaph on the tomb of Duns Scotus (c.1265–1308), in
> Cologne, Germany*

Lament him, Mauchline husbands a',
He aften did assist ye;
For had ye staid hale weeks awa',
Your wives they ne'er had missed ye.
Ye Mauchline bairns, as on ye press
To school in bands together,
O tread ye lightly on his grass –
Perhaps he was your father!

> *Robert Burns (1759–1796)*, Epitaph for a Wag in Mauchline

Here lie Willie Michie's banes,
O Satan, when ye tak him,
Gie him the schulin o' your weans,
For clever deils he'll mak them!
> *Robert Burns*, Epitaph for William Michie

Sen she is deid, I speak of her no more.
> *Robert Henryson (c.1425–1500)*, The Testament of Cresseid

Here lie I, Martin Elginbrodde:
Hae mercy o' my soul, O God,
As I wad do, gin I were God
And ye were Martin Elginbrodde
> *George Macdonald (1824–1905)*, David Elginbrod

MacGregor Despite Them
> *Modern inscription above the grave of Rob Roy MacGregor (died 1734),*
> *in Balquhidder Churchyard, Stirlingshire*

Here lies of sense bereft –
But sense he never had.
Here lies, by feeling left –
But that is just as bad.
Here lies, reduced to dirt –
That's what he always was
> *George Outram (1805–1856)*, Here Lies

In peace and war he suffer'd overmuch:
War stole away his strength, and peace his crutch.
> *William Soutar (1898–1943)*, Epitaph for a Disabled Ex-Serviceman

This be the verse you grave for me:
Here he lies where he longed to be,
Home is the sailor, home from sea,
And the hunter home from the hill.
> *Robert Louis Stevenson (1850–1894)*, Requiem

Family and Social Life

'O hold your hand, Lord William,' she said,
'For your strokes they are wondrous sair;
True lovers I can get many an ane,
But a father I can never get mair.'
    Anonymous, The Douglas Tragedy

Ye maun gang to your father, Janet,
Ye maun gang to him sune;
Ye maun gang to your father, Janet,
In case that his days are dune.
    Anonymous, Fair Janet

'And what will ye leave to your bairns and your wife,
Edward, Edward?
And what will ye leave to your bairns and your wife,
When ye gang owre the sea, O?'
'The warld's room – let them beg through life,
Mither, mither;
The warld's room – let them beg through life,
For them never mair will I see, O.'
    Anonymous, Edward

Ye daurna swear aboot the toon,
It is against the law,
An' if ye use profanities,
Then ye'll be putten awa'.
    Traditional, Drumdelgie

Fame is rot: daughters are the thing.
    Sir J.M. Barrie (1860–1937), Dear Brutus

Baloo, baloo, my wee, wee thing,
O saftly close thy blinkin' e'e!
Baloo, baloo, my wee, wee thing,
For thou are doubly dear to me.
Thy daddy now is far awa',
A sailor laddie o'er the sea;

But hope ay hechts his safe return
To you my bonnie lamb and me.
  'Cradle Song', from Allan Cunningham, Songs of Scotland *(1825)*

When the noisy ten hours drum
Gar's your trades gae dandering hame,
Gie a' to merriment and glee,
Wi' sang and glass they fley the power
O' care that wad harass the hour.
  Robert Fergusson (1750–1774), Auld Reekie

'I' my grandfather's time, as I have heard him tell, ilka maister o' a
faamily had his ain sate in his ain hoose; aye, an' sat wi' his hat on
his heed afore the best in the land; an' had his ain dish, an' wus aye
helpit first, an' keepit up his authority as a man should do. Paurents
were paurents then – bairns daurdna set upo' their gabs afore them
as they dae noo.'
  Susan Ferrier (1782–1854), Marriage

The awe and dread with which the untutored savage contemplates
his mother-in-law are amongst the most familiar facts of
anthropology.
  Sir James G. Frazer (1854–1941), The Golden Bough

I can make a lord, but only God Almighty can make a gentleman.
  King James VI (1566–1625)

In circumstances roughly similar to this one, in certain tribes of
chimpanzees, individuals bare their arses to each other, a method
of pacifying the aggressor. But this wasnt the place to display arses.
This was family.
  James Kelman (1946–), A Disaffection

Poor mother, she thought, she's had five children and she's as barren
as Rannoch Moor. What did she know of life with her church
committees and her Madeira cakes and her husband who was more
Calvinistic than Calvin himself?
  Joan Lingard (1932–), The Prevailing Wind

And the atmosphere warm with that lovely heat,
The warmth of tenderness and loving souls, the smiling anxiety,
That rules a house where a child is about to be born.
  Hugh MacDiarmid (C.M. Grieve, 1892–1978), Lo! A Child is Born

Wi' every effort to be fair
And nae undue antagonism
I canna but say that my sweethheart's mither
Is a moolie besom, a moolie besom,
Naething but a moolie besom!
Hugh MacDiarmid, A Moolie Besom

Women do not find it difficult nowadays to behave like men, but
they often find it extremely difficult to behave like gentlemen.
Compton Mackenzie (1883–1972), Literature in My Time

You waitit for me to be born
I wait for you to dee.
Alastair Mackie (1925–1995), For My Father

Gracious acceptance is an art – an art which most never bother to
cultivate.
Alexander McCall Smith (1948–), Love over Scotland

the urban misery, the architectural degradation, the raw, alcohol-
riddled despair, the petty criminal furtiveness, the bleak violence of
living in many parts of industrial Scotland.
John McGrath (1935–2002), Naked Thoughts That Roam About
(with Nadine Holdsworth), 2001

Marriage is one long conversation, chequered by disputes.
Robert Louis Stevenson (1850–1894)

Matrimony . . . no more than a sort of friendship recognised by the
police.
Robert Louis Stevenson

My children from the youngest to the eldest loves me and fears me
as sinners dread death. My look is law.
Lady Strange, quoted in H.G. Graham, The Social Life of Scotland
in the Eighteenth Century *(1899)*

She thought that her relatives were so boring. They hung onto
the mundane for grim life; it was a glum adhesive binding them
together.
Irvine Welsh (1957–), Trainspotting

Fantasy, Visions and Magic

It fell about the Martinmas
When nights are lang and mirk,
The carline wife's three sons cam' hame,
And their hats were o' the birk.
It neither grew in syke nor ditch,
Nor yet in any sheugh;
But in the howe o' Paradise
That birk grew fair eneuch.
    Anonymous, The Wife of Usher's Well

The cock doth craw, the day doth daw,
The channerin' worm doth chide
    The Wife of Usher's Well

Wae's me, wae's me,
The acorn's not yet
Fa'n from the tree,
That's to make the wood,
That's to make the cradle,
That's to rock the bairn,
That's to grow a man,
That's to lay me.
    Anonymous, The Wandering Spectre

My mouth it is full cold, Margaret,
It has the smell now of the ground;
And if I kiss thy comely mouth,
Thy days of life will not be lang.
    Anonymous, Clerk Saunders

Then up and crew the milk white cock,
And up and crew the grey,
Her lover vanished in the air,
And she gaed weeping away.
    Clerk Saunders

'Harp and carp, Thomas,' she said,
'Harp and carp along wi' me.'
    Anonymous, Thomas the Rhymer

'And see ye not that bonnie road
That winds about the ferny brae?
That is the road to fair Elfland,
Where thou and I this night maun gae.'
    Thomas the Rhymer

For forty days and forty nichts
He wade thro' red blude to the knee,
He saw neither sun nor mune,
But he heard the roarin' o' the sea.
    Thomas the Rhymer

She cam' tripping adown the stair,
And a' her maids before her;
As soon as they saw her weel-faur'd face,
They cast the glamourie owre her.
    Anonymous, Johnnie Faa

'I saw the new moon late yestreen,
Wi' the auld moon in her arm;
And if we gang to sea, master,
I fear we'll come to harm.'
    Anonymous, Sir Patrick Spens

'But I hae dreamed a dreary dream,
Beyond the Isle of Skye:
I saw a dead man win a fight,
And I think that man was I.'
    Anonymous, The Battle of Otterbourne

Yit scho wanderit and yeid by to ane elriche well,
Scho met thar, as I wene,
Ane ask rydand on a snaill,
And cryit, 'Ourtane fallow, haill!'
And raid ane inch behind the taill,
Till it wes neir evin.
    Anonymous, Kynd Kittok

Gin ye ca' me imp or elf,
I rede ye look well to yourself;
Gin ye ca' me fairy,
I'll work ye muckle tarry;
Gin guid neibour ye ca' me,
Then guid neibour I will be.
But gin ye ca' me seelie wicht,
I'll be your friend both day and nicht.
> *Traditional, from Chambers'* Popular Rhymes

When the first baby laughed for the first time, his laugh broke into a million pieces, and they all went skipping about. That was the beginning of fairies.
> *Sir J.M. Barrie (1860–1937),* The Little White Bird

The shore was cold with mermaids and angels
> *George Mackay Brown (1921–1996),* Beachcomber

So in Scotland witches used to raise the wind by dipping a rag in water and beating it thrice on a stone, saying:
'I knok this rag upon this stane
To raise the wind in the divellis name,
It sall not lye till I please againe.'
> *Sir James G. Frazer (1854–1941),* The Golden Bough

. . . a strange dream came to her as they plodded up through the ancient hills.
For out of the night ahead of them came running a man, father didn't see him or heed to him, though old Bob in the dream that was Chris's snorted and shied. And as he came he wrung his hands, he was mad and singing, a foreign creature, black-bearded, half-naked he was; and he cried in the Greek The ships of Pytheas! The ships of Pytheas! and went by into the smore of the sleet-storm on the Grampian hills.
> *Lewis Grassic Gibbon (James Leslie Mitchell, 1901–1935),* Sunset Song

In 1845 it could seriously be written in the new Statistical Account that a late Principal of Aberdeen University had contributed 'by his benevolent exertions in an eminent degree to the expulsion of fairies from the Highland Hills'.
> *I.F. Grant,* Highland Folk Ways *(1961)*

The Second Sight is an unwelcome gift. To whoever has it, visions come not of his own seeking, and their significance is almost invariably tragic.

    I.F. Grant, Highland Folk Ways

O doulie place and groundless deep dungeoun,
Furnace of fire, with stink intolerable,
Pit of despair, without remissioun

    Robert Henryson (c.1425–1500), Orpheus and Eurydice

Late, late in a gloamin' when all was still,
When the fringe was red on the westlin' hill,
The wood was sere, the moon i' the wane,
The reek o' the cot hung over the plain,
Like a little wee cloud in the world its lane;
When the ingle glowed wi' an eiry leme –
Late, late in the gloaming Kilmeny came hame!

    James Hogg (1770–1835), Kilmeny

Kilmeny look'd up wi' a lovely grace,
But nae smile was seen on Kilmeny's face;
As still was her look, and as still was her e'e,
As the stillness that lay on the emerant lea

    James Hogg, Kilmeny

A murmuring sough is on the wood,
And the witching star is red as blood.
And in the cleft of heaven I scan
The giant form of a naked man;
His eye is like the burning brand,
And he holds a sword in his right hand.

    James Hogg, A Witch's Chant

O there are doings here below
That mortal ne'er should ken;
For there are things in this fair world
Beyond the reach o' men!

    James Hogg, May of the Moril Glen

And underneath the wheele saw I there
An ugly pit as deep as ony hell,
That to behold thereon I quoke for fear;
Bot o thing heard I, that who there-in fell
Come no more up again tidings to tell.

 King James I (1394–1437), The Kingis Quair

Across the silent stream
Where the dream-shadows go,
From the dim blue Hill of Dream
I have heard the West Wind blow.

 Fiona MacLeod (William Sharp, 1855–1905), From the Hills
 of Dream

I have no playmate but the tide
The seaweed loves with dark brown eyes:
The night waves have the stars for play,
For me but sighs.

 Fiona MacLeod, The Moon-Child

Last night I dreamed a ghastly dream,
Before the dirl o' day.
A twining worm cam out the wast,
Its back was like the slae.
It ganted wide as deid men gant,
Turned three times on its tail,
And wrapped itsel the warld around
Til ilka rock did wail.

 Edwin Muir (1887–1959), Ballad of the Flood

And, dancing on each chimney top,
I saw a thousand darling imps
Keeping time with skip and hop.

 William Bell Scott (1811–1890), The Witch's Ballad

And on the provost's brave ridge-tile,
On the provost's grand ridge-tile,
The Blackamooor first to master me
I saw, I saw that winsome smile,
The mouth that did my heart beguile,
And spoke the great Word over me,
In the land beyond the sea.

 William Bell Scott, The Witch's Ballad

. . . thru the flicherin' floichan-drift
A beast cam doun the hill.
It steppit like a stallion,
Wha's heid hauds up a horn,
And weel the men o' Scotland kent
It was the unicorn.

    William Soutar (1898–1943), Birthday

For there was Janet comin' doun the clachan – her or her likeness, nane could tell – wi' her neck thrawn, an' her heid on ae side, like a body that has been hangit, an' a girn on her face like an unstreakit corp.

    Robert Louis Stevenson (1850–1894), Thrawn Janet

. . . when a' o' a sudden, he heard a laigh, uncanny steer up-stairs; a foot gaed to an' fro in the chalmer whaur the corp was hangin'; syne the door was opened, though he minded weel that he had lockit it; an' syne there was a step upon the landin', an' it seemed to him as if the corp was lookin' ower the rail and doun on him whaur he stood.

    Robert Louis Stevenson, Thrawn Janet

Food and Drink

O gude ale comes and gude ale goes,
Gude ale gars me sell my hose,
Sell my hose and pawn my shoon,
Gude ale hauds my heart aboon.
  Anonymous

Moderation, sir, aye. Moderation is my rule. Nine or ten is
reasonable refreshment, but after that it's apt to degenerate into
drinking.
  Anonymous

For if you feed your good man well
He'll love you all your life, oh!
And then to all the world he'll tell
There ne'er was such a wife, oh!
  Anonymous, The Quaker's Wife

Not too high, not too low, not too fast, and not too slow.
  *Traditional rhyme for working the 'fro' stick' to mix cream, whey and
  oatmeal.*

Tatties an' pint
  *Traditional phrase for a meal consisting only of potatoes. Eaters could
  'point' at fowls outside, or fish hanging to dry.*

Its fried I'm fired for:
Sober Black Pudding
on a broad bay of bacon
with an egg like a solar flare
  John Aberdein (1947–), Sabbath Breakfast

On the ferry I also have Cal Mac curry and chips with lots of
tomato sauce. This is, I realise, your basic poor/horribilist cuisine
. . . mass-production time-warp pseudo-curry
  Iain Banks (1954–), Raw Spirit

In dinner talk it is perhaps allowable to fling any faggot rather than let the fire go out.

    Sir J.M. Barrie (1860–1937)

I once saw an English guy in Glasgow trying to order a pint of lager and lime and the barman went: 'We don't do cocktails.'

    Frankie Boyle (1972–)

'Dish or no dish,' rejoined the Caledonian, 'there's a deal o' fine confused feedin' about it, let me tell you.'

    John Brown (1810–1882), Horae Subsecivae, *on Haggis.*

Some hae meat and canna eat,
And some hae nane that want it;
But we hae meat, and we can eat,
And sae the Lord be thankit.

    'The Selkirk Grace', attributed to Robert Burns (1759–1796)

See Social-life and Glee sit down
All joyous and unthinking,
Till, quite transmogrified, they've grown
Debauchery and Drinking.

    Robert Burns, An Address to the Unco Guid

Go fetch to me a pint o' wine,
And fill it in a silver tassie;
That I may drink before I go,
A service to my bonie lassie.

    Robert Burns, The Silver Tassie

We are na fou, we're nae that fou,
But just a drappie in our e'e

    Robert Burns, O Willie Brew'd a Peck o' Maut

Fast by an ingle, bleezin' finely,
Wi' reamin' swats that drank divinely . . .
The night drave on wi' sangs and clatter,
And aye the ale was growing better

    Robert Burns, Tam o' Shanter

We'll tak' a richt gude-willie waught
For Auld Lang Syne.

    Robert Burns, Auld Lang Syne

Food fill the wame, and keeps us livin';
But, oiled by thee,
The wheels o' life gang down-hill scrievin',
Wi' rattlin' glee.
  Robert Burns, Scotch Drink

Freedom an' whisky gang thegither
  Robert Burns, The Author's Earnest Cry and Prayer to the Right
  Honourable and Honourable, the Scotch Representatives in the
  House of Commons

Few go away sober at any time, and for the greatest part of his
guests, in the conclusion, they cannot go at all.
  Edmund Burt (c.1695–1752), Letters from a Gentleman in the
  North of Scotland, *on Forbes of Culloden*

Liquid madness
  Thomas Carlyle (1795–1881), On Chartism

Nip-pint, Nip-pint –
Mustn't-get-drunk, mustn't-get-drunk.
Nip-pint, Nip-pint –
Tae pot wi' it a', tae pot wi' it a'.
  Robin Cockburn, The Galliard *(1948)*

Advocaat: the alcoholic's omelette.
  Billy Connolly (1942–), Gullible's Travels

There is no finer breakfast than flounders fried in oatmeal with a
little salt butter, as ever they came out of the water, with their tails
jerking 'flip-flop' in the frizzle of the pan.
  S.R. Crockett (1859–1914), The Raiders

The proper drinking of Scotch whisky is more than indulgence; it
is a toast to a civilisation, a tribute to the continuity of culture, a
manifesto of man's determination to use the resources of nature to
refresh mind and body and enjoy to the full the senses with which
he has been endowed.
  David Daiches (1912–2005), Scotch Whisky *(1969)*

I am not fond of devilled stoat.
  Donald Dewar (1937–2000) (a curry enthusiast) on being asked if he
  had enjoyed a meal in a certain Indian restaurant

the grossly overrated potato, that marvel of insipidity.
    Norman Douglas (1868–1952), Together

Than culit thai thair mouthis with confortable drinkis;
And carpit full cummerlik with cop going round.
    William Dunbar (c.1460–c.1520), The Tretis of the Twa Mariit
    Wemen and the Wedo

A double Scotch is about the size of a small Scotch before the War,
and a single Scotch is nothing more than a dirty glass.
    Lord Dundee (1872–1924)

There's nothing as good as a pot of kale with an auk in it.
    Old man from Deerness, Orkney, quoted in Alexander Fenton, Scottish
    Country Life *(1976)*. Kale: *broth*; auk: *guillemot*.

The cure for which there is no disease
    John Ferguson (fl. 19th century), on whisky

Whan big as burns the gutters rin,
Gin ye hae catcht a droukit skin,
To Luckie Middlemist's loup in,
And sit fu' snug
O'er oysters and a dram o' gin,
Or haddock lug
    Robert Fergusson (1750–1774), Auld Reekie

And they'd broth, it was good, and the oatcakes better; and then
boiled beef and potatoes and turnip; and then rice pudding with
prunes; and then some tea.
    Lewis Grassic Gibbon (James Leslie Mitchell, 1901–1935), Sunset Song

. . . when days of refinement came, old topers mourned over these
departed times when 'there were fewer glasses and more bottles'.
    H. Grey Graham, The Social Life of Scotland in the Eighteenth
    Century *(1899)*

Single malts must be drunk with circumspection. Contrary to the
old joke about the Highlander liking two things to be naked, one of
them whisky, malts are best drunk with a little water to bring out
the aroma and flavour.
    Neil M. Gunn (1891–1973), Whisky and Scotland

Oh, the dreadfu' curse o' drinkin'!
Men are ill, but to my thinkin',
Lookin' through the drucken fock,
There's a Jenny for ilk Jock.
> *Janet Hamilton (1795–1873)*, Oor Location

They drank the water clear,
Instead of wine, but yet they made good cheer.
> *Robert Henryson (c.1425–c.1500)*, The Town Mouse and the Country Mouse

In good company you need not ask who is the master of the feast.
The man who sits in the lowest place, and who is always industrious
in helping everyone, is certainly the man.
> *David Hume (1711–1776)*, Essays

He was a bold man who first swallowed an oyster.
> *Attributed to King James VI (1566–1625)*

But he does have a packet of potato crisps which he can stuff
between two slices of margarined bread. A piece on crisps. Aye
beautiful. Crunchy and munchy. And a cup of good strong coffee.
> *James Kelman (1946–)*, A Disaffection

How beit we want the spices and the winis,
Or uther strange fructis delicious,
We have als gude, and more needfull for us.
> *Sir David Lindsay (c.1490–1555)*, The Dreme of the Realme of Scotland

'He's dead now, but he lived to a great age. I mind him saying once
– he was fou' at the time – "Man, I've only got one vice, but it's
given me more pleasure than all my virtues." '
> *Eric Linklater (1899–1974)*, Magnus Merriman

Sausages is the boys!
> *Jimmy Logan (1928–2001), catch-phrase from the radio show 'It's All Yours'*

O English Food! How I adore looking forward
to you, Scotch trifle at the North British Hotel,
Princes Street, Edinburgh. Yes, it is good, very good,
the best in Scotland.
> *George Macbeth (1935–)*, An Ode to English Food

If it was raining, it was 'We'll have a dram to keep out the wet'; if it was cold, 'We'll have a dram to keep out the cold'; and if it was a fine day why then, 'We'll drink its health.'

> *J.A. MacCulloch, on Skye in the 19th century*

The majority of Glasgow pubs are for connoisseurs of the morose, for those who relish the element of degradation in all boozing . . . It is the old story of those who prefer hard-centre chocolates to soft, storm to sunshine, sour to sweet. True Scots always prefer the former of these opposites.

> *Hugh MacDiarmid (C.M. Grieve, 1892–1978)*, The Dour Drinkers of Glasgow

John: I tell you what, when I'm dead will you pour a bottle of the Talisker over my dead body?
Alex: Certainly, certainly, you won't mind if I pass it through the kidneys first.

> *John McGrath (1935–2002)*, The Cheviot, The Stag and the Black, Black Oil

Love makes the world go round? Not at all. Whisky makes it go round twice as fast.

> *Compton Mackenzie (1883–1972)*, Whisky Galore

When I came to my friend's house of a morning, I used to be asked if I had my morning draught yet? I am now asked if I have had my tea? And in lieu of the big quaigh with strong ale and toast, and after a dram of good wholesome Scots spirits, there is now the tea-kettle put to the fire, the tea table and silver and china equipage brought in, and marmalade and cream.

> *William Mackintosh of Borlum (1662–1743)*, Essay on Ways and Means of Enclosing

. . . it is a thoroughly democratic dish, equally available and equally honoured in castle, farm and croft. Finally, the use of the paunch of the animal as the receptacle of the ingredients gives the touch of romantic barbarism so dear to the Scottish heart.

> *F. Marian McNeill (1885–1973)*, The Scots Kitchen, *on haggis*

Just a wee deoch an doruis,
Just a wee drop, that's a';
Just a wee deoch an doruis,
Afore ye gang awa'.
There's a wee wifie waitin'
In a wee but-and-ben;
But if ye can say 'It's a braw bricht moonlicht nicht',
It's a' richt, ye ken.

    R.F. Morrison, sung by Sir Harry Lauder (1911)

'That's the thing that angers me aboot an egg,' continued the
Captain. 'It never makes ye gled to see it on the table; ye know at
once the thing's a mere put-by because your wife or Jum could not
be bothered makin' something tasty.'

    'We'll hae to get the hens to put their heids together and invent a
new kind o' fancy egg for sailors,' said Sunny Jim.

    Neil Munro (1864–1930), The Vital Spark

. . . though we're a' fearfu' fond o' oor parritch in Scotland, and
some men mak' a brag o' takin' them every mornin' just as if they
were a cauld bath, we're gey gled to skip them at a holiday and just
be daein' wi' ham and eggs.

    Neil Munro, Erchie, My Droll Friend

'The honestest thing I ever saw said aboot tea was in a grocer's
window in Inverness – Our Unapproachable: 2s6d.'

    Neil Munro, Jimmy Swan, The Joy Traveller

Fat say ye till a dram?

    Charles Murray (1864–1941), Docken Afore his Peers

Wha'll buy caller herrin'?
They're bonny fish and halesome fairin':
Wha'll buy caller herrin'
New-drawn frae the Forth?

    Lady Nairne (1766–1845), Caller Herrin'

A month without an R in it has nae richt being in the year.

    Christopher North (John Wilson, 1785–1854), Noctes Ambrosianae

He found that learnin', fame,
Gas, philanthropy, and steam,
Logic, loyalty, gude name,
Were a' mere shams;
That the source o' joy below,
An' the antidote to woe,
An' the only proper go,
Was drinkin' drams.

    George Outram (1805–1856), Drinkin' Drams

If the good Lord had wanted us to know about cuisine, he would never have given us crispy pancakes.

    Ian Pattison (1950–), The Rab C. Nesbitt Scripts *(1990)*

Good claret best keeps out the cauld,
And drives away the winter soon,
It makes a man baith gash and bauld,
And heaves his saul beyond the moon.

    Allan Ramsay (1686–1758), To the Phiz, an Ode

'Ach, it's sair cheenged times at Castle Grant, when gentlemans can gang to bed on their ain feet.'

    Dean E.B. Ramsay (1793–1872), Reminiscences of Scottish Life and Character

Here we are, progressing tenfold, buying the right bread, real croissants, we're making fresh muesli and we understand what a great cup of coffee is. And then some idiot brings out a deep-fried chocolate sandwich.

    Gordon Ramsay (1966–), chef

I had always an unbreakeable rule, and that was when things were looking thoroughly bad to go out to a restaurant and have a good dinner and a bottle of wine.

    John M. Robertson (1856–1933), 60th birthday speech

The boy flew at the oranges with the enthusiasm of a ferret finding the rabbit family at home after a long day of fruitless subterranean research.

    Saki (H.H. Munro, 1870–1916), The Toys of Peace

The cook was a good cook, as cooks go; and as good cooks go, she went.

    Saki, Reginald

'Lord, for what we are about to receive
Help us to be truly thankful – Aimen –
Wumman, ye've pit ingans in't again.'
     Tom Scott (1918–1995), Auld Sanct-Aundrians

A glass of wine is a glorious creature, and it reconciles poor
humanity to itself: and that is what few things can do.
     Sir Walter Scott (1771–1832)

. . . an overdose of the creature
     Sir Walter Scott, Guy Mannering

And there will be fadges and brochen,
Wi' fouth o' good gabbocks o' skate,
Powsowdie, and drammock and crowdie,
An' caller nowtfeet in a plate.
An' there will be partens and buckies,
And whitin's and speldin's enew,
And singit sheep's heid, and a haggis,
And scadlips to sup till ye spue.
     Attributed to Francis Sempill (c.1616–1682), The Wedding of Maggie
     and Jock

kys milk is best for butter, and yows milk best for cheiss, for kys
milk will give both mor butter and better butter than yows milk,
and yows milk will give both mor and better cheiss than kys milk.
     Skene of Hallyards, Manuscript of Husbandrie, *1665*

Tattie-scones, and the mealy-dot,
And a whack o' crumpy-crowdie;
And aye a bit pickle in the pat
For onie orra body.
     William Soutar (1898–1943), Hamely Fare

. . . drunk as owls
     Robert Louis Stevenson (1850–1894), Treasure Island

Fifteen men on a dead man's chest –
Yo-ho-ho, and a bottle of rum!
Drink and the devil had done for the rest –
Yo-ho-ho, and a bottle of rum!
     Robert Louis Stevenson, Treasure Island

Friends and Enemies

Friends are lost by calling often; and by calling seldom.
Anonymous

And may I ever have a friend,
In whom I safely may depend,
To crack a joke, or tell a tale,
Or share a pint of napppy ale.
Anonymous, The Frugal Wish

There is no treasure which may be compared
Unto a faithful friend.
Anonymous, Roxburghe Ballads

For much better it is
To bide a friend's anger than a foe's kiss.
Alexander Barclay (c.1475–1552), The Mirrour of Good Manners

To find a friend one must close one eye. To keep him – two.
Norman Douglas (1868–1952), Almanac

Here's to the friends we can trust
When storms of adversity blaw;
May they live in our songs and be nearest our hearts,
Nor depart like the year that's awa'.
John Dunlop (1755–1820), The Year That's Awa'

Here am I, who have written on all sorts of subjects calculated to
arouse hostility, moral, political, and religious; and yet I have no
enemies, except indeed, all the Whigs, all the Tories, and all the
Christians.
David Hume (1711–1776), quoted in Lord Brougham's Men of Letters
and Science in the Reign of George III

I do not know him quite so well
As he knows me.
Robert F. Murray (1863–1894), Adventure of a Poet

Should auld acquaintance be forgot, and never thought upon?
> *Francis Sempill (c.1616–1685), 'Auld Lang Syne', from James Watson's* Choice Collection of Scots Poems, *1711*

So long as we are loved by others I should say that we are almost indispensable; and no man is useless while he has a friend.
> *Robert Louis Stevenson (1850–1894)*

. . . the dearest friends are the auldest friends,
And the young are just on trial.
> *Robert Louis Stevenson,* It's an Owercome Sooth

When I came into Scotland I knew well enough what I was to expect from my enemies, but I little foresaw what I meet with from my friends.
> *Prince Charles Edward Stuart (1720–1788), letter, quoted in Blaikie,* Itinerary of Prince Charles Stuart *(1897)*

Human Nature

And muckle thocht our gudewife to hersell,
But never a word she spak.
Anonymous, Get Up and Bar the Door

It's pride puts a' the country doun,
Sae tak' your auld cloak about ye.
Anonymous, Tak' Your Auld Cloak About Ye

If happiness hae not her seat
An' centre in the breast,
We may be wise, or rich, or great,
But never can be blest.
Robert Burns (1759–1796), Epistle to Davie

But human bodies are sic fools,
For a' their colleges and schools,
That when nae real ills perplex them,
They mak enow themsels to vex them.
Robert Burns, The Twa Dogs

But, och, I backwards cast my e'e
On prospects drear!
And forward, though I canna see,
I guess, and fear.
Robert Burns, To a Mouse

I have everything here to make me happy except the faculty of
being happy.
Jane Welsh Carlyle (1801–1866), Letters

The greatest of faults, I should say, is to be conscious of none.
Thomas Carlyle (1795–1881), On Heroes, Hero-Worship, and the
Heroic in History

In all times and places the Hero has been worshipped. It will ever be so. We all love great men.

> *Thomas Carlyle*, On Heroes, Hero-Worship, and the Heroic in History

The barrenest of all mortals is the sentimentalist.

> *Thomas Carlyle*, Characteristics

We have not the love of greatness, but the love of the love of greatness.

> *Thomas Carlyle*, Essays

It is the restriction placed on vice by our social code which makes its pursuit so peculiarly agreeable.

> *Kenneth Grahame (1859–1932)*

The heart of man is made to reconcile contradictions.

> *David Hume (1711–1776)*, Essays, Moral, Political, and Literary

It is not contrary to reason to prefer the destruction of the whole world to the scratching of my finger.

> *David Hume*, A Treatise Upon Human Nature

a lie so obvious it was another way
of telling the truth

> *Norman MacCaig (1910–1996)*, Queen of Scots

The great men sayis that their distress
Comis for the peoples wickedness;
The people sayis for the transgressioun
Of great men, and their oppressioun:
Bot nane will their awin sin confess.

> *Sir Richard Maitland (1496–1586)*, How Suld Our Commonweill Endure

While exploring a particularly wild and uncultivated region of Africa, Mungo Park unexpectedly came across a gibbet. 'The sight of it', he later remarked, 'gave me infinite pleasure, as it proved that I was in a civilised society.'

> *Mungo Park (1771–1806)*, *quoted in C. Fadiman*, The Little, Brown Book of Anecdotes *(1985)*

Who grasped at earthly fame
Grasped wind
 Robert Pollok (1798–1827), The Course of Time

Oh, what a tangled web we weave,
When first we practice to deceive.
 Sir Walter Scott (1771–1832), Marmion

The sickening pang of hope deferr'd
 Sir Walter Scott, The Lady of the Lake

The cruellest lies are often told in silence.
 Robert Louis Stevenson (1850–1894), Virginibus Puerisque

I hate cynicism a great deal worse than I do the Devil; unless,
perhaps, the two were the same thing?
 Robert Louis Stevenson, Walt Whitman

The conscience has morbid sensibilities; it must be employed but
not indulged, like the imagination or the stomach.
 Robert Louis Stevenson, Ethical Studies

If it is for fame that men do brave actions, they are only silly fellows
after all.
 Robert Louis Stevenson, The English Admirals

But I strode on austere;
No hope could have no fear.
 James Thomson (1834–1882), The City of Dreadful Night

Insults

This is the savage pimp without dispute
First bought his mother for a prostitute;
Of all the miscreants ever went to hell,
this villain rampant bears away the bell.
> *Anonymous, on the first Duke of Lauderdale (1616–1682), Secretary for*
> *Scotland*

O Bute, if instead of contempt and of odium,
You wish to obtain universal eulogium,
From your breast to your gullet transfer the blue string,
Our hearts are all yours from the very first swing.
> *Anonymous pasquinade against Lord Bute (1713–1792), Prime Minister;*
> *quoted in Alan Lloyd,* The Wickedest Age

Wha called ye partan-face, my bonnie man?
> *John Buchan (1875–1940),* Prester John

Bright ran thy line, o Galloway,
Thro' many a far-fam'd sire;
So ran the far fam'd Roman way,
So ended in a mire.
> *Robert Burns (1759–1796), on the Earl of Galloway*

She tauld thee weel thou wast a skellum,
A blethering, blustering, drunken blellum
> *Robert Burns,* Tam o' Shanter

. . . a cursed old Jew, not worth his weight in cold bacon.
> *Thomas Carlyle (1795–1881), on Benjamin Disraeli, recorded in*
> *Monypenny and Buckle,* The Life of Benjamin D'Israeli, Lord
> Beaconsfield

It seldom pays to be rude. It never pays to be only half-rude.
> *Norman Douglas (1868–1952)*

Thae tarmegantis, with tag and atter,
Full loud in Ersche began to clatter,
And rowp lyk revin and ruke.
The devil sa devit was with thair yell,
That in the depest pot of hell
He smorit thame with smuke.

    William Dunbar (c.1460–c.1520), The Daunce of the Sevin Deidly
    Sinnis

I have ane wallidrag, ane worm, ane auld wobat carle.
A wastit wolroun, nae worth but wordis to clatter;
Ane bumbart, ane drone bee, ane bag full of flewme,
Ane skabbit skarth, ane scorpioun, ane scutard behind.

    William Dunbar, The Tretis of the Twa Mariit Wemen and the
    Wedo

He dois as dotit dog that damys on all bussis,
And liftis his leg apone loft, thoght he nought list pische

    William Dunbar, The Tretis of the Twa Mariit Wemen and the
    Wedo

Mandrag, mymmerkin, maid maister but in mows,
Thrys scheild trumpir with ane threid bair goun,
Say Deo mercy, or I cry the doun.
– Quod Kennedy to Dunbar
Iersche brybour bard, vyle beggar with thy brattis
Cuntbittin crawdoun Kennedy, coward of kynd . . .
Thy trechour tung hes tane ane heland strynd –
Ane lawland ers wald mak a bettir noyis.
–Quod Dunbar to Kennedy

    William Dunbar, The Flyting of Dunbar and Kennedie

One day, sitting opposite Charlemagne at a meal, that jester cruelly
asked: 'What is there betwixt Sottum and Scottum?' Quick came
the reply of John: 'The breadth of this table, Sire.'

    Arnold Fleming, The Medieval Scots Scholar in France, *on John
    Scotus (c.810–c.877)*

Today I pronunced a word which should never come out of a ladys
lips it was that I called John an Impudent Bitch

    Marjory Fleming (1803–1811), Journals

As for Gordon Brown – I've described him and Tony Blair as two cheeks of the same arse.
  George Galloway (1954–), 'Comment is Free', 9 May 2006

Something unique in natural history: the first-ever metamorphosis of a butterfly into a slug.
  George Galloway, on the writer Christopher Hitchens's support for the Iraq war, 14 September 2005

Weill, gin they arena deid, it's time they were.
  Robert Garioch (Robert Garioch Sutherland, 1909–1981), Elegy

You are, sir, a presumptuous, self-conceited pedagogue . . . a mildew, a canker-worm in the bosom of the Reformed Church
  James Hogg (1770–1835), The Private Memoirs and Confessions of a Justified Sinner

Though thou're like Judas, an apostate black,
In the resemblance thou dost one thing lack;
When he had gotten his ill-purchased pelf,
He went away and wisely hanged himself:
This thou may do at last, but yet I doubt
If thou hast any bowels to gush out.
  Charles Lamb (1775–1834), Epigram on Sir James Mackintosh

Servile and impertinent, shallow and pedantic, a bigot and a sot, bloated with family pride, and eternally blustering about the dignity of a born gentleman, yet stooping to be a talebearer, an eavesdropper, a common butt in the taverns of London.
  Lord Macaulay (1800–1859), on James Boswell

Ablachs, and scrats, and dorbels o' a' kinds
Aye'd drob me wi' their puir eel-dronin' minds,
Wee drochlin' craturs drutling their bit thochts
The dorty bodies! Feech! Nae Sassunach drings
'll daunton me.
  Hugh MacDiarmid (1892–1978), Gairmscoile *(on some contemporary versifiers)*

In spite of all their kind some elements of worth
With difficulty persist here and there on earth.
  Hugh MacDiarmid, Another Epitaph on an Army of Mercenaries

Here's your likeness again:
a wisp-headed scowler,
without hat or wig,
without headpiece or crest,
you're plucked bald and bare;
with mange at your elbows
and the scratch marks of itch at your arse.

> *Duncan Bàn MacIntyre (1724–1812),* Oran do'n Taillear *(Song for the Tailor)*

Ya knee-crept, Jesus-crept, swatchin' little fucker, ah'll cut the bliddy scrotum aff ye! Ah'll knacker and gut ye, ah'll eviscerate ye! Ya hure-spun, bastrified, conscrapulated young prick, ah'll do twenty years for mincin' you . . . ya parish-eyed, perishin' bastart.

> *Roddy Macmillan (1923–1979), The Bevellers (1973)*

The fattest hog in Epicurus' sty.

> *William Mason (1724–1797),* An Heroic Epistle to Sir William Chambers, *on David Hume*

Jemmy . . . in recording the noble growlings of the Great Bear, thought not of his own Scotch snivel.

> *Christopher North (John Wilson, 1785–1854), 'Noctes Ambrosianae', on James Boswell*

I was present in a large company at dinner, when Bruce was talking away. Someone asked him what musical instruments were used in Abyssinia. Bruce hesitated, not being prepared for the question, and at last said, 'I think I saw one lyre there.' George Selwyn whispered his next man, 'Yes, and there is one less since he left the country.'

> *Recorded of James Bruce (1730–1794), in John Pinkerton,* Walpoliana

Tommy, your mother should have kept her legs together.

> *Bill Shankly (1914–1981), when keeper Tommy Lawrence let in a goal*

Sin a' oor wit is in oor wame
Wha'll flyte us for a lack o' lair;
Oor guts maun glorify your name
Sin a' oor wit is in oor wame.

> *William Soutar (1898–1943),* From Any Burns Club to Scotland

... up to his death three years earlier she had been living with Lord Alfred Douglas, the fatal lover of Oscar Wilde, an arrangement which I imagine would satisfy any woman's craving for birth control ... I used to think it a pity that her mother rather than she had not thought of birth control.

Muriel Spark (1918–2006), Curriculum Vitae *(on Marie Stopes)*

These deathless names by this dead snake defiled
Bid memory spit upon him for their sake.

Algernon Swinburne (1837–1909), After Looking Into Carlyle's Reminiscences

The thermometer having been stolen from his sanctum, the said worthy editor announced that the mean cuss who took it might as well bring or send it back (no questions asked) for it could not be any use to him in the place where he was going, as it only registered up to 212 degrees.

James Thomson (1834–1882), Religion in the Rocky Mountains

People say that the Souness revolution was responsible for the rise in Rangers support but I think it's more to do with the Government Care in the Community policies, which threw these unfortunates on to the streets.

Irvine Welsh (1957–), interview on Erin Web, 1997

Journalism and News

The printing-press is either the greatest blessing or the greatest curse of modern times, one sometimes forgets which.
   Sir J.M. Barrie (1860–1937), Sentimental Tommy

The Press is the Fourth Estate of the realm.
   Thomas Carlyle (1795–1881), On Heroes, Hero-Worship, and the Heroic in History

The tyrant on the throne
Is the morning and evening press.
   John Davidson (1857–1909), Fleet Street Eclogues

Would you find that news in the Mearns Chief? – you wouldn't, so you knew it couldn't be true . . . Ay, the Mearns Chief was aye up-to-date, and showed you a photo of Mrs MacTavish winning the haggis at a Hogmanay dance.
   Lewis Grassic Gibbon (James Leslie Mitchell, 1901–1935), Cloud Howe

No news is better than evil news.
   King James VI (1566–1625), quoted in Loseley Manuscripts

He joined the *Daily Record* as Art editor – a position, he recalls, which had extremely little to do with art, and almost nothing to do with editing.
   Magnus Magnusson and others, The Glorious Privilege *(1979), on Sir Alastair Dunnett, editor of the* Scotsman, *1956–72*

As far as I'm concerned, Scotland will be reborn when the last minister is strangled with the last copy of the Sunday Post.
   Tom Nairn (1932–1963), 'The Three Dreams of Scottish Nationalism', in K. Miller, Memoirs of a Modern Scotland (1970)

We cultivate literature on a little oatmeal.
   Sydney Smith (1771–1845), proposed motto for the Edinburgh Review, but 'too near the truth to be admitted' quoted in Lady Holland, Memoir of the Rev. Sydney Smith

As a journalist, I rely on two qualifications, a congenital laziness, and a poor memory.
   Wilfred Taylor, Scot Free (1953)

Lamentations

When Alysandyr our King was dede
That Scotland led in luf and le,
Away was sons of ale and brede,
Of wine and wax, of gamyn and gle;
Our gold was changyd into lead.
Christ born into Virginitie
Succour Scotland and remede
That stad is in perplexytie.

 Anonymous

Half owre, half owre to Aberdour
'Tis fifty fathoms deep,
And there lies gude Sir Patrick Spens,
Wi' the Scots lords at his feet.

 Anonymous, Sir Patrick Spens

Ohone, alas, for I was the youngest,
And aye my weird it was the hardest.

 Anonymous, Cospatrick

O there is nane in Galloway,
There's nane at a' for me.
I ne'er lo'ed a lad but ane,
And he's drooned in the sea.

 Anonymous, The Lawlands o' Holland

Yestreen the Queen had four Maries,
The night she'll hae but three:
There was Marie Seton, and Marie Beaton,
And Marie Carmichael, and me.
O, little did my mither ken,
The day she cradled me,
The lands I was to travel in;
The death I was to dee.

 Anonymous, The Queen's Marie

To seek het water beneith cauld ice,
Surely it is a great folie –
I have asked grace at a graceless face,
But there is nane for my men and me!

 Anonymous, Johnie Armstrong

O Helen fair, beyond compare!
I'll mak' a garland o' thy hair,
Shall bind my heart for evermair,
Until the day I dee!
> *Anonymous*, Helen of Kirkconnel

I took his body on my back,
And whiles I gaed, and whiles I sat;
I digg'd a grave, and laid him in,
And happ'd him with the sod sae green.
> *Anonymous*, The Lament of the Border Widow

To have, to hold, and then to part
Is the great sorrow of the human heart
> *Inscription from St Monans Churchyard, Fife*

Dinna speak tae me o' the guid auld days,
For wha mair than me kens better;
Wha ran barefitted in ragged claes,
In summer days and winter.
> *Mary Brooksbank (1897–1980)*, 18 Dempster Street – The Guid
> Auld Bad Days

Farewell, ye dungeons dark and strong,
The wretch's destinie!
McPherson's time will not be long
On yonder gallows tree.
> *Robert Burns (1759–1796)*, McPherson's Farewell

They make a desert, and they call it peace.
> *Words about the Romans, ascribed to Calgacus, Caledonian war leader, at*
> *Mons Graupius, AD84, in Tacitus*, Agricola

Few, few shall part where many meet!
The snow shall be their winding-sheet,
And every turf beneath their feet
Shall be a soldier's sepulchre!
> *Thomas Campbell (1777–1844)*, Hohenlinden

I've seen the smiling of Fortune beguiling,
I've felt all its favours and found its decay
> *Alison Cockburn (1712–1794)*, The Flowers of the Forest

Quhome to sall I complene my wo,
And kyth my kairis ane or mo,
I knaw nocht amang rich nor pure
Quha is my freynd, quha is my fo;
For in the warld may none assure
    William Dunbar (c.1460–1520), None May Assure in This Warld

Now they are moaning on ilka green loaning,
The flowers o' the Forest are a' wede away.
    Jane Elliott (1727–1805), The Flowers o' the Forest

And aye the owercome o' his lilt
Was 'Wae's me for Prince Charlie!'
    William Glen (1789–1826), Wae's Me for Prince Charlie

My ae fald friend when I was hardest stad!
My hope, my heal, thou wast in maist honour!
. . . Though I began and took the war on hand.
I vow to God, that has the warld in wauld,
Thy deid sall be to Southeron full dear sauld.
    'Blind Harry' (fl.1490s), Wallace *(Lament for the Graham)*

Alas, Scotland, to whom sall thou complain:
Alas, fra pain who sall thee now restrain!
Alas, thy help is fastlie brought to ground,
Thy best chieftain in braith bandis is bound.
    'Blind Harry', Wallace

Ochane!
Now is my breist with stormy stoundis stad,
Wrappit in woe, ane wretch full of wane.
    Robert Henryson (c.1425–c.1500), The Testament of Cresseid

Woe to the realm that has owre young a king.
    Sir David Lindsay (c.1490–1555), Complaynt of the Common Weill
    of Scotland

Alas! How easily things go wrong!
A sigh too deep or a kiss too long,
And then comes a mist and a weeping rain,
And life is never the same again.
    George Macdonald (1824–1905), Phantastes

No more, no more, no more for ever
In war or peace shall return MacCrimmon;
No more, no more, no more for ever
Shall love or gold bring back MacCrimmon!

> *Norman MacLeod (1812–1872)*, Cumha mhic Criomein
> *('MacCrimmon's Lament') to a tune of Donald Bàn MacCrimmon*
> *(d. 1746), translated by J. S. Blackie*

He fell as the moon in a storm; as the sun from the midst of his
course, when clouds rise from the waste of the waves, when the
blackness of the storm inwraps the rocks of Ardannidir. I, like an
ancient oak on Morven, I moulder alone in my place. The blast has
lopped my branches away; and I tremble at the wings of the north.
Prince of warriors, Oscur my son! Shall I see thee no more.

> *James Macpherson (1736–1796)*, Fragments of Ancient Poetry

Roll on, ye dark-brown years, for ye bring no joy on your course.
Let the tomb open to Ossian, for his strength has failed. The sons
of the song are gone to rest; my voice remains, like a blast, that
roars, lonely, on a sea-surrounded rock, after the winds are laid.
The dark mist whistles there, and the distant mariner sees the
waving trees.

> *James Macpherson*, Ossian: Last Songs of Selma

In this new yeir I see but weir,
Nae cause to sing;
In this new yeir I see but weir,
Nae cause there is to sing.

> *Sir Richard Maitland (1496–1586)*, On the New Yeir 1560

Anis on a day I seemed a seemly sicht.
Thou wants the wight that never said thee nay:
Adieu for ay! This a lang gude nicht!

> *Alexander Montgomerie (c.1545–c.1611)*, A Lang Gude Nicht

I'll sing thine obsequies with trumpet sounds,
And write thine epitaph in blood and wounds.

> *Marquis of Montrose (1612–1650)*, Lines on the Execution of King
> Charles I

Mony a hert will brak in twa,
Should he ne'er come back again . . .
Sweet's the laverock's note, and lang,
Lilting wildly up the glen,
But aye to me he sings ae sang,
Will ye no' come back again?
. . . Better lo'ed ye canna be:
Will ye no' come back again?
> *Lady Nairne (1766–1845)*, Will Ye No' Come Back Again?

But woe awaits a country when
She sees the tears of bearded men.
> *Sir Walter Scott (1771–1832)*, Marmion

He is gone on the mountain,
He is lost to the forest,
Like a summer-dried fountain,
When our need was the sorest . . .
Fleet foot on the correi,
Sage counsel in cumber,
Red hand in the foray,
How sound is thy slumber!
> *Sir Walter Scott*, *'Coronach'*, *from* The Lady of the Lake

That year we thatched the house with snowflakes
> *Derick Thomson (1921–)*, *'Strathnaver'* (Srath Nabhair)

The Land

Tweed says to Till
Whit gars ye rin sae still?
Till says to Tweed,
Tho' ye rin fast
And I rin slaw,
For ae man that ye droon,
I droon twa.
Traditional

Ownership in land exists for the sake of the people; not the people
for the sake of the ownership.
John Stuart Blackie (1809–1895), The Scottish Highlanders and the
Land Laws

Then come and scour the Bens with me, ye jolly stalkers all,
With lawyers to defend your rights, and gillies at your call!
Those crofter carles may cross the sea, but we are masters here,
And say to all, both great and small, Let none disturb the deer.
John Stuart Blackie, The Scottish Highlanders and the Land Laws

. . . land of the omnipotent No
Alan Bold (1943–1998), A Memory of Death

Scotland the wee
Tom Buchan (1931–1995), Scotland the Wee

And well know within that bastard land
Hath wisdom's goddess never held command . . .
Whose thistle well betrays the niggard earth,
Emblem of all to whom the land gives birth:
Each genial influence nurtured to resist:
A land of meanness, sophistry, and mist.
Lord Byron (1788–1824), The Curse of Minerva

Our fathers fought, so runs the glorious tale,
To save you, country mine, from tyrants rash,
And now their bones and you are up for sale,
The smartest bidder buys for ready cash.
  J.R. Christie, My Native Land *(c.1910)*

But these I saw while you to butts were striding
Guided by servile ghillies to your sport.
Fast-rooted bracken where the corn once ripened;
Roofless and ruined homesteads by the score
  Helen B. Cruickshank (1886–1975), Shooting Guest, Nonconformist

Hame, hame, hame, hame, fain wad I be!
Hame, hame, hame, hame, to my ain countrie!
  Allan Cunningham (1784–1842) Hame, Hame, Hame

. . . ownership is really custodianship.
  Sir Frank Fraser Darling (1903–1979), Island Farm

Did not strong connections draw me elsewhere, I believe Scotland
would be the country I should choose to end my days in.
  Benjamin Franklin (1706–1790)

. . . and a darkness down on the land he loved better than his soul or
God.
  Lewis Grassic Gibbon (James Leslie Mitchell, 1901–1935), Sunset Song

Sea and sky and the folk who wrought and fought and were learned,
teaching and saying and praying, they lasted but as a breath, a mist
of fog in the hills, but the land was forever, it moved and changed
below you, but was forever, you were close to it and it to you, not at
a bleak remove it held you and hurted you.
  Lewis Grassic Gibbon, Sunset Song

This is my country
The land that begat me,
These windy spaces
Are surely my own.
  Sir Alexander Gray (1882–1967), Scotland

My name is Norval; on the Grampian hills
My father feeds his flocks
  John Home (1724–1808), Douglas

And oh! What grand's the smell ye'll get
Frae the neep-fields by the sea!

    Violet Jacob (1863–1946), The Neep Fields by the Sea

Once you get the hang of it, and apprehend the type, it is a most
beautiful and admirable little country – fit, for distinction etc., to
make up a trio with Italy and Greece.

    Henry James (1843–1916), Letter to Alice James (1878)

. . . in Scotland I felt as if in a second home, and that I was received
as a son, and never repudiated . . . The chief national characteristics
of the Scots are constancy and an unwearied perseverance.
These qualities have made that dreary and barren land a home of
prosperity, a flourishing paradise.

    Lajos Kossuth (1802–1894)

So this is your Scotland. It is rather nice, but dampish and Northern
and one shrinks a trifle under one's skin. For these countries, one
should be amphibian.

    D.H. Lawrence (1885–1930), Letter to Dorothy Brett, 1926

Scotland's an attitude of mind.

    Maurice Lindsay (1918–2009), Speaking of Scotland

Scotland small? Our multiform, our infinite Scotland small?
Only as a patch of hillside may be a cliché corner
To a fool who cries 'Nothing but heather!'

    Hugh MacDiarmid (C.M. Grieve, 1892–1978), Scotland Small?

We are the men
Who own your glen
Though you won't see us there –
In Edinburgh clubs
And Guildford pubs
We insist how much we care.

    John McGrath (1935–2002), The Cheviot, the Stag and the Black,
Black Oil

So – picture it, if you will, right there at the top of the glen,
beautiful vista – the Crammem Inn, High-Rise Motorcroft – all
finished in natural, washable, plastic granitette. Right next door, the
'Frying Scotsman' All Night Chipperama – with a wee ethnic bit,
Fingal's Café – serving seaweed suppers in the basket and draught
Drambuie.
　　John McGrath, The Cheviot, the Stag and the Black, Black Oil

And heavy on the slumber of the moorland
The hardship and poverty of the thousands
of crofters and the lowly of the lands
　　Sorley Maclean (1911–1996), The Cuillin

It's the far Cuillins that are puttin' love on me,
As step I wi' the sunlight for my load . . .
Sure, by Tummel and Loch Rannoch an' Lochaber I will go,
By heather tracks wi' heaven in their wiles . . .
It's the blue Islands that are pullin' me away,
Their laughter puts the leap upon the lame.
　　Kenneth MacLeod (1871–1955), The Road to the Isles

The place commanded us by God,
where we can't travel moor or strand,
and every bit of fat or value
they have grabbed with Land Law from us.
　　Mary Macpherson (1821–1898), Brosnachadh nan Gaidheal
　　(Incitement of the Gaels, translated by William Neill)

This is a difficult country, and our home.
　　Edwin Muir (1887–1959), The Difficult Land

Scotland is bounded on the South by England, on the East by the
rising sun, on the North by the arory-bory-Alice and on the West
by Eternity.
　　Nan Shepherd (1893–1981), Quarry Wood

This is the land God gave to Andy Stewart –
　　Iain Crichton Smith (1928–1998), The White Air of March

The earth eats everything there is.
　　Iain Crichton Smith, The Earth Eats Everything

That garret of the earth – that knuckle-end of England – that land
of Calvin, oatcakes, and sulphur.

> *Sydney Smith (1771–1845), quoted in Lady Holland,* A Memoir of the
> Rev. Sydney Smith *(1855)*

When shall I see Scotland again? Never shall I forget the happy
days I passed there, amidst odious smells, barbarian sounds, bad
suppers, excellent hearts, and most enlightened and cultivated
understanding.

> *Sydney Smith*

Blows the wind today, and the sun and the rain are flying,
Blows the wind on the moors today and now,
Where about the graves of the martyrs the whaups are crying,
My heart remembers how!

> *Robert Louis Stevenson (1850–1894),* Blows the Wind Today

I have never seen such an unspoiled and dramatic sea side landscape
and the location makes it perfect for our development.

> *Donald Trump, in Trump International Golf Links website, 2011*

Scotland is the country above all others that I have seen, in which
a man of imagination may carve out his own pleasures; there are so
many inhabited solitudes.

> *Dorothy Wordsworth (1771–1855),* Recollections of a Tour Made in
> Scotland

The Law

Let them bring me prisoners, and I'll find them law.
> Lord Braxfield (1722–1799), Tory judge of the Court of Session

Muckle he made o' that – he was hanget.
> Lord Braxfield, in a political trial, in reply to the plea that Jesus Christ too was a reformer, quoted by Lord Cockburn in Memorials of His Time (1856)

Ye're a verra clever chiel', man, but ye'll be nane the waur o' a hanging.
> Lord Braxfield, to a defendant, quoted by J.G. Lockhart, Memoirs of the Life of Sir Walter Scott (1837–8)

A fig for those by law protected!
Liberty's a glorious feast!
Courts for cowards were erected,
Churches built to please the priest
> Robert Burns (1759–1796), The Jolly Beggars

I knew a very wise man . . . he believed that if a man were permitted to make all the ballads, he need not care who should make the laws of a nation.
> Andrew Fletcher of Saltoun (1653–1716), An Account of a Conversation Concerning a Right Regulation of Governments for the Common Good of Mankind

. . . when a poor man was found guilty by his master, the proprietor of Ballindalloch, and put into the pit until the gallows was prepared, he drew a short sword and declared he would kill the first man that put a hand on him, his wife remonstrated and prevailed on him with the argument, 'Come up quietly and be hanged, and do not anger the laird.'
> 'Hall's Travels in Scotland', quoted in Graham, The Social Life of Scotland in the Eighteenth Century

We advocates are trained to laugh at judges' jokes. It's the way they tell them.

> *Ian Hamilton QC (1925–), blog, 30 September 2011*

Justice may nocht have dominatioun,
But where Peace makis habitatioun.

> *Sir David Lindsay (c.1490–1555),* The Dreme of the Realme of Scotland

A Judge has sentenced himself to a suicide's grave?
– The nearest to a just sentence any judge ever gave.

> *Hugh MacDiarmid (C.M. Grieve, 1892–1978),* A Judge Commits Suicide

When ane of them sustenis wrang,
We cry for justice' heid, and hang;
But when our neichbours we owr-gang
We lawbour justice to delay.

> *Sir Richard Maitland (1496–1586),* Satire on the Age

Never give your reasons; for your judgement will probably be right, but your reasons almost certainly will be wrong.

> *Lord Mansfield (1705–1793),* Advice to Judges

Here enter not Attorneys, Barristers,
Nor bridle-champing law-Practitioners:
Clerks, Commissaries, Scribes nor Pharisees,
Wilful disturbers of the People's ease:
Judges, destroyers, with an unjust breath,
Of honest men, like dogs, ev'n unto death.
Your salary is at the gibbet-foot:
Go drink there.

> *François Rabelais,* Gargantua and Pantagruel, *translated by Sir Thomas Urquhart (1611–1660)*

. . . that bastard verdict, Not proven. I hate that Caledonian medium quid. One who is not proven guilty is innocent in the eye of law.

> *Sir Walter Scott (1771–1832),* Journal, *1827*

There are two sides to every story and one loses. Why do we not have perjury trials every day?

> *Tommy Sheridan (1964–), on trial for perjury, 2010*

No laws, however stringent, can make the idle industrious, the thriftless provident, or the drunken sober.
   Samuel Smiles (1812–1904) Self-Help

. . . you are a most notorious offender. You stand convicted of sickness, hunger, wretchedness, and want.
   Tobias Smollett (1721–1771), The Expedition of Humphrey Clinker

Love

Follow love, and it will flee:
Flee it, and it follows ye.
    Anonymous

It is a pity I was not with the Black-haired Lad on the brow of the
hill under the rainstorms, in a small hollow of the wilds or in some
secret place; and I'll not take a greybeard while you come to my
mind.
    Anonymous, from Gaelic, translated by Kenneth Jackson

The white bloom of the blackthorn, she;
The small sweet raspberry blossom, she;
More fair the shy, rare glance of her eye
Than the world's wealth to me.
    From Gaelic

My heart is heich abufe,
My body is full of bliss,
For I am set in lufe,
As weil as I wald wiss.
    Anonymous, My Heart is Heich Abufe

Ane lad may luve ane lady of estate
Ane lord ane lass: luve has no uthir law.
Wha can undo that is predestinate?
    Anonymous

I lean'd my back unto an aik,
I thought it was a trusty tree;
But first it bow'd, and syne it brak,
Sae my true love did lightly me.
O waly, waly! but love be bonnie
A little time, while it is new;
But when 'tis auld, it waxeth cauld,
And fades away like morning dew.
    Anonymous, O Waly, Waly

And wow! but they were lovers dear,
And lov'd fu' constantlie;
But ay the mair when they fell out,
The sairer was their plea.

Anonymous, Young Benjie

Why weep ye by the tide, ladye,
Why weep ye by the tide?
I'll wed ye to my youngest son,
And ye shall be his bride.
And ye shall be his bride, ladye,
Sae comely to be seen:
But aye she loot the tear doon fa'
For Jock o' Hazeldean.

Anonymous, Jock o' Hazeldean

Willie's rare, and Willie's fair;
And Willie's wondrous bonny:
And Willie hecht to marry me,
Gin e'er he married ony.

Anonymous, Willie's Rare

Tho' his richt e'e doth skellie, an' his left leg doth limp ill,
He's won the heart and got the hand of Kate Dalrymple.

Anonymous, Kate Dalrymple

Kissed yestreen, and kissed yestreen,
Up the Gallowgate, down the Green:
I've woo'd wi' lords, and woo'd wi' lairds
I've mool'd wi' carles, and mell'd wi' cairds

Anonymous

A fine wee lass, a bonnie wee lass, is bonnie wee Jeannie McColl;
I gave her my mother's engagement ring and a bonnie wee tartan
shawl.
I met her at a waddin' in the Co-operative Hall;
I wis the best man and she was the belle of the ball.

Twentieth-century music hall song

My beloved sall ha'e this he'rt tae break,
Reid, reid wine and the barley cake,
A he'rt tae break, and a mou' tae kiss,
Tho' he be nae mine, as I am his.

Marion Angus (1866–1946), Mary's Song

Gif she to my desire wad listen,
I wadna caa the king my cuisin.
    J.K. Annand (1908–1993), My Weird Is Comforted

Yes, I have died for love, as others do;
But praised be God, it was in such a sort
That I revived within an hour or two.
    Sir Robert Ayton (1570–1638), On Love

If I ever really love it will be like Mary Queen of Scots, who said
of her Bothwell that she could follow him round the world in her
nighty.
    Sir J.M. Barrie (1860–1937), What Every Woman Knows

But twice unhappier is he, I lairn,
That feedis in his hairt a mad desire,
And follows on a woman throw the fire,
Led by a blind and teachit by a bairn.
    Mark Alexander Boyd (1563–1601), Cupid and Venus

. . . a certain delicious Passion, which in spite of acid
Disappointment, gin-horse Prudence and bookworm Philosophy, I
hold to be the first of human joys, our dearest pleasure here below
. . . Thus with me began Love and Poesy.
    Robert Burns (1759–1796), Letter to Dr John Moore

What can a young lassie, what shall a young lassie,
What can a young lassie do wi' an auld man?
    Robert Burns, What Can a Young Lassie Do Wi' an Auld Man?

She is a winsome wee thing,
She is a handsome wee thing,
She is a lo'esome wee thing,
This dear wee wife o' mine.
    Robert Burns, My Wife's a Winsome Wee Thing

Bonie wee thing, cannie wee thing,
Lovely wee thing, wert thou mine,
I would hold thee in my bosom,
Lest my jewel I should tine.
    Robert Burns, Bonie Wee Thing

My luve is like a red, red rose,
That's newy sprung in June;
My luve is like a melody,
That's sweetly play'd in tune.
But fair thou art, my bonie lass,
So deep in luve am I;
And I will luve thee still, my dear,
Till a' the seas gang dry.
Till all the seas gang dry, my dear,
And the rocks melt wi' the sun,
And I will love thee still, my dear,
While the sands o' life shall run.

Robert Burns, My Luve is Like a Red, Red Rose

Yestreen, when to the trembling string
The dance gaed through the lighted ha',
To thee my fancy took its wing,
I sat, but neither heard nor saw:
Tho' this was fair, and that was braw,
And yon the toast of a' the town,
I sigh'd, and said amang them a',
Ye are na Mary Morison.

Robert Burns, Mary Morison

I'll meet thee on the lea-rig,
My ain kind dearie, O

Robert Burns, My Ain Kind Dearie

My love she's but a lassie yet;
My love she's but a lassie yet:
We'll let her stand a year or twa:
She'll nae be half sae saucy yet.

Robert Burns, My Love She's But a Lassie Yet

Wi' lightsome heart I pu'd a rose
Fu' sweet upon its thorny tree:
But my fause lover staw my rose,
But oh! he left the thorn wi' me.

Robert Burns, Ye Banks and Braes o' Bonnie Doon

But steal me a blink o' your bonnie black e'e,
Yet look as if ye werena lookin' at me . . .
O whistle and I'll come to you, my lad.

Robert Burns, O Whistle and I'll Come to You

Had we never lov'd sae kindly,
Had we never lov'd sae blindly,
Never met – or never parted,
We had ne'er been broken-hearted.
> *Robert Burns*, Parting Song to Clarinda

If doughty deeds my lady please,
Right soon I'll mount my steed . . .
Then tell me how to woo thee, Love,
O tell me how to woo thee!
> *R.B. Cunninghame Graham (1852–1936)*, Tell Me How to Woo
> Thee

Her brow is like the snaw-drift,
Her neck is like the swan;
Her face it is the fairest
That e'er the sun shone on.
That e'er the sun shone on,
And dark blue is her e'e:
And for bonnie Annie Laurie
I'd lay me doun and dee.
> *William Douglas (fl. c.1700)*, Annie Laurie

The flow'rs did smile, like those upon her face,
And as their aspen stalks those fingers band,
That she might read my case,
A hyacinth I wish'd me in her hand.
> *William Drummond (1585–1649)*, Like the Italian Queen

How silly and how dear, how very dear
To send a dehydrated porcupine
By letter post, with love.
> *Ian Hamilton Finlay (1925–1996)*, Gift

So it was she knew she liked him, loved him as they said in the
soppy English books, you were shamed and a fool to say that in
Scotland.
> *Lewis Grassic Gibbon (James Leslie Mitchell, 1901–1935)*, Sunset Song

At lufis lair gif thou will lear,
Tak there ane a b c:
Be heynd, courtass, and fair of feir,
Wyse, hardy and free
> *Robert Henryson (c.1425–c.1500)*, Robene and Makyne

Give me the highest joy
That the heart o' man can frame:
My bonnie, bonnie lassie,
When the kye come hame.
  James Hogg (1770–1835), When the Kye Come Hame

But O, her artless smile's mair sweet,
Than hinny or than marmalete.
  James Hogg, My Love She's But a Lassie Yet

'Oh Mary, ye're wan in a million.'
'Oh, oh, and so's yer chances.'
  Ron Clark and Carl McDougall, Cod Liver Oil and the Orange Juice

So ferre I falling into lufis dance,
That sodeynly my wit, my contenance,
My hert, my will, my nature and my mynd,
Was changit clene rycht in ane other kind.
  King James I (1394–1437), The Kingis Quair

How they strut about, people in love,
How tall they grow, pleased with themselves
  Jackie Kay (1961–), Late Love

Art ye on sleip, quod she. O fye for shame!
Haf ye nocht tauld that luifaris takis no rest?
  Alexander Montgomerie (c.1545–c.1611), A Dream

'If you're goin' to speak aboot love, be dacent and and speak aboot it
in the Gaalic. But we're no talkin' aboot love: we're talkin' aboot my
merrage.'
  Neil Munro (1864–1930), The Vital Spark

Ye're a bonny lad, and I'm a lassie free,
Ye're welcomer to tak' me than to let me be.
  Allan Ramsay (1686–1758), The Gentle Shepherd

The Yellow-haired Laddie sat doon on yon brae,
Cries – Milk the ewes, Lassie! Let nane o' them gae!
And ay she milked, and aye she sang –
The Yellow-haired Laddie shall be my gudeman!
  Allan Ramsay, The Yellow-Haired Laddie

While hard and fast I held her in my grips,
My very saul came lowping to my lips.
   Allan Ramsay, The Gentle Shepherd

Love is ane fervent fire
Kendillit without desire;
Short pleasure, lang displeasure,
Repentence is the hire
   Alexander Scott (c.1520–c.1590), A Rondel of Luve

Whatten ane glaikit fule am I
To slay myself with melancholy,
Sen weill I ken I may nocht get her?
   Alexander Scott, To Luve Unluvit

O ye'll tak' the high road,
And I'll tak' the low road:
And I'll be in Scotland afore ye;
But me and my true love will never meet again,
By the bonnie, bonnie banks o' Loch Lomond.
   Lady John Douglas Scott (1810–1900), Loch Lomond

Love swells like the Solway, but ebbs like its tide.
   Sir Walter Scott (1771–1832), Lochinvar

Love rules the court, the camp, the grove,
And men below and saints above;
For love is heaven, and heaven is love.
   Sir Walter Scott, The Lay of the Last Minstrel

Thy fatal shafts unerring move,
I bow before thine altar, Love.
   Tobias Smollett (1721–1771), The Adventures of Roderick Random

A' thru the nicht we spak nae word
Nor sinder'd bane frae bane:
A' thru the nicht I heard her hert
Gang soundin' wi' my ain.
   William Soutar (1898–1943), The Tryst

I will make you brooches and toys for your delight
Of bird-song at morning and star-shine at night.
   Robert Louis Stevenson (1850–1894), Romance

Absences are a good influence in love, and keep it bright and delicate.

    Robert Louis Stevenson, Virginibus Puerisque

We always believe our first love is our last, and our last love our first.

    George Whyte-Melville (1821–1878)

Men and Women

Though all the wood under the heaven that growis
Were crafty pennis convenient to write . . .
All the men were writtaris that ever took life
Could not not write the false dissaitful despite
And wicketness contenit in a wife.
    Anonymous

When Aberdeen and Ayr are baith ae toun,
And Tweed sall turn and rinnis into Tay . . .
When Paradise is quit of heavenly hue,
She whom I luve sall steadfast be and true.
    Anonymous

Gif ye'll not wed a tocherless wife,
A wife will ne'er wed ye.
    Anonymous, Lord Thomas and Fair Annet

'A bed, a bed,' Clerk Saunders said,
'A bed for you and me.'
'Fye na, fye na,' said may Margaret,
'Till anes we married be.'
    Anonymous, Clerk Saunders

I'll wager, I'll wager, I'll wager wi' you
Five hundred merks and ten,
That a maid shanna gae to the bonny broom
And a maiden return again.
    Anonymous, The Broomfield Hill

Word is to the kitchen gane,
And word is to the ha'.
And word is to the noble room
Amang the ladies a',
That Marie Hamilton's brought to bed,
And the bonny babe's miss'd and awa'.
    Anonymous, The Queen's Marie

Then up sho gat ane meikle rung
And the gudeman made to the door;
Quoth he, 'Dame, I sall hauld my tongue,
For, an we fecht, I'll get the waur.'
> *Anonymous*, The Wife of Auchtermuchty

Bell, my wife, she lo'es nae strife,
But she would guide me if she can;
And to maintain an easy life,
I aft maun yield, though I'm gudeman.
> *Anonymous*, Tak' Your Auld Cloak About Ye

Rosebery to his lady says,
'My hinnie and my succour,
O shall we dae the thing ye ken.
Or shall we hae our supper?'
Wi' modest face, sae fu' o' grace
replies the bonnie lady,
'My lord, ye may do as ye please:
But supper is na ready.'
> *Anonymous, 18th century*

Can spirit from the tomb, or fiend from Hell,
More hateful, more malignant be than man?
> *Joanna Baillie (1762–1851)*, Orra

You see, dear, it is not true that woman was made from man's rib;
she was really made from his funny bone.
> *Sir J.M. Barrie (1860–1937)*, What Every Woman Knows

Wisdom hath no sex.
> *John Stuart Blackie (1809–1895)*, The Wise Men of Greece

Ye stupid auld bitch . . . I beg your pardon, mem, I mistook ye for
my wife.
> *Attributed to Lord Braxfield (1722–1799), to his partner at whist*

Lissy, I am looking out for a wife, and I thought you just the person
that would suit me. Let me have your answer, aff or on, the morn,
and nae mair about it.
> *Lord Braxfield's proposal to his second wife, recorded in John Kay,*
> Original Portraits *(1877)*

O gie the lass her fairin, lad,
O gie the lass her fairin,
An' something else she'll gie to you
That's waly worth the wearin
> *Robert Burns (1759–1796)*, Gie the Lass Her Fairin

O wha my babie-clouts will buy,
O wha will tent me when I cry;
Wha will kiss me where I lie,
The rantin' dog the daddie o't.
> *Robert Burns*, The Rantin' Dog the Daddie O't.

... our hame
Where sits our sulky, sullen dame,
Gathering her brows like gathering storm,
Nursing her wrath to keep it warm.
> *Robert Burns*, Tam o' Shanter

Ah, gentle dames! it gars me greet,
To think how mony counsels sweet,
How mony lengthen'd, sage advices,
The husband frae the wife despises!
> *Robert Burns*, Tam o' Shanter

Fra my tap-knot to my tae, John,
I'm like the new fa'n snow:
And it's a' for your convenience,
John Anderson, my Jo.
> *Robert Burns*, John Anderson, My Jo, *bawdy version*

There's some are fou' o' love divine;
There's some are fou' o' brandy;
And many jobs that day begin,
May end in 'houghmagandie'
Some ither day.
> *Robert Burns*, The Holy Fair

Gin a body meet a body,
Comin' through the rye;
Gin a body kiss a body,
Need a body cry?
Ilka lassie has her laddie,

Nane, they say, ha'e I:
Yet a' the lads they smile at me,
When comin' through the rye.
    Robert Burns, Comin' Through the Rye

Clever men are good; but they are not the best.
    Thomas Carlyle (1795–1881), Goethe

What is man? A foolish baby;
Vainly strives, and fights, and frets;
Demanding all, deserving nothing,
One small grave is all he gets.
    Thomas Carlyle, Cui Bono

Thus does society naturally divide itself into four classes:
Noblemen, Gentlemen, Gigmen, and Men.
    Thomas Carlyle, Essays

There was a singular race of excellent Scotch old ladies. They were
a delightful set; strong-headed, warm-hearted and high-spirited;
the fire of their temper not always latent; merry even in solitude;
very resolute; indifferent about the modes and habits of the modern
world
    Henry Thomas Cockburn (1779–1854), Memorials

The souls of men that pave their hell-ward path
With women's souls lose immortality.
    John Davidson (1857–1909), Smith

There is not a maid, wife or widow, whose fancy any man, if he set
himself to it, could not conquer; nor any man whom any woman
could not subdue if she chose.
    John Davidson, A Romantic Farce

Man thinks more, woman feels more. He discovers more but
remembers less; she is more receptive and less forgetful.
    Sir Patrick Geddes (1854–1932), The Evolution of Sex *(with J. Arthur*
    Thomson)

Lie over to me from the wall or else
Get up and clean the grate.
    W.S. Graham (1918–1986), Baldy Bane

Donnchadh Bàn Mac an t-Saoir, commonly known as Duncan
Bàn MacIntyre, wrote a song to his fair young Mhàiri after their
marriage saying that he had put his net into the clear fresh water,
drawn it ashore and landed from it a sea-trout as shining as a swan
on the sea. Then one morning Donnchadh Bàn (who could neither
read nor write) lay in bed in their heather-thatched cabin in Glen
Orchy, composing.

It was raining, rain came in, drip, drip, drip on to the bed. Not to
be interrupted in the inexorability of composition, the inexorability
of the poem (perhaps it was his 'Misty Corrie'), Donnchadh Bàn
called 'Out with you and put some heather on, fair young Mhàiri.
It's raining.'

Or so it is said.

> *Geoffrey Grigson (1905–1985)*, The Private Art: A Poetry Notebook
> *(1982)*

What better school for manners than the company of virtuous
women?

> *David Hume (1711–1776)*, Essays

. . . as I took a particular pleasure in the company of modest women,
I had no reason to be displeased with the reception I got from them.

> *David Hume*, My Own Life

Women, destined by nature to be obedient, ought to be disciplined
early to bear wrongs without murmuring. This is a hard lesson; and
yet it is necessary even for their own sake.

> *Lord Kames (1696–1782)*, Loose Hints Upon Education

For men were just a perfect nuisance – wasn't that so, now? My
goodness me! No wonder women always aged much quicker than
their menfolk, considering all they had to put up with

> *Jessie Kesson (Jessie Grant Macdonald, 1916–1994)*, A Glitter of Mica

To promote a Woman to beare rule, superioritie, dominion, or
empire above any Realme, Nation or Citie, is repugnant to Nature;
contumelie to God, a thing most contrary to his revealed will and
approved ordinance; and finallie it is the subversion of good Order,
of all equitie and justice.

> *John Knox (c.1513–1572)* The First Blast of the Trumpet Against the
> Monstrous Regiment of Women

I gang like a ghaist, and I carena to spin;
I daurna think on Jamie, for that wad be a sin;
But I'll do my best a gude wife aye to be,
For auld Robin Gray he is kind unto me,
    Lady Anne Lindsay (1750–1826), Auld Robin Gray

Oh I am wild-eyed, unkempt, hellbent, a harridan.
My sharp tongue will shrivel any man.
    Liz Lochhead (1947–), Harridan

Oh, we spill the beans and we swill our gin,
and discover we're Sisters Under The Skin.
    Liz Lochhead, True Confessions

I must say here that the race of true Scotswomen, iron women,
hardy, indomitable, humorous, gay, shrewd women with an amazing
sense of values, seems to be facing extinction too in today's
Scotland.
    Hugh MacDiarmid (C.M. Grieve, 1892–1978), Lucky Poet

And you sall hae my breists like stars,
My limb like willow wands,
And on my lips ye'll heed nae mair,
And in my hair forget,
The seed o' a' the men that in
My virgin womb ha'e met.
    Hugh MacDiarmid, A Drunk Man Looks at the Thistle

'Buffers like yon would stop the Flying Scotsman going full tilt at
Longniddry,' Binnie said. 'Fine I'd like a wee sit-out with her.'
    Bruce Marshall (1889–1987), Teacup Terrace

For there's nae luck aboot the hoose,
There's nae luck at a';
There's little pleasure in the hoose,
When our gudeman's awa'.
    W.J. Mickle (1734–1788), The Mariner's Wife

'Is't a laddie or a lassie?' said the gardener. 'A laddie,' said the maid.
'Weel,' says he, 'I'm glad o' that, for there's ower many women in
the world.' 'Hech, man,' said Jess, 'div ye no ken there's aye maist
sawn o' the best crap?'
    Dean E.B. Ramsay (1793–1872), Reminiscences of Scottish Life and
    Character

Frae flesher Rab that lived in Crieff,
A bonnie lassie wanted to buy some beef;
He took her in his arms, and doun they did fa',
And the wind blew the bonnie lassie's plaidie awa'.
> *'Blind Rob' (early 19th century)*, The Wind Blew the Bonnie Lassie's
> Plaidie Awa'

O woman! in our hours of ease
Uncertain, coy and hard to please . . .
When pain and anguish wring the brow,
A ministering angel thou!
> *Sir Walter Scott (1771–1832)*, Marmion

Woman's faith and woman's trust,
Write the characters in dust.
> *Sir Walter Scott*, The Betrothed

I no great Adam and you no bright Eve
> *Iain Crichton Smith (1928–1998)*, At the Firth of Lorne

The brooding boy and sighing maid,
Wholly fain and half afraid.
> *Robert Louis Stevenson (1850–1894)*, Underwoods

To marry is to domesticate the Recording Angel.
> *Robert Louis Stevenson*, Virginibus Puerisque

She oped the door, she loot him in:
He cuist aside his dreepin' plaidie:
'Blaw your warst, ye wind and rain,
Since Maggie, now, I'm in aside ye.'
> *Robert Tannahill (1774–1810)*, Oh! Are Ye Sleepin', Maggie?

He saw her charming, but he saw not half
The charms her downcast modesty concealed.
> *James Thomson (1700–1748)*, The Seasons

He worried about her, however; thinking that anyone who would
sleep with him would sleep with anybody.
> *Irvine Welsh (1957–)*, Trainspotting

The Mind and Medicine

Up the close and doun the stair,
But an' ben wi' Burke an' Hare.
Burke's the butcher, Hare's the thief,
Knox the boy that buys the beef.
  Anonymous, 19th century, The West Point Murders

I find I'm haunted with a busie mind . . .
O what a wandring thing's the Mind!
What contrares are there combin'd?
  John Barclay (late 17th century)

'What are ye gaun to get frae her?'
'A big cup o' Greegory's Mixtur' wi' a Queen Anne Pooder in it.'
'Will ye tak' that?'
'I'll get naething else to eat till I dae.'
  J.J. Bell (1871–1934), Wee McGreegor

Any really good doctor ought to be able to tell before a patient has
fairly sat down, a good deal of what is the matter with him or her.
  Joseph Bell (1837–1911), quoted in Joseph Bell: An Appreciation by an
  Old Friend *(1913)*

My curse upon your venom'd stang,
That shoots my tortur'd gooms alang,
An' thro' my lug gies mony a twang.
  Robert Burns (1759–1796), Address to the Toothache

I am more and more persuaded that there is no complete misery in
the world that does not emanate from the bowels.
  Jane Welsh Carlyle (1801–1866), Letter to Eliza Stoddart (1834)

I'm schizophrenic, and so am I.
  Billy Connolly (1942–)

Minds are like parachutes. They only function when they are open.
  James Dewar (1842–1923), physicist (attributed)

Whenever patients come to I,
I physics, bleeds and sweats 'em;
If after that they choose to die,
What's that to me! – I letts 'em.
> *Thomas, Lord Erskine (1750–1823)*, Epigram on Dr John Lettsom

I've never met a healthy person who worried much about his health,
or a good person who worried about his soul.
> *J.B.S. Haldane (1892–1964)*

Herein is not only a great vanity, but a great contempt of God's
good gifts, that the sweetness of men's breath, being a good gift of
God, should be wilfully corrupted by this stinking smoke.
> *King James VI (1566–1625)*, A Treatise Against Tobacco

There is no seventh sense of the mystic kind . . . But if there is not a
distinct magnetic sense, I say it is a very great wonder that there is
not.
> *Lord Kelvin (1824–1907), presidential address to the Birmingham and
> Midland Institute*

The fumes rose hotly from the new-tarred surface. 'Best cure in the
world for whooping-cough,' her mother always said. 'Nonsense,'
her father had countered, for he had no faith in miracles. You went
when your time came. Tar or no tar.
> *Jessie Kesson (Jessie Grant Macdonald, 1916–1994)*, Where the Apple
> Ripens

We are born into a world where alienation awaits us.
> *R.D. Laing (1927–1989)*, The Politics of Experience

Madness need not be all breakdown. It may also be breakthrough.
> *R.D. Laing*, The Politics of Experience

There is no such condition as 'schizophrenia'; but the label is a
social fact and the social fact a political event.
> *R.D. Laing, The Politics of Experience*

As the chill snow is friendly to the earth,
And pain and loss are friendly to the soul,
Shielding it from the black heart-killing frost;
So madness is but one of God's pale winters.
> *George Macdonald (1824–1905)*, A Story of the Sea-Shore

I wrote to my wife, 'I have seen something very promising indeed in my new mosquitoes' and I scribbled the following unfinished verses in one of my In Exile notebooks, in pencil:

This day designing God
Hath put into my hand
a wondrous thing. And God
Be praised. At His command
I have found thy secret deeds,
O million-murdering Death.

> *Sir Ronald Ross (1857–1932)*, Memoirs

I think for my part one-half of the nation is mad – and the other not very sound.

> *Tobias Smollett (1721–1771)*, The Adventures of Sir Launcelot Greaves

Sic a hoast hae I got:
Sic a hoast hae I got:
I dout my days are on the trot

> *William Soutar (1898–1943)*, Sic a Hoast

Every man has a sane spot somewhere.

> *Robert Louis Stevenson (1850–1894)*, The Wrecker *(with Lloyd Osbourne)*

Ah'm no sick yet, but it's in the fuckin post, that's fir sure.

> *Irvine Welsh (1957–)*, Trainspotting

Monsters

The side was steep, and the bottom deep;
From bank to bank the water pouring;
The bonny grey mare she swat for fear,
For she heard the water-kelpie roaring.
    Anonymous, Annan Water

'What wae hae ye sic a sma' sma' neck?'
'Aih-h-h! – late – and wee-e-e moul.'
'What way hae ye sic a muckle, muckle heid?'
'Muckle wit, muckle wit.'
'What do you come for?'
'For you.'
    Anonymous, An Old Wife Sat at her Reel

The Great Grey Man of Ben Macdhui, or Ferlas Mor as he is called
in the Gaelic, is Scotland's Abominable Snowman . . . he has been
seen by responsible people who have reputations to lose, most of
them expert mountaineers accustomed to hills at night and not
given to imagining things.
    Alastair Borthwick, Always a Little Further

Ghost, kelpie, wraith,
And all the trumpery of vulgar faith.
    Thomas Campbell (1777–1844), The Pilgrim of Glencoe

. . . the monsters which inhabited the three large and deep Highland
lochs, Ness, Shiel and Morar, were so well known by the old Gaelic-
speaking people that they had distinctive names. The Loch Ness
Monster was spoken of as An Niseag, the Loch Shiel Monster as An
Seileag, and the Loch Morar Monster as A' Mhorag.
    Seton Gordon (1886–1977), A Highland Year

My stalker, John Stuart at Achnacarry, has seen it twice and both times at sunrise in summer, when there was not a ripple on the water. The creature was basking on the surface; he saw only the head and hind-quarters, proving its back was hollow, which is not the shape of any fish, or of a seal. Its head resembled that of a horse.

Earl of Malmesbury, Memoirs *(1857), on a monster in Loch Arkaig*

Downward we drift through shadow and light,
Under yon rock the eddies sleep,
Calm and silent, dark and deep.
The Kelpy has risen from the fathomless pool,
He has lighted his candle of death and of dool

Sir Walter Scott (1771–1832), On Tweed River

It's all humbug.

Professor Peter Tait (1831–1901)

Mountains and Climbers

Any fool can climb good rock, but it takes craft and cunning to get up vegetatious schist and granite.

> *J.H.B. Bell, quoted in W.H. Murray*, Mountaineering in Scotland

By the time you have topped a hundred Munros (the incurable stage usually), you will know Scotland – and yourself – in a fuller, richer way.

> *Hamish Brown (1934–), 'The Munros: A Personal View', in D. Bennet,* The Munros *(1985)*

Once a week the sun shines, and then the mountain peaks are revealed in all the inexpressible tints of blue; and there is blueness which is azure, mother-of-pearl, foggy or indigo, clouded like vapours, a hint or mere reminder of something beautifully blue . . . I tell you, unknown and divine virtues arose within me at the sight of this unbounded blueness.

> *Karel Capek (1890–1938),* Letters from England

When he some heaps of hills hath overwent,
Begins to think on rest, his journey spent,
Till, mounting some tall mountain he do find
More heights before him than he left behind.

> *William Drummond (1585–1649),* Flowers of Sion

'Look, the peaks of Arran.' I saw a low dark smudge against a pale patch of clear sky but was not much impressed. On a clear day in central Scotland you can see Arran from any high place West of Tinto.

> *Alasdair Gray (1934–),* 1982 Janine

. . . the Mountains are extatic & ought to be visited in pilgrimage once a year. None but these monstrous creatures of God know how to join so much beauty with so much horror.

> *Thomas Gray (1716–1771),* Letters

The reality is that 99% of trad ascents are scarcely more adventurous than getting lost in the aisles of Ikea. Adventure happens when the outcome is uncertain.

Dave Macleod, Climber *magazine, 2005, on the controversy between 'traditional,' and 'adventure' modes.*

There is hardly any bad luck in the mountains, only good.

Gwen Moffat (1924–), Two Star Red

Ben Nevis looms the laird of a'

Charles Murray (1864–1941), Bennachie

A mystic twilight, like that of an old chapel at vespers, pervaded these highest slopes of Buachaille. We stood at the everlasting gates, and as so often happens at the end of a great climb, a profound stillness came upon my mind, and paradoxically the silence was song and the diversity of things vanished. The mountains and the world and I were one. But that was not all: a strange and powerful feeling that something as yet unknown was also within my grasp, was trembling into vision.

W.H. Murray (1913–1996), Mountaineering in Scotland

'How do you know this rope is safe, Hamish?'
'I don't,' he replied in his abstract way.
'Well, how are we to find out whether it's safe, if you can't tell us from up there?'
MacInnes was the model of patience. 'Try climbing up the rope,' he remarked, encouragingly. 'I'll be most surprised if it comes away.'

Tom Patey (1932–1970), One Man's Mountains

The rock is like porridge – in consistency though not quality, for porridge is part of our national heritage and a feast fit for a king. This was not.

Tom Patey, One Man's Mountains

The word 'impossible' has no permanent place in a climber's vocabulary.

Tom Patey, One Man's Mountains

The rocky summits, split and rent,
Formed turret, dome or battlement,
Or seemed fantastically set
With cupola or minaret.
> *Sir Walter Scott (1771–1832)*, The Lady of the Lake

'The Hielan' hills, the Hielan' hills – I never see them but they gar
me grew.'
> *Sir Walter Scott*, Rob Roy

All are aspects of one entity, the living mountain. The
disintegrating rock, the nurturing rain, the quickening sun, the
seed, the root, the bird – all are one. Eagle and alpine veronica are
part of the mountain's wholeness.
> *Nan Shepherd (1893–1981)*, The Living Mountain

You cannot feel comfortable at Loch Coruisk, and the discomfort
rises in a great degree from the feeling that you are outside of
everything – that the thunder-smitten peaks have a life with which
you cannot intermeddle. The dumb monsters sadden and perplex.
> *Alexander Smith (1830–1867)*, A Summer in Skye

It was towards evening when by a steep but safe passage I outwitted
the mountain's formidable defences, reaching the curious top that
makes it resemble a cockatoo and gives it the name Stack Polly.
> *Andrew Young (1885–1971)*, A Retrospect of Flowers

Above all was Suilven, throwing its dark shadow, a mountain huger
than itself.
> *Andrew Young*, A Retrospect of Flowers

And mist like hair hangs over
One barren breast and me,
Who climb, a desperate lover,
With hand and knee,
> *Andrew Young*, The Paps of Jura

Music, Dance and Song

Let sum go drink, and sum go dance;
Menstrallis blaw up ane brawll of France:
Lat see quha hobbilis best.
> *Anonymous*, The Fader, Founder of Faith and Felicite *(1500). brawll:*
> *a kind of dance*

There's some come here for to see me hang,
And some to buy my fiddle:
But ere I see it amang them fa',
I'll brak it doon the middle.
> *Anonymous*, Macpherson's Rant

O sing to me the auld Scotch sangs
In the braid Scottish tongue,
The sangs my father loved to hear,
The sangs my mother sung.
> *Traditional*, The Auld Scotch Sangs

I asked the piper 'How long does it take to learn to play a pibroch?'
He answered 'It takes seven years to learn to play the pipes, and
seven years to learn to play a pibroch. And then you need the
poetry.'
> *George Bruce (1909–2002), radio interview with Pipe Major Robert U.*
> *Brown, from* The Land Out There

Blast upon blast they blew,
Each clad in tartan new,
Bonnet and blackcock feather:
And every Piper was fou' –
Twenty Pipers together!
> *Robert Buchanan (1845–1901)*, The Wedding of Shon Maclean

There's threesome reels, there's foursome reels,
There's hornpipes and strathspeys, man,
But the ae best dance e'er cam to the land
Was the deils awa wi' th' Exciseman.
> *Robert Burns (1759–1796)*, The Deil's Awa Wi' Th' Exciseman

There sat Auld Nick, in shape o' beast . . .
He screw'd the pipes, and gart them skirl,
Till roof and rafters a' did dirl.
  Robert Burns, Tam o' Shanter

Those who think that composing a Scotch song is a trifling business
– let them try.
  Robert Burns, Letter to James Hoy, 1787

I couldn't talk to people face to face, so I got on stage and started
screaming and squealing and twitching.
  David Byrne (1952–), Scottish-born US musician

'It's impossible the bagpipe could frighten any body,' said Miss
Jackie in a high voice: 'nobody with common sense could be
frightened at a bagpipe.'
Mrs Douglas here mildly interposed, and soothed down the
offended pride of the Highlanders, by attributing Lady Juliana's
agitation entirely to surprise. The word operated like a charm; all
were ready to admit, that it was a surprising thing when heard for
the first time.
  Susan Ferrier (1782–1854), Marriage

When I have talked for a hour I feel lousy –
Not so when I have danced for a hour,
The dancers inherit the party.
  Ian Hamilton Finlay (1925–1996), The Dancers Inherit the Party

I have heard the story that MacCrimmon would write down a tune
on the wet sand as the tide began to ebb, and would expect his
pupils to be able to play it before the flood tide once more flowed
over the sand and washed away the marks.
  Seton Gordon (1886–1977), A Highland Year

Lady Anne Lindsay heard her own ballad 'Auld Robin Gray' sung to
the accompaniment of the harp, and applauded by companies who
were unaware that the bright blushing girl in the corner had written
it
  H. Grey Graham, The Social Life of Scotland in the Eighteenth
  Century *(1899)*

He heard a heavenly melody and sound,
Passing all instrumentis musical,
Causit be the rolling of the spheris round
    Robert Henryson (c.1425–c.1500), Orpheus and Eurydice

Of sic music to write I do but dote,
Therefore of this matter a straw I lay,
For in my life I couth never sing a note
    Robert Henryson, Orpheus and Eurydice

The way a seated jazz musician gets him or herself and the
instrument prepared, these wee glimmers of a smile to the fellow
musicians, the friends and acquaintances in the audience, but also
taking great care not to confront directly the stares from members
of the ordinary people – otherwise enter irony: the kind that leads
to a lack of overall control.
    James Kelman (1946–), A Disaffection

one thing he had learned this afternoon:
playing the pipes was not a substitute for sex!
    James Kelman, A Disaffection

I will nae priest for me shall sing,
Nor yet nae bells for me to ring,
But ae Bag-pipe to play a spring.
    Walter Kennedy (1460–1500)

I will try to follow you on the last day of the world,
And pray I may see you all standing shoulder to shoulder
With Patrick Mor Macrimmon and Duncan Ban Macrimmon in
the centre . . .
And you playing: 'Farewell to Scotland, and the rest of the earth'
    Hugh MacDiarmid (C.M. Grieve, 1892–1978)

The God-imprisoned harmonies
That out in gracious motions go.
    George Macdonald (1824–1905), Organ Songs

'And good pipers iss difficult nooadays to get; there's not many in
it. You'll maybe get a kind of a plain piper going aboot the streets of
Gleska noo and then, but they're like the herrin', and the turnips,
and rhubarb, and things like that – you don't get them fresh in
Gleska.'
    Neil Munro (1864–1930), The Vital Spark

He filled the bag at a breath and swung a lover's arm round about it. To those who know not the pipes, the feel of the bag in the oxter is a gaiety lost. The sweet round curve is like a girl's waist; it is friendly and warm in the crook of the elbow and against a man's side, and to press it is to bring laughing or tears.

Neil Munro, The Lost Pibroch

I remember asking Bert, 'When you were doing it, did you know you were like . . . heavy? Heavier than all these bands that were heavy?' He nodded this thoroughly appropriate nod and passed me a biscuit – as if to say, 'Yes, and I'm too heavy to even talk about it.'

Pete Paphides, on Bert Jansch, musician (1943–2011), Guardian, 6 October 2011

He touched his harp and nations heard, entranced,
As some vast river of unfailing source,
Rapid, exhaustless, deep, his numbers flowed,
And opened new fountains in the human heart.

Robert Pollok (1798–1827), The Course of Time

Westering home, and a song in the air,
Light in the eye, and it's goodbye to care

Sir Hugh S. Roberton (1874–1952), Westering Home

The whole was so uncouth and extraordinary; the impression which this wild music made on me contrasted so strongly with that which it made upon the inhabitants of the country, that I am convinced we should look upon this strange composition not as essentially belonging to music, but to history

B.F. St Fond (1741–1819), Travels in England and Scotland

Hearken, my minstrels! Which of ye all
Touched his harp with that dying fall,
So sweet, so soft, so faint,
It seemed an angel's whispered call
To an expiring saint?

Sir Walter Scott (1771–1832), The Bride of Triermain

I'm a piper to my trade,
My name is Rob the Ranter:
The lassies loup as they were daft,
When I blaw up my chanter.

Francis Sempill (c.1616–1682), Maggie Lauder

. . . d fidl
wee aa dat soonds
still laukit insyd
waitin
fur a tym
whin im aibl
to pirswaid
dm oot.

    Mark R. Smith, a meideetashun upu lairnin d fidl

One cannot but be conscious of an underlying melancholy in
Scotswomen. This melancholy is particularly attractive in the
ballroom, where it gives a singular piquancy to the enthusiasm and
earnestness they put into their national dances.

    Stendhal (Henri Beyle, 1783–1842)

The important thing is what happens at the moment of
performance, for the people who make the effort to be there: it lives
with them.

    Judith Weir (1954–)

I'm sick to death of people saying we've made eleven albums that all
sound exactly the same. In fact we've made twelve albums that all
sound exactly the same.

    Angus Young (1959–), rock musician

Nature

O Nature! A' thy shows an' forms
To feeling, pensive hearts hae charms!
   Robert Burns (1759–1796), Epistle to William Simpson

Nature, which is the time-vesture of God, and reveals Him to the
wise, hides Him from the foolish.
   Thomas Carlyle (1795–1881), Sartor Resartus

The daisy did onbreid her crownell small,
And every flour unlappit in the dale
   Gavin Douglas (1475–1522), Prologue to the Aeneid

the leaf is the chief product and phenomenon of life: this is a green
world, with animals comparatively few and small, and all dependent
on the leaves. By leaves we live.
   Sir Patrick Geddes (1854–1932), lecture in Dundee, 1927

The muirlan' burnie, purple-fringed
Wi' hinny-scented heather,
Whaur gowden king-cups blink aneath
The brecken's waving feather.
   Janet Hamilton (1795–1873), Auld Mither Scotland

There's gowd in the breast of the primrose pale,
An' siller in every blossom;
There's riches galore in the breeze of the vale,
And health in the wild wind's bosom.
   James Hogg (1770–1835), There's Gowd in the Breast

Let them popple, let them pirl,
Plish-plash and plunk and plop and ploot,
In quakin' quaw or fish-currie,
I ken a' they're aboot.
   Hugh MacDiarmid (C.M. Grieve, 1892–1978), Water Music

Bountiful Primroses,
With outspread heart that needs the rough leaves' care.
  George Macdonald (1824–1905), Wild Flowers

The curled young bracken unsheath their green claws
  Fiona MacLeod (William Sharp, 1855–1905)

And what saw ye there
At the bush aboon Traquair?
Or what did you hear that was worth your heed?
I heard the cushat croon
Thro' the gowden afternoon,
And the Quair burn singin' doun to the Vale o' Tweed.
  J.C. Shairp (1819–1885), The Bush Aboon Traquair

Silence is, perhaps, the greatest Hallelujah; the silent hosannas
of the sun, the stars, the trees and the flowers. But silence is
not enough – the innumerable songs of earth mingle with the
acclamations of the serene witnesses. The wind, the water, the cries
of bird and beast and the thoughful utterance of humanity: each day
is life's messiah and at its feet are leaves and about its head are the
canticles of joy.
  William Soutar (1898–1943), Diary

Anyone who aspires to being made a mummy, need only arrange to
be buried in a bog.
  Andrew Young (1885–1971), A Retrospect of Flowers

Primula Scotica might be an even better emblem for Scotland. It is
not common everywhere like the Thistle; it is confined to Scotland,
growing nowhere else.
  Andrew Young, A Retrospect of Flowers

The People

Saint Peter said to God, in ane sport word –
'Can ye nocht mak a Hielandman of this horse turd?'
God turned owre the horse turd with his pykit staff,
And up start a Hielandman as black as ony draff.

    Anonymous, How the First Hielandman was Made

God send the land deliverance
Frae every reiving, riding Scot;
We'll sune hae neither cow nor ewe,
We'll sune hae neither staig nor stot.

    Anonymous, The Death of Parcy Reed

. . . there are no finer Gentlemen in the World, than that Nation
can justly boast of; but then they are such as have travelled, and are
indebted to other Countries for those Accomplishments that render
them so esteemed, their own affording only Pedantry, Poverty,
Brutality, and Hypocrisy.

    Anonymous, Scotland Characterised, *1701*

See how they press to cross the Tweed,
And strain their limbs with eager speed!
While Scotland from her fertile shore
Cries, On my sons, return no more.
Hither they haste with willing mind,
Nor cast one longing look behind.

    Anonymous

Nowhere beats the heart so kindly
As beneath the tartan plaid.

    W.E. Aytoun (1818–1865), Charles Edward at Versailles

As Dr Johnson never said, Is there any Scotsman without charm?

    Sir J.M. Barrie (1860–1937), address to Edinburgh University

The two classes that mek ahl the mischief of the kintry are weemen
and meenisters.

    William Black (1841–1898), Highland Cousins

Trust yow no Skott.
Andrew Boord, English spy, to Thomas Cromwell, 1536

Really, we are getting horribly like our neighbours.
John Buchan (1875–1940), The Scots Tongue

The truth is that we are at bottom the most sentimental and emotional people on earth.
John Buchan, The Scots Tongue

From scenes like these, old Scotia's grandeur springs,
That makes her lov'd at home, rever'd abroad:
Princes and lords are but the breath of kings:
An honest man's the noblest work o' God.
Robert Burns (1759–1796), The Cottar's Saturday Night

Had Cain been Scot, God would have changed his doom,
Not forc'd him wander, but confin'd him home.
J. Cleveland, Poems, 1647

Of the overseers of the slave plantations in the West Indies three out of four are Scotsmen, and the fourth is generally observed to have very suspicious cheekbones.
Samuel Taylor Coleridge (1772–1834), 1812, quoted in T.M. Devine, Scotland's Empire, 2011

Argument to the Scot is a vice more attractive than whisky.
Walter Elliott (1888–1958), speech to the House of Commons, 1942

They plume themselves on their skill in dialectic subtleties.
Desiderius Erasmus (c.1466–1536), on Scottish scholars

If the Scots knew enough to go indoors when it rained, they would never get any exercise.
Simeon Ford (1855–1933), My Trip to Scotland

This is certainly a fine country to grow old in. I could not spare a look to the young people, so much was I engrossed in contemplating their grandmothers.
Ann Grant (1755–1838), Letters from the Mountains

They hate every appearance of comfort themselves, and refuse it to others.
William Hazlitt (1778–1830), Essays

a country whose ethnic multiplicity has been one of the chief
sources of its energy and resilience, as well as of its vulnerability.

> *Hamish Henderson (1919–2002), quoted in Timothy Neat*, Hamish
> Henderson: A Biography *(2009)*

One of the great delusions of Scottish society is the widespread
belief that Scotland is a tolerant and welcoming community and
that racism is a problem confined to England's green and unpleasant
land.

> *John Horne, 'Racism, Sectarianism and Football in Scotland'*, Scottish
> Affairs *No. 12, 1995*

Permit me to begin with paying a just tribute to Scotch sincerity
wherever I find it. I own, I am not apt to confide in the professions
of gentlemen of that country; and when they smile, I feel an
involuntary emotion to guard myself against mischief.

> *'Junius'*, Letters *(1770)*

From a physical point of view, the Celt and the Saxon are one;
whatever may be the source of their mutual antagonism, it does not
lie in a difference of race.

> *Sir Arthur Keith (1866–1955)*, Nationality and Race, *1919*

A glance at their history or literature . . . reveals what lies under the
slow accent, the respectability and the solid flesh. Under the cake
lies Bonny Dundee.

> *James Kennaway (1928–1968)*, Household Ghosts

I have been trying all my life to like Scotchmen, and am obliged to
desist from the experiment in despair.

> *Charles Lamb (1775–1834)*, Essays of Elia

For I marvel greatlie, I you assure,
Considderand the people and the ground,
That riches suld nocht in this realm redound.

> *Sir David Lindsay (c.1490–1555)*, The Dreme of the Realme of
> Scotland

Our gentyl men are all degenerate;
Liberalitie and Lawtie, both, are loste;
And cowardice with Lordis is laureate;
And knichtlie curage turnit in brag and boast.

> *Sir David Lindsay*, The Complaint of the Commoun Weill of
> Scotland

'We arra peepul', is the strange, defiant cry heard from some of
Scotland's football terraces in the late twentieth century. But which
people? A foreign visitor might well be confused.
  Michael Lynch, Scotland, A New History *(1991)*

. . . a' the dour provincial thocht
That merks the Scottish breed
  Hugh MacDiarmid (C.M. Grieve, 1892–1978), A Drunk Man Looks
  at the Thistle

. . . though no news came
Of their destruction's night
to reach the world agony of grief,
the fall of the Asturians in their glory,
their lot was the lot of all poor people,
hardship, want and injury,
ever since the humble of every land
were deceived by ruling class, State and Civil Law,
and by every prostitute
who sold their soul for that price
that the bitches of the world have earned
  Sorley Maclean (1911–1996), The Cuillin

Far frae my hame I wander, but still my thoughts return
To my ain folk ower yonder, in the sheiling by the burn . . .
And it's oh! but I'm longing for my ain folk,
Though they be but lowly, poor and plain folk
  Wilfrid Mills (W.A. Braund, 1857–1938), My Ain Folk

Our fathers all were poor,
Poorer our fathers' fathers;
Beyond, we dare not look.
  Edwin Muir (1887–1959), The Fathers

The Scots have always been an unhappy people; their history
is a varying record of heroism, treachery, persistent bloodshed,
perpetual feuds, and long-winded and sanguine arguments.
  Edwin Muir, Scottish Journey

In all companies it gives me pleasure to declare that the English, as
a people, are very little inferior to the Scots.
  Christopher North (John Wilson, 1785–1854), Noctes Ambrosianae

The Scots are not at home unless they are abroad.
   George Orwell (Eric Blair, 1903–1950), The Lion and the Unicorn

Professor Palmer hasn't arrived yet. But there's a black guy here who wants to see you – I've told him to wait.
   Godfrey Palmer, Scotland's first black Professor, on keeping an appointment in Edinburgh, Times Higher Education Supplement, *15 August 2003*

Such Mediocrity was ne'er on view,
Bolster'd by tireless Scottish Ballyhoo –
Nay! In two Qualities they stand supreme;
Their Self-advertisement and Self-esteem.
   Anthony Powell (fl.18th century), Caledonia

proud as Scots
   François Rabelais, Gargantua and Pantagruel, *translated by Sir Thomas Urquhart (1611–1660)*

Walking into town, I saw, in a radiant raincoat,
the woman from the fish-shop. 'What a day it is!'
cried I, like a sunstruck madman.
And what did she have to say for it?
Her brow grew bleak, her ancestors raged in their graves
as she spoke with their ancient misery:
'We'll pay for it, we'll pay for it, we'll pay for it.'
   Alastair Reid (1926–), Weathering

The perfervid Scot (Proefervidum ingenium Scotorum)
   André Rivet (fl. 16th century)

Where are the folk like the folk o' the West?
Canty, and couthy, and kindly, the best
   Sir Hugh S. Roberton (1874–1952), Westering Home

I have heard higher sentiments from the lips of poor, uneducated men and women . . . than I ever yet met with out of the Bible.
   Sir Walter Scott (1771–1832), quoted by J.G. Lockhart in Life of Scott

The Celt . . .
From out the sunrise, evermore has felt,
Like a religion, ties and dues of blood.
   Alexander Smith (1830–1867), Torquil and Oona

Who knows now what it was like to be fed only on three meals
of potatoes a day? Or to experience as a child the rigours of the
Scottish sabbath, where the highlight was a visit to the cemetery?

    T.C. Smout (1933–), A Century of the Scottish People *(1986)*

For the Lord has pity on the bairns
Wha belang to Caledonie.
Her likely lads are wurlin weans
And cudna be onie ither,
Sin a toom howe is in the breist
O' their sair forjaskit mither.

    William Soutar (1898–1943), Second Childhood

Why do you softly, richly speak
Rhythm so sweetly scanned?
Poverty hath the Gaelic and Greek
In my land.

    Rachel Annand Taylor (1876–1900), The Princess of Scotland

The stamp-peyin self-employed ur truly the lowest form ay vermin
oan god's earth.

    Irvine Welsh (1957–), Trainspotting

It is never difficult to distinguish between a Scotsman with a
grievance and a ray of sunshine.

    P.G. Wodehouse (1881–1975), quoted in Richard Usborne, Wodehouse
    at Work *(1961)*

The Scotch are great charmers, and sing through their noses like
musical tea-kettles.

    Virginia Woolf (1882–1941), Letters

Places

(in alphabetical order)

Far's Strawberry Bank? Far's the auld Wallace Tour?
Fat's come owre the Denburn ablow and abeen?
An' dammit, ye've flittit oor Tarnty Ha'
rugged doon the New Market and muckt up the Green.

> *A.M. Davidson (1897–1979*, Vandalism, *on 'civic improvement' in*
> *Aberdeen*

Aberdeen impresses the stranger as a city of granite palaces,
inhabited by people as definite as their building material.

> *H.V. Morton (1892–1979)*, In Search of Scotland

Aberdeen a thin-lipped peasant woman who has borne eleven and
buried nine.

> *Lewis Grassic Gibbon (James Leslie Mitchell, 1901–1935)*, Scottish
> Scene

Glitter of mica at the windy corners
. . . the sleek sun flooding
The broad abundant dying sprawl of the Dee

> *G.S. Fraser (1915–1980)*, Hometown Elegy, *on Aberdeen*

It is an ageless sang this auld isle sings
In the burn born alang the scree fute
By riven craigs where the black raven brings
The still-born lamb to its nest by the rowan-rute

> *Robert Maclellan (1907–1985)*, Arran

Cam' ye by Athol, lad wi' the philabeg?
Down by the Tummel or banks o' the Garry?
Saw ye the lads wi' their bonnets and white cockades
Leaving their mountains to follow Prince Charlie?

> *Traditional*, Cam' Ye By Athol?

It was a true, sterling, gospel sermon – it was striking, sublime, and awful in the extreme. He finally made out the IT, mentioned in the text, to mean, properly and positively, the notable town of Auchtermuchty. He proved all the people in it, to their perfect satisfaction, to be in the gall of bitterness and the bond of iniquity.

> *James Hogg (1770–1835)*, The Private Memoirs and Confessions of a Justified Sinner

Auld Ayr, wham ne'er a toon surpasses,
For honest men and bonny lasses.

> *Robert Burns (1759–1796)*, Tam o' Shanter

Happy the man who belongs to no party,
But sits in his ain house, and looks at Benarty.

> *Sir Michael Malcolm of Lochore, at the time of the French Revolution, 1789*

In all the Hebrides, Benbecula is the sea's dearest child. That is why the returning tide races so quickly over the sand, hurrying with pouted lips to kiss its shore. And when the night's embraces are over, the sea leaves Benbecula again, like a mother bird going to forage for its young.

> *Hector MacIver (1910–1966)*, 'The Outer Isles', in G. Scott-Moncrieff, Scottish Country *(1936)*

'We're buryin' Annie,' says I.
'Whatna Annie?' says Mr Sutherland.
'Animosity,' says I – ony auld baur'll pass in Brora.

> *Neil Munro (1864–1930)*, Jimmy Swan, The Joy Traveller

I am glad to have seen the Caledonian Canal, but don't want to see it again.

> *Matthew Arnold (1822–1888)*, Letters

Carrick for a man,
Kyle for a coo,
Cunningham for corn and bere,
Galloway for woo'.

> *Old saying*

From Glasgow to Greenock, with towns on each side,
The hammers' ding-dong is the song of the Clyde.

> *R.Y. Bell and Ian Gourley*, The Song of the Clyde *(c.1963)*

Ye lover of the picturesque, if ye wish to drown your grief,
Take my advice and visit the ancient town of Crieff.
    William McGonagall (1825–1902), Beautiful Crieff

Dundee . . . As men have made it, it stands today perhaps the
completest monument in the entire continent of human folly,
avarice and selfishness.
    Fionn McColla (Thomas Douglas Macdonald, 1906–1975)

Dundee, a frowsy fisherwife addicted to gin and infanticide.
    Lewis Grassic Gibbon (James Leslie Mitchell, 1901–1935), Scottish
Scene

What Benares is to the Hindu, Mecca to the Mohammedan,
Jerusalem to the Christian, all that is Dunfermline to me.
    Andrew Carnegie (1835–1918)

Duns dings a'.
    Traditional Duns saying

Your burgh of beggaris is ane nest,
To shout the swengouris will nocht rest,
All honest folk they do molest,
Sa piteously they cry and rame
    William Dunbar (c.1460–c.1520), Satire on Edinburgh

The impression Edinburgh has made on me is very great; it is quite
beautiful, totally unlike anything else I have ever seen; and what is
even more, Albert, who has seen so much, says it is unlike anything
he ever saw.
    Queen Victoria (1819–1901), Letters

Who indeed, that has once seen Edinburgh, with its couchant lion
crag, but must see it again in dreams, waking or sleeping?
    Charlotte Bronte (1816–1855), Letters

This braw, hie-heapit toun
    Lewis Spence (1874–1955), The Prows o' Reekie

The Castle looms – a fell, a fabulous ferlie.
Dragonish, darksome, dourly grapplan the Rock
wi' claws o' stane.
    Alexander Scott (1920–1989), Haar in Princes Street

To none but those who have themselves suffered the thing in the body, can the gloom and depression of our Edinburgh winters be brought home.
  Robert Louis Stevenson (1850–1894)

To imagine Edinburgh as a disappointed spinster, with a hare-lip and inhibitions, is at least to approximate as closely to the truth as to image the Prime Mover as a Levantine Semite.
  Lewis Grassic Gibbon (James Leslie Mitchell, 1901–1935), Scottish Scene

Isna Embro a glorious city!
  James Hogg (1770–1835)

Three crests against the saffron sky
Beyond the purple plain
  Andrew Lang (1844–1912), Twilight on Tweed, *on the Eildon Hills*

We seemed to stand an endless while,
Though still no word was said,
Three men alive on Flannan Isle,
Who thought on three men dead.
  Wilfred Gibson (1878–1962), Flannan Isle

'For the sake o' business I've had to order suits in places no' the size o' Fochabers, where they put rabbit-pouches in your jacket whether ye poach or no'.
  Neil Munro (1864–1930), Jimmy Swan, The Joy Traveller

'What', I inquired of my companion, 'are these kind people pitying me so very much for?'
'For your want of Gaelic, to be sure. How can a man get on in the world that wants Gaelic?'
'But do not they themselves,' I asked, 'want English?'
'Oh, yes,' he said. 'But what does that signify? What is the use of English in Gairloch?'
  Hugh Miller (1820–1856), My Schools and Schoolmasters

This is the tree that never grew
This is the bird that never flew
This is the fish that never swam
This is the bell that never rang
  Traditional rhyme associated with Glasgow's coat of arms

Glasgow is one of the few places in Scotland which defy
personification ... The monster of Loch Ness is probably the
lost soul of Glasgow, in scales and horns, disporting itself in the
Highlands after evacuating finally and completely its mother-
corpse.

>   *Lewis Grassic Gibbon (James Leslie Mitchell, 1901–1935)*, Scottish
>   Scene

City! I am true son of thine ...
From terrace proud to alley base
I know thee as my mother's face.

>   *Alexander Thomson (1830–1867)*, Glasgow

A sacredness of love and death
Dwells in thy noise and smoky breath

>   *Alexander Smith (1830–1867)*, Glasgow

Glasgow, that damned sprawling evil town

>   *G.S. Fraser (1915–1980)*, Meditation of a Patriot

'Heaven seems vera little improvement on Glesga,' a Glasgow
man is said to have commented, after death, to a friend who had
predeceased him. 'Man, this is no' Heaven,' the other replied.

>   *Anonymous*

I belong to Glasgow,
Dear old Glasgow town ...
But when I get a couple o' drinks on a Saturday,
Glasgow belongs to me!

>   *Will Fyffe (1885–1947)*, I Belong to Glasgow

It's Scotland's Friendliest Market-Place.
Watch Your Handbags, Ladies, Please.

>   *Gerald Mangan (1951–)*, Heraclitus at Glasgow Cross

'... all the wise men in Glasgow come from the East – that's to say,
they come from Edinburgh.'
'Yes, and the wiser they are the quicker they come.'

>   *Neil Munro (1864–1930)*, Erchie, My Droll Friend

It all looks a bit like somebody's mouth just after they've had most
of their teeth removed.

>   *Iain Banks (1954–), on Gourock, in* Raw Spirit

I will arise now, and go to Inverness,
And a small villa rent there, of lath and plaster built;
Nine bedrooms will I have there, and I'll don my native dress,
And walk around in a damned loud kilt.
  Harry Graham (1874–1936), The Cockney of the North

Iona of my heart, Iona of my love, instead of monks' voices shall be
lowing of cattle, but ere the world comes to an end, Iona shall be as
it was.
  Saint Columba (521–597)

That man is little to be envied, whose patriotism would not gain
force upon the plain of Marathon, or whose piety would not grow
warmer among the ruins of Iona.
  Samuel Johnson (1709–1784), A Journey to the Western Islands

I ken mysel' by the queer-like smell
That the next stop's Kirkcaddy!
  M.C. Smith (c.1869–1949), The Boy in the Train

But the far-flung line o' the Lang Whang Road,
Wi' the mune on the sky's eebree,
An' naething but me an' the wind abroad,
Is the wuss that's hauntin' me.
  Hugh Haliburton (J. Logie Robertson, 1846–1922), The Lang Whang
  Road

I have nowhere seen loveliness so intense and so diverse crowded
into so small a place. Langholm presents the manifold and
multiform grandeur and delight of Scotland in miniature.
  Hugh MacDiarmid (C.M. Grieve, 1892–1978), The Thistle Rises

For Lochaber no more, Lochaber no more,
We'll maybe return to Lochaber no more.
  Allan Ramsay (1686–1758), Lochaber No more

It is a far cry to Lochow
  Traditional Campbell slogan, quoted by Sir Walter Scott (1771–1832) in
  Rob Roy

If thou wouldst view fair Melrose aright,
Go visit it by the pale moonlight.
  Sir Walter Scott, The Lay of the Last Minstrel

O Alva hills is bonny,
Tillicoultry hills is fair,
But to think on the Braes o' Menstrie
It maks my heart fu' sair.
>   *Anonymous*

Goodbye Glasgow, we're gonna go, way down by-o,
Out tae the west tae get the best that money can buy-o,
A shangrila that's no too far fae the toon-o
Just far enough tae keep you scruff fae comin' roon-o.
>   *Sean Tierney (d.2000)*, The Milngavie Song

No bloody sport, no bloody games,
No bloody fun: the bloody dames
Won't even give their bloody names
In bloody Orkney
>   *'Hamish Blair'*, Bloody Orkney, *written in the Second World War*

As everyone is well aware, the chief crop of Orkney is wireless poles.
>   *Ian Hamilton Finlay (1925–1996)*, The Chief Crop of Orkney

St Johnstoun is a merry toun
Whaur the water rins sae schire;
And whaur the leafy hill looks doun
On steeple and on spire.
>   *William Soutar (1898–1943)* St Johnstoun *(Perth)*

Some towns have quietly died. Some have been murdered. The most
striking case of murder is Roxburgh. On the map of Scotland one
finds Roxburghshire, but the town is gone, sacked by the armies of
Edward I of England.
>   *Stephen Bone*, Albion: an Artist's Britain *(1939)*

St Andrews by the northern sea,
A haunted town it is to me!
A little city, worn and grey,
The grey North Ocean girds it round.
And o'er the rocks, and up the bay,
The long sea-rollers surge and sound.
>   *Andrew Lang (1844–1912)*, Almae Matres

And the sea below is still as deep
As the sky above.
Alexander Stewart (1829–1901), The St Kilda Maid's Song

What struck me in these islands was their bleakness, the number of ridiculous little churches, the fact that bogs do not require a level surface for their existence but can also run uphill, and that ponies sometimes have a black stripe like the wild ass
Norman Douglas (1868–1952), Looking Back *(on Shetland and Orkney)*

And there was Stonehaven itself, the home of the poverty toffs, folk said, where you might live in sin as much as you pleased but were damned to hell if you hadn't a white sark.
Lewis Grassic Gibbon (James Leslie Mitchell, 1901–1935), Sunset Song

. . . on the road to Thurso there is a low suavity of line, a smoothness of texture, a far light-filled perspective that holds the mind to wonder and a pleasant silence.
Neil Gunn (1891–1973), Highland Pack

Wick is . . . the meanest of men's towns, set on what is surely the baldest of God's bays.
Robert Louis Stevenson (1850–1894)

Poets and Poetry

Who would not be
The Laureate bold,
With his butt of sherry
To keep him merry
And nothing to do but pocket his gold?
> *W.E. Aytoun (1818–1865)*, The Laureate

Gie me ae spark o' Nature's fire,
That's a' the learning I desire;
Then, tho' I drudge thro' dub and mire
At pleugh or cart,
My Muse, tho' hamely in attire,
May touch the heart.
> *Robert Burns (1759–1796)*, Epistle to J. Lapraik

The said Hogg is a strange being, but of great, though uncouth, powers.
> *Lord Byron (1788–1824), Letter to Thomas Moore, on James Hogg*

A vein of poetry exists in the hearts of all men.
> *Thomas Carlyle (1795–1881)*, On Heroes, Hero-Worship, and the Heroic in History

Mr Thomson makes one of his characters address Sophonisba in a line which some critics reckoned the false pathetic:
O! Sophonisba! Sophonisba, oh!
Upon which a smart from the pit cried out:
Oh! Jamey Thomson! Jamey Thomson, oh!
> *Colley Cibber (1671–1757), Lives, on James Thomson's 'Sophonisba'*

Beis weill advisit my werk or ye reprief;
Consider it warely, read ofter than anis,
Weill, at ane blenk, slee poetry nocht ta'en is.
> *Gavin Douglas (1475–1522)*, Prologue to the Aeneid

So me behovit whilom, or than be dumb,
Some bastard Latin, French or Inglis use,
Where scant were Scottis; I had na other choiss.
　Gavin Douglas, Prologue to the Aeneid

Therefore, guid friendis, for ane gymp or a bourd,
I pray you, note me not at every word.
　Gavin Douglas, Prologue to the Aeneid

He shouldn't have written in such small print.
　O. Douglas (1877–1948), The Setons, *on Walter Scott*

Poetry and prayer are very similar.
　Carol Ann Duffy (1955–)

On Waterloo's ensanguined plain
Lie tens of thousands of the slain,
But none by sabre or by shot
Fell half so flat as Walter Scott.
　Thomas, Lord Erskine (1750–1823), on Scott's The Field of Waterloo

The best a writer writes is Beautiful
He should ignore the mad and dutiful.
　Ian Hamilton Finlay (1925–1996), The Writer and Beauty

I am only a wee Scottish poet on the outside of everything.
　Ian Hamilton Finlay

The Scottish poets all felt competent to teach the art of government
to their rulers
　M.M. Gray, Scottish Poetry from Barbour to James VI *(1935)*

He offers the Muse no violence. If he lights upon a good thought,
he immediately drops it in fear of spoiling a good thing.
　William Hazlitt (1778–1830), Lectures on the English Poets, *on
Thomas Campbell (1777–1844)*

Och, I wish you hadn't come right now,
You've put me off my balance:
I was just translating my last wee poem
Into the dear old Lallans.
　Alan Jackson (1938–), A Scotch Poet Speaks

Stanzas are always noteworthy things; they are never mere diagrams or patterns. In this Scottish poetry it comes out how much of thought the different stanzas bring along with them – they are tunes setting the mind of the poet dancing in a particular measure.

   W.P. Ker (1855–1923), On the Poetry of Burns

Search Scotland over, from the Pentland to the Solway, and there is not a cottage-hut so poor and wretched as to be without its Bible; and hardly one that, on the same shelf, and next to it, does not treasure a Burns.

   John Gibson Lockhart (1794–1854), Life of Burns

Here lies the peerless peer Lord Peter
Who broke the laws of God and man and metre

   John Gibson Lockhart, Epitaph for Lord Robertson

Are my poems spoken in the factories and fields,
In the streets o' the toon?
Gin they're no', then I'm failin' to doe
What I ocht to ha' dune.

   Hugh MacDiarmid (C.M. Grieve, 1892–1978), Second Hymn to
   Lenin

. . . men wha through the ages sit,
And never move frae aff the bit,
Wha hear a Burns or Shakespeare sing,
Yet still their ain bit jingles string,
As they were worth the fashioning

   Hugh MacDiarmid, A Drunk Man Looks at the Thistle

A Scottish poet maun assume
The burden o' his people's doom,
And dee to brak' their livin' tomb.

   Hugh MacDiarmid, A Drunk Man Looks at the Thistle

The essential beginning of all national uprisings is that poets should believe.

   A.G. Macdonell (1895–1941), My Scotland

I know the sharp bitterness of the spirit
better than the swift joy of the heart.

   Sorley Maclean (1911–1996), 'When I Speak of the Face' (An Uair a
   Labhras Mi Mu Aodann)

Every critic in the town
Runs the minor poet down;
Every critic – don't you know it!
Is himself a minor poet.
> *Robert F. Murray (1863–1894)*

They say I'm only a poet,
Whose fate is as dead as my verse
(His father's a packman, you know it;
His father, in turn, couldn't boast).
They'd take a good field and plough it.
I can cut better poems than most.
> *William Ross (1762–1790)*, Oran Gaoil *(Love Song), translated by Iain Crichton Smith*

Ne'er
Was flattery lost on poet's ear;
A simple race! they waste their toil
For the vain tribute of a smile.
> *Sir Walter Scott (1771–1832)*, The Lay of the Last Minstrel

Many a clever boy is flogged into a dunce; and many an original composition corrected into mediocrity . . . Somehow he wants audacity – fears the public, and, what is worse, fears the shadow of his own reputation.
> *Sir Walter Scott*, Journal, *referring to Thomas Campbell (1777–1844)*

Poetry drives its lines into her forehead
like an angled plough across a bare field.
> *Iain Crichton Smith (1928–1998)*, A Young Highland Girl Studying Poetry

Lea him at least outgang wi mockerie,
The Makar macironical!
A sang on his perjurit lips
And naething i the pouch
– Or i the hert, for that!
> *Sydney Goodsir Smith (1915–1975)*, 23rd Elegy: Farewell to Calypso

There are mair sangs that bide unsung
nor aa that hae been wrocht.
> *William Soutar (1898–1943)*, The Makar

Of all my verse, like not a single line;
But like my title, for it is not mine.
That title from a better man I stole;
Ah, how much better, had I stol'n the whole!

> *Robert Louis Stevenson (1850–1894)*, Underwoods

Oh! If by any unfortunate chance I should happen to die,
In a French field of turnips or radishes I'll lie.
But thinking of it as really Scottish all the time,
Because my patriotic body will impart goodness to the slime.

> *J.Y. Watson*, A Pastiche of Rupert Brooke in the style of William
> McGonagall *(prize-winner in a parody competition, 1950s?)*

Politics and Protest

Four and twenty blacklegs, working night and day,
Fed on eggs and bacon, getting double pay;
Helmets on their thick heads, bayonets gleaming bright,
If someone burst a sugar bag, the lot would die of fright.

> *Anonymous, student magazine of 1928, quoted in Roy M. Pinkerton,*
> *'Of Chambers and Communities', in G. Donaldson,* Four Centuries:
> Edinburgh University Life *(1983)*

All political parties die at last of swallowing their own lies.

> *John Arbuthnot (1667–1735), quoted in R. Garnett,* Life of Emerson
> *(1988)*

'A millionaire communist?'
'Why not? You've got penniless capitalists.'
'What'll happen to him when the Revolution comes?'
'He'll be commissar for Scotland, and you'll be sent to the salt
mines of Ross and Cromarty.'

> *Chaim Bermant (1929–1998),* Jericho Sleep Alone

Insolence in the few begets
Hate in the many; hatred breeds revolt,
Revolt where all are free to rise and rule
Breeds anarchy, whose wild chaotic reign
Calls in the despot . . . thus we reel
From vassalage to vassalage, through fits
Of drunken freedom, – glorious for an hour.

> *J.S. Blackie (1809–1895),* The Wise Men of Greece

I want to lead a Government humble enough to know its place.

> *Gordon Brown, on standing for the Labour Party leadership, May 2007*

Class-conscious we are, and class-conscious will be
Till our fit's on the neck o' the boor-joysie

> *Socialist hymn quoted or parodied by John Buchan (1875–1940) in*
> Huntingtower

Now Sark rins over Solway sands,
And Tweed rins to the ocean,
To mark where England's province stands –
Such a parcel of rogues in a nation!
    Robert Burns (1759–1796), Such a Parcel of Rogues in a Nation

Who will not sing 'God Save the King'
Shall hang as high's the steeple;
But while we sing 'God Save the King',
We'll ne'er forget the people.
    Robert Burns, Does Haughty Gaul Invasion Threat?

In Politics if thou wouldst mix,
And mean thy fortunes be;
Bear this in mind, be deaf and blind,
Let great folk hear and see.
    Robert Burns, In Politics if Thou Wouldst Mix

Aristocracy of Feudal Parchment has passed away with a mighty
rushing; and now, by a natural course, we arrive at Aristocracy of
the Moneybag.
    Thomas Carlyle (1795–1881), The French Revolution

Wha the deil hae we got for a King,
But a wee, wee German lairdie!
    Allan Cunningham (1784–1842), The Wee, Wee German Lairdie

Devolution is a motorway to independence with no exits.
    Tam Dalyell (1932–), Labour politician

Cynicism, together with unrealistic expectation, are the two great
bugbears of politics.
    Donald Dewar (1937–2000)

Distrust of authority should be the first civic duty.
    Norman Douglas (1868–1952), An Almanac

Socialism? These days? There's the tree that never grew. Och, a
shower of shites. There's the bird that never flew.
    Carol Ann Duffy (1955–), Politico

'The late Oliver Brown . . . put it well. He said that when I won Hamilton, you could feel a chill along the Labour back benches, looking for a spine to run up.'

Winnie Ewing (1933–), quoted in Kenneth Roy, Conversations in a Small Country *(1989)*

We are not in Afghanistan for the sake of the education policy in a broken 13th-century country. We are there so the people of Britain and our global interests are not threatened.

Liam Fox (1961–), Tory politician.

I think the disappearance of the Soviet Union is the biggest catastrophe of my life.

George Galloway (1954–), quoted in The Guardian, *16 September 2002*

We say to young Muslims: we know that you're angry, you're right to be angry. But the best way to be angry is to hit the government where it hurts, through politics, through the ballot-box, through elections, through engaging with non-Muslims to build a broad front to bring about a change in politics at home and abroad.

George Galloway, Talksport Radio, 3 September 2006

You can no more be independence lite than pregnant lite.

Annabel Goldie (1950–), Scottish Tory leader, quoted by Stuart Crawford on 'Caledonian Mercury', 31 May 2011

When they get into Parliament they are at once bitten with the absurd idea that they are no longer working men, but statesmen, and they try to behave as such.

R.B. Cunninghame Graham (1852–1936), on his fellow Labour MPs, letter to Wilfrid Blunt, 1908

The Scottish Tories are an extreme case of necrophilia.

Christopher Harvie (1944–), Cultural Weapons

A good nationalist must first of all be a good internationalist.

Hamish Henderson (1919–2002), quoted in Timothy Neat, Hamish Henderson: A Biography *(2009)*

A regard for liberty, though a laudable passion, ought commonly to be subordinate to a reverence for established government.

David Hume (1711–1776), Essays Moral and Political

I will govern according to the common weal, but not according to the common will.

King James VI, Reply to the House of Commons, 1621

Were it no for the workin man what wad the rich man be?
What care some gentry if they're weel though a' the puir wad dee?

Ellen Johnston (c.1835–c.1874), The Last Sark

The first step in reform, either of the Land Laws or of the House of Lords, is to destroy these superstitions. Show the people that our Old Nobility is not noble, that its land are stolen lands - stolen either by force or fraud; show people that the title-deeds are rapine, murder, massacre, cheating, or Court harlotry; dissolve the halo of divinity that surrounds the hereditary title; let the people clearly understand that our present House of Lords is composed largely of descendants of successful pirates and rogues; do these things and you shatter the Romance that keeps the nation numb and spellbound while privilege picks its pockets.

Tom Johnston (1881–1965) Our Scots Noble Families

It's quite remarkable really the different ways whereby the state requires its artists to suck dummytits.

James Kelman (1946–), lecture to the Glasgow School of Art, 1996

While all the Middle Classes should
With every vile Capitalist
Be clean reformed away for good
And vanish like a morning mist!

Andrew Lang (1844–1912), The New Millennium

Ah! splendid Vision, golden time,
An end of hunger, cold and crime.
An end of Rent, and end of Rank,
An end of balance at the Bank,
An end of everything that's meant
To bring Investors five per cent.

Andrew Lang, The New Millennium

I must follow them. I am their leader.

Andrew Bonar Law (1858–1923), quoted in E. Raymond, Mr Balfour *(1920)*

All government is a monopoly of violence
> *Hugh MacDiarmid (C.M. Grieve, 1892–1978)*, The Glass of Pure
> Water

. . . if I had my way
I would melt your gold payment,
pour it into your skull,
till it reached to your boots.
> *Iain Lòm Macdonald (c.1620–c.1707)*, Oran an Aghaidh an Aonaidh
> *(Song Against the Union), citing the alleged bribe-takers*

We will not get true independence in a oner. People will want to see
how a parliament or assembly works before going for what we want
for Scotland.
> *Robert McIntyre, letter to Gordon Wilson (1989), quoted in Andrew*
> *Marr,* The Battle for Scotland *(1996)*

The Commons, faithful to their system, remained in a wise and
masterly inactivity.
> *Sir James Mackintosh (1765–1832)*, Vindiciae Gallicae

I am not here, then, as the accused; I am here as the accuser of
capitalism dripping with blood from head to foot.
> *John MacLean (1879–1923), at his trial for sedition, 1919*

Scottish separation is part of England's imperial disintegration.
> *John Maclean, Election Address, 1922*

some, by no means all, organisations appear to have lost sight of
the basic fact that public services are the people's services and
that providers exist to deliver these on behalf of the public. The
public are more than just customers of public authorities – they are
owners, shareholders and stakeholders rolled into one.
> *Jim Martin, Scottish Ombudsman, quoted in* Holyrood, *17 October*
> *2011*

Toryism is an innate principle o' human nature – Whiggism but an
evil habit.
> *Christopher North (John Wilson, 1785–1854)*, Noctes Ambrosianae

What is called 'Communism' in backward countries is hunger
becoming articulate.
> *John Boyd Orr (1880–1971), quoted by Ritchie Calder in* Science
> Profiles

By the time the civil service has finished drafting a document to give effect to a principle, there may be little of the principle left.
 Lord Reith (1889–1971), Into the Wind

What is the matter though we all fall? The cause shall not fall.
 James Renwick (1662–1688), letter to his fellow-Covenanters, 1683

You suddenly realise you're no longer in government when you get into the back of your car and it doesn't go anywhere.
 Sir Malcolm Rifkind (1946–), Tory politician

A diplomat is someone who can tell you to go to hell and leave you looking forward to the trip.
 Attributed to Alex Salmond (1954–)

I believe passionately in English independence.
 Alex Salmond, on BBC Newsnight, 10 January 2007

I think the English are well capable of self-government and should be given the opportunity.
 Alex Salmond, on BBC Newsnight, 10 January 2007

It is lawful to prevent the murder of ourselves or our brethren, when no other way is left, by killing the murderers before they accomplish their wicked design, if they be habitually prosecuting it . . . It is lawful – to kill Tories or open murderers, as devouring beasts.
 Alexander Shields (c.1660–1700), A Hind Let Loose, *Cameronian tract*

Glasgow doesnae accept this; if you come tae Glasgow we'll set about ye.
 John Smeaton (1976–), one of those who helped to frustrate a terrorist attack at Glasgow Airport, quoted in Time *Magazine, 11 July 2007*

A'body kens oor nationalism
Is yet a thing o' sect and schism
 William Soutar (1898–1943), Vision

. . . the vulgar, mean-minded politically-correct clones in the abysmal Scottish Parliament in Holyrood.
 Gerald Warner (1945–), quoted in @cusackandrew blog, September 2008

Religion and the Church

A cold Church,
A thin wretched cleric;
The body in subjection shedding tears:
Great their reward in the eyes of the King of Heaven.

> *Anonymous, 12th century verse from Gaelic, quoted in Hugh Cheape
> and I. F. Grant, 'Periods in Highland History' (1987), from Donald
> MacKinnon,* A Descriptive Catalogue of Gaelic Manuscripts *(1912)*

Lufe God abufe al, and yi nychtbour as yi self

> *Inscription on 'John Knox's House', High Street, Edinburgh (16th
> century)*

Better keep the devil out, than have to put him out.

> *Anonymous*

There is more knavery among kirkmen than honesty among
courtiers.

> *Anonymous*

Elspeth Buchan: Come and toil in the garden of the Lord!
Old man: Thank ye, but He wasna ower kind to the first gairdner
that he had.

> *Apocryphal anecdote of 'The Woman of Revelation' (1738–1791)*

I do believe in stone and lime,
    a manse of large dimension,
Broad acres for a glebe and farm,
    that is my church extension.
My folk may perish if they like –
    Christ's name I rarely mention;
I take the stipend due by right
    to men of good intention.

> *Anonymous, 18th century, quoted in Gordon Donaldson,* The Faith of
> the Scots *(1990)*

The Free Kirk, the wee kirk,
The kirk without the steeple;
The Auld Kirk, the cauld kirk,
The kirk without the people.

> *Anonymous, rhyme on the Disruption of 1843*

O Lord! Thou art like a mouse in a drystane dyke, aye keekin' out
at us frae holes and crannies, but we canna see Thee.

> *Anonymous Western minister, quoted in Charles Mackay, 'Poetry and
> Humour of the Scottish Language' (1882), from Rogers'* Illustrations of
> Scottish Life

'We thank thee, O Lord, for all Thy mercies; such as they are.'

> *Anonymous Aberdeen minister, quoted in William Power,* Scotland and
> the Scots *(1934)*

I thought God was actually floating somewhere overhead, a
stern man with a beard, something like Papa only of enormous
dimension, infinitely powerful and fearsome. Fear indeed hung over
me like a dark cloud in my childhood.

> *John Logie Baird (1888–1946),* Sermons, Soap and Television

If there is no future life, this world is a bad joke. But whose joke?

> *A.J. Balfour (1848–1930), Attributed death-bed remark*

Nothing to pay,
No, nothing to pay . . .
Coatbridge to Glory,
And nothing to pay.

> *Baptist hymn, quoted by David Donaldson, in 'Coatbridge to Glory',
> from A. Kamm and A. Lean,* A Scottish Childhood *(1985)*

Religion fails if it cannot speak to men as they are.

> *William Barclay (1907–1978)*

There are two great days in a person's life – the day we are born,
and the day we discover why.

> *William Barclay*

Man's extremity is God's opportunity

> *Lord Belhaven (1656–1708), Speech to the Scottish Parliament, 1706*

Few are thy days and full of woe,
O man of woman born;
Thy doom is written, 'Dust thou art,
And shalt to dust return.'
Michael Bruce (1746–1767), also claimed by John Logan (1748–1788)

An atheist is a man with no invisible means of support.
John Buchan (1875–1940), quoted in H.E. Fosdick, On Being a Real
Person

'Is it true that under the Act there's a maternity benefit, and that a
woman gets the benefit whether she's married or no?'
'That is right.'
'D'ye approve of that?'
'With all my heart.'
'Well, sir, how d'ye explain this? The Bible says the wages of sin is
death and the Act says thirty shillin's.'
John Buchan, Memory-Hold-the-Door

When the Scotch Kirk was at the height of its power, we may search
history in vain for any institution that can compete with it, except
the Spanish Inquisition
Henry Thomas Buckle (1821–1862), History of Civilisation in
England

But Lord, remember me and mine
Wi' mercies temporal and divine,
That I for grace and gear may shine
Excelled by none:
And all the glory shall be thine,
Amen! Amen!
Robert Burns (1759–1796), Holy Willie's Prayer

The sire turns o'er, with patriarchal grace,
The big ha'-Bible, ance his father's pride:
His bonnet reverently is laid aside,
His lyart haffets wearing thin and bare:
Those strains that once did sweet in Zion glide,
He wales a portion with judicious care;
And 'Let us worship God!' he says with solemn air.
Robert Burns, The Cottar's Saturday Night

They never sought in vain that sought the Lord aright!
Robert Burns, The Cottar's Saturday Night

O thou! Whatever title suit thee –
Auld 'Hornie', 'Satan', 'Nick', or 'Clootie'
   Robert Burns, Address to the Deil

'Our neighbour nation will say of us, poor Scotland! beggarly
Scotland! scabbed Scotland! Lousy Scotland! yea, but Covenanted
Scotland! that makes amends for all.'
   Robert Calder, 17th century minister, quoted in Scots Presbyterian
   Eloquence Displayed

the Church of Scotland has been high in her time, fair as the moon,
clear as the sun, and terrible as an army with banners. The day has
been when Zion was stately in Scotland. The terror of the Church
of Scotland once took hold of all the kings and great men that
passed by . . . our Lord is to set up a standard, and oh! that it may
be carried to Scotland. When it is set up it shall be carried through
the nations, and it shall go to Rome, and the gates of Rome shall be
burned with fire. . .
   Richard Cameron (1648–1680), Covenanting leader, his last sermon

I fear I have nothing original in me
Excepting original sin.
   Thomas Campbell (1777–1844)

The Lord knows I go up this ladder with less fear and perturbation
of spirit than ever I entered the pulpit to preach.
   Donald Cargill (1619–1681), Covenanter minister, at his execution

Man's unhappiness, as I construe, comes of his Greatness, it is
because there is an Infinite in him, which with all his cunning he
cannot quite bury under the Finite.
   Thomas Carlyle (1795–1881)

His religion is at best an anxious wish – like that of Rabelais: a great
Perhaps.
   Thomas Carlyle, Essays *(on Robert Burns)*

For me as an individual the worst thing in this unhappy age in
which I have grown old is that one was born into a faith which could
not, without deceit or strain, be maintained.
   Catherine Carswell (1879–1946), Lying Awake

Then the folk were sair pitten aboot,
An' they cried, as the weather grew waur:
'Oh Lord! We ken we hae sinn'd,
But a joke can be carried owre far!'
Then they chapped at the ark's muckle door,
To speir gin douce Noah had room;
But Noah never heedit their cries;
He said, 'This'll learn ye to soom.'
> *W.D. Cocker (1882–1970),* The Deluge

It is a mistaken belief that priestdom died when they spelled it
Presbytery.
> *S.R. Crockett (1859–1914),* Bog Myrtle and Peat

. . . the North, where Time stands still
and Change holds holiday, where Old and New
welter upon the border of the world,
and savage faith works woe.
> *John Davidson (1857–1909),* Ballad of the Making of a Poet

The wark gangs bonnily on.
> *Attributed to David Dickson (c.1583–1663) in Henry Guthry,* Memoirs
> of Scottish Affairs, Civil and Ecclesiastical *(1702), on executions of*
> *opponents of the Covenanters, 1645*

Hot Burning Coals of Juniper shall be
Thy Bed of Down, and then to Cover thee
A Quilt of Boyling Brimstone thou must take,
And Wrap thee in till thou full Payment make
> *James Donaldson (late 17th century),* The Voice of God

Whenever a young man was recommended to old Lord Stormont
for one of his kirks, he used allways to ask, 'Is he good-natured in
his drink?' and if that was the case he said he should be his man.
> *Quoted of Lord Stormont (d. 1748), by Sir John Douglas in Charles*
> *Rodger,* Boswelliana *(1874)*

The gods take wondrous shapes, sometimes.
> *Norman Douglas (1868–1952),* Old Calabria

The test of Religion, the final test of Religion, is not Religiousness
but Love. Greatest thing in the world.
> *Henry Drummond (1851–1897),* Beautiful Thoughts

Ave Maria, gratia plena!
Thy birth has with his blude
Fra fall mortall originall
Us raunsound on the rude.
>   *William Dunbar (c.1460–c.1520)*, Ane Ballat of Our Ladye

Nearly every great evil, religious, political, social and commercial, which Alba labours under owes its existence or its continuation to Protestantism.
>   *Ruaraidh Erskine of Mar (1869–1960), in* Guth na Bliadhna *(Voice of the Time)*

The truth is, my friends, you might as weel expect to see my red coo climb the muckle pear tree in the manse garden tail first and whistle like a laverock!
>   *William Faichney (1805–1854), in a sermon about the rich entering the Kingdom of Heaven, quoted in Hugh MacDiarmid*, Lucky Poet *(1943)*

It was the saying, sir, of one of the wisest judges who ever sat on the Scottish bench, that a poor clergy made a pure clergy; a maxim which deserves to be engraven in letters of gold on every manse in Scotland.
>   *Susan Ferrier (1782–1854)*, Destiny

An annibabtist is a thing I am not a member of: – I am a Pisplikan just now and a Prisbetern at Kercaldy my native town which though dirty is clein in the country.
>   *Marjory Fleming (1803–1811)*, Journals

. . . a base impudent brazen-faced villain, a spiteful ignorant pedant, a gross idolator, a great liar, a mere slanderer, an evil man, hardened against all shame . . . full of insolence and abuse, chicanery and nonsense, detestable, misty, erroneous, wicked, vile, pernicious, terrible and horrid doctrines, tending to corrupt the mind and stupefy the conscience, with gross iniquity, audacious hostility, pitiful evasion, base, palpable and shocking deceit
>   *The Rev Adam Gib (fl. 17th century), anti-Burgher leader, reviewing a work by the Rev Archibald Hill, a Burgher minister, from a pamphlet printed in Perth (1782)*

Religion – a Scot know religion? Half of them think of God as a Scot with brosy morals and a penchant for Burns. And the other half are over damned mean to allow the Almighty even existence.
Lewis Grassic Gibbon (James Leslie Mitchell, 1901–1935), Cloud Howe

I confess that, as an impartial outsider, I hope that as long as there are an appreciable number of Protestants, they will be balanced by some Catholics; for, while both bodies have been about equally hostile to truth, the Catholics have on the whole been kinder to beauty.
J.B.S. Haldane (1892–1964), Science and Ethics

O for the days when sinners shook
Aneth the true Herd's righteous crook.
Henry Henderson (1873–1957), The Northern Muse

Nothing in the world delights a truly religious people so much as consigning them to eternal damnation.
James Hogg (1770–1835), The Private Memoirs and Confessions of a Justified Sinner

Upon the whole, we may conclude, that the Christian Religion not only was at first attended by miracles, but even to this day cannot be believed by any reasonable person without one.
David Hume (1711–1776), An Enquiry Concerning Human Understanding

What strange objects of adoration are cats and monkies? says the learned doctor. They are a least as good as the relics or rotten bones of martyrs
David Hume, The Natural History of Religion

revelation when it condescended to describe the manner of man's creation went sadly astray.
Sir Arthur Keith (1866–1955), Evolution and Ethics

Do not be afraid of being free-thinkers. If you think strongly enough you will be forced by science to the belief in God, which is the foundation of all Religion. You will find science not antagonistic, but helpful to Religion.
Lord Kelvin (1824–1907), *Address to the Rev. Professor Henslow, London, 1903*

It was only later I came to the conclusion that Eve had been framed.
   Helena Kennedy (1950–), Eve Was Framed: Women and British Justice

A man with God is always in the majority
   Attributed to John Knox (c.1513–1572); quoted also as 'God and one are always a majority' by Mary Slessor, in James Buchan, The Expendable Mary Slessor *(1980)*

Seeing that impossible it is, but that either I shall offend God or else that I shall displease the world, I have determined to obey God, notwithstanding that the world shall rage thereat.
   John Knox (c.1513–1572)

Some goes to church just for a walk,
Some go there to laugh and talk . . .
Some go there to doze and nod,
It's few goes there to worship God.
   Sir James Cameron Lees (1834–1913), The Sabbath

There was a smug, trim, smooth little minister, making three hundred a year pimping for a God in whom his heart was too small to believe.
   Eric Linklater (1899–1974), Magnus Merriman

Anxiety, sickness, suffering, or danger now and then with a foregoing of the common conveniences and charities of this life, may make us pause and cause the spirit to waver and the soul to sink; but let this only be for a moment. All these are nothing when compared with the glory which shall be revealed in and for us.
   David Livingstone (1813–1873), speech at Cambridge University, 4 December 1857

. . . the reik of Maister Patrik Hammyltoun hes infected as many as it blew upoun.
   John Lyndsay (fl. 16th century), Letter to Archbishop Beaton on the burning of Patrick Hamilton, 1528, quoted in John Knox, History of the Reformation in Scotland

Abide with me: fast falls the eventide;
The darkness deepens; Lord, with me abide
   Henry Francis Lyte (1793–1847), Abide With Me

Change and decay in all around I see
   Henry Francis Lyte, Abide With Me

Ransomed, healed, restored, forgiven,
Who like me His praise should sing?
   Henry Francis Lyte, Praise My Soul the King of Heaven

. . . the minister's voice
spread a pollution of bad beliefs
   Norman MacCaig (1910–1996), Highland Funeral

Let men find the faith that builds mountains
Before they seek the faith that moves them.
   Hugh MacDiarmid, (C.M. Grieve, 1892–1978), On a Raised Beach

The principal part of faith is patience
   George Macdonald (1824–1905)

Love of our neighbour is the only door out of the dungeon of self.
   George Macdonald

The Lord is my Shepherd!
I'm a puir man, I grant,
But I am weel neiboured!
   George Macdonald, The Lord is my Shepherd

I find doing the will of God, leaves me no time for disputing about
His plans.
   George Macdonald, The Marquis of Lossie

Courage, brother! do not stumble
Though the path be dark as night
There's a star to guide the humble,
Trust in God, and do the right.
   Norman Macleod (1812–1872), Trust in God

O Love that will not let me go
   George Matheson (1842–1906), O Love That Will Not Let Me Go

Make me a captive, Lord,
And then I shall be free
   George Matheson, Make Me a Captive, Lord

The Reformation was a kind of spiritual strychnine of which
Scotland took an overdose.

    Willa Muir (1890–1970), Mrs Grundy in Scotland

'No man wi' any releegion aboot him would caal his canary a Wee
Free.'

    Neil Munro (1864–1930), The Vital Spark

The gude auld Kirk o' Scotland,
She's nae in ruins yet!

    George Murray (1819–1868), The Auld Kirk o' Scotland

We can't for a certainty tell
What mirth may molest us on Monday,
But at least to begin the week well,
We can all be unhappy on Sunday.

    Lord Neaves (1800–1876), Songs and Verses

I cannot praise the Doctor's eyes,
I never saw his glance divine;
He always shuts them when he prays,
And when he preaches, he shuts mine.

    George Outram (1805–1856), Lines on the Doctor

The Devil was sick – the Devil a monk would be;
The Devil was well – the Devil a monk was he.

    François Rabelais, Gargantua and Pantagruel, *translated by Sir
Thomas Urquhart (1611–1660)*

A young girl sat upon the cutty-stool at St Andrews . . . was asked
who was the father of her child? How can I tell, she replied artlessly,
amang a wheen o' Divinity students?

    Dean E.B. Ramsay (1793–1872), Reminiscences of Scottish Life and
Character

Being in a minister's house, there was the minimum of religious
consolation.

    John Macnair Reid (1895–1954), Homeward Journey

Every conjecture we form with regard to the works of God has as little probability as the conjectures of a child with regard to the works of a man.

Thomas Reid (1710–1796), Inquiry into the Human Mind

a kind of systematic insanity

John M. Robertson (1856–1933), on trinitarian theology

in large measure a compilation of simple Semitic myth and tradition, forged priestly codes, fabulous and falsified history, and books written by anybody other than those whose names they bear: its cosmology is in the terms of the case mere barbaric fantasy, and its ethic frequently odious.

John M. Robertson, Explorations, *on the Bible*

it was not, as it is generally supposed to be, a spontaneous movement, if there can be such a thing, of the religious conscience of the Scottish people, but was largely engineered by vested interests that stood to profit by the changes that took place.

John M. Robertson, The Perversion of Scotland, *on the Reformation*

Suffering is the professor's golden garment.

Samuel Rutherford (c.1600–1661), Letter to Marion McNaught, 1637

Scotland's judgement sleepeth not: awake and repent.

Samuel Rutherford, Letter to his parishioners at Anwoth, 1637

No man can be an unbeliever nowadays. The Christian apologists have left one nothing to disbelieve.

Saki (H.H. Munro, 1870–1916)

I've read the secret name o' Knox's God.
The gowd calf 'Getting On'

Tom Scott (1918–1995), Fergus

What has the Kirk given us? Ugly churches and services, identifying in the minds of the churchgoers ugliness with God, have stifled the Scottish arts almost out of existence . . . until the Kirk as it has been is dead Scotland will continue to be the Home of Lost Causes.

George Scott-Moncrieff (1910–1974), in D.C. Thomson, Scotland in Quest of her Youth: A Scrutiny *(1932)*

The soul of man is like the rolling world,
One half in day, the other dipt in night;
The one has music and the flying cloud,
The other, silence and the wakeful stars.
  Alexander Smith (1830–1867), Horton

Covenanters. Hopeless cases committed to hopeless causes. Ten
thousand martyrs, but no saints. The sad thing is, there's practically
no point now in trying to explain what they fought and died for.
  W. Gordon Smith (1928–1996), Mr Jock (1987)

The Pope was Giovanni, good Pope John. The Moderator was
the great Dr Archie Craig. He'd gone to Rome to support the
ecumenical movement. They had a cordial meeting, but both men
realised the way ahead was rocky. As Dr Craig rose to go, the Pope
shook him warmly by the hand. 'Arrivaderci, Erchie.' Dr Craig
turns at the door, 'Aye, an ca' canny, Giovanni.'
  W. Gordon Smith, Mr Jock

The god can no more exist without his people than the nation
without its god.
  William Robertson Smith (1846–1894), The Religion of the Semites

in particular, it requires an effort to reconcile our imagination to
the bloody ritual which is prominent in almost every religion which
has a strong sense of sin.
  William Robertson Smith, The Religion of the Semites

Nothing has afforded me so convincing a proof of the unity of
the Deity as these purely mental conceptions of numerical and
mathematical science which have been by slow degrees vouchsafed
to man, and are still granted in these latter times by the Differential
Calculus, now superseded by the Higher Algebra, all of which must
have existed in that sublimely omniscient Mind from eternity.
  Mary Somerville (1780–1872), Personal Recollections

We have been making a tub these forty years, and now the bottom
thereof is fallen out.
  Archbishop Spottiswoode on the National Covenant, 1638

A generous prayer is never presented in vain.
  Robert Louis Stevenson (1850–1894), The Merry Men

Nae schauchlin' testimony here –
We were a' damned, an' that was clear.
I owned, wi' gratitude an' wonder,
He was a pleisure to sit under.
  Robert Louis Stevenson, The Scotsman's Return from Abroad

whosoever will not seek the Lord God of Israel shall be put to
death, whether small or great, whether Man or woman
  Sir James Stewart (1645–1713), Ius Populi Vindicatum *(1669)*,
  proposal for a new Covenant

Work as though work alone thy end would gain,
But pray to God as though all work were in vain.
  Sir D'Arcy Wentworth Thompson (1860–1948), Sales Attici

You can make of men a machine militant, but not a machine human
through and through; just so you can make of men a Church
militant, but not a Church human through and through.
  James Thomson (1834–1882), Sympathy

You can't endure an hour of their society here, and they pester you
to come and spend eternity with them!
  James Thomson, Principal Tulloch on Personal Immortality, *on
  converters*

God was the private property of a chosen few
Whose lives ran carefully and correctly to the grave.
  Ruthven Todd (1914–1978), In Edinburgh

The Lord God is my Pastor gude,
Abundantlie for me to feid:
Then how can I be destitute
Of ony gude thing in my neid?
  James, John and Robert Wedderburn (fl. 16th century), Psalm 23 *from*
  The Gude and Godlie Ballatis

John, cum kis me now,
John, cum kis me now,
John, cum kis me by and by,
And mak no moir ado.
The Lord thy God I am,
That John dois the call;
John representis man
By grace celestiall . . .

> *James, John and Robert Wedderburn, remaking of an old song into a*
> *'Gude and Godlie Ballat'*

The Eleventh Commandment: Thou shalt not be found out.

> *George Whyte-Melville (1821–1878)*

There is a happy land,
Far, far away,
Where saints in glory stand,
Bright, bright as day.

> *Andrew Young (1807–1889)*

There is a happy land
Down in Duke Street Jail,
Where all the prisoners stand
Tied to a nail.

> *Children's burlesque of the preceding item*

Science and the Scientific Approach

Operations were started by the purchase of a tea chest, an old hat box, some darning needles, and a bullseye lens from a local shop, also a plentiful supply of sealing wax and Seccotine glue.

John Logie Baird (1888–1946), Sermons, Soap and Television

Science is of no party.

A.J. Balfour (1848–1930), Politics and Political Economy

The scientific man is the only person who has anything new to say and who does not know how to say it.

Sir J.M. Barrie (1860–1937)

The only machine I ever understood was a wheelbarrow, and that imperfectly.

E.T. Bell (1883–1960), Scottish-born US mathematician

'Obvious' is the most dangerous word in mathematics.

E.T. Bell

Millions, millions – did I say millions?
Billions and trillions are more like the fact.
Millions, billions, trillions, quadrillions,
Make the long sum of creation exact,

J.S. Blackie (1809–1895),' Song of Geology', quoted in C.P. Finlayson, 'The Symposium Academicum', in G. Donaldson, Four Centuries: Edinburgh University Life *(1983)*

He devoured every kind of learning. Not content with chemistry and natural philosophy, he studied anatomy, and was one day found carrying home for dissection the head of a child that had died of some hidden disorder.

Lord Brougham (1778–1868), Lives of Men of Literature and Science in the Age of George III, *on James Watt (1736–1819)*

To assert that a body received heat without its temperature rising, was to make the understanding correct the touch, and defy its dictates. It was a bold and beautiful paradox, which required courage as well as insight to broach, and the reception of which marks an epoch in the human mind, because it was an immense step towards idealizing matter into force.

> *Henry Thomas Buckle (1821–1862)*, The History of Civilization in England, *Vol. 2, on Joseph Black's discovery of latent heat*

A trend is a trend is a trend,
But the question is, will it bend?
Will it alter its course
Through some unforeseen force
And come to a premature end?

> *Sir Alexander Cairncross (1911–1998)*, 'Stein Age Forecaster', *in* Economic Journal, *1969*

The citizen is told that ignorance of the law is no excuse; ignorance of science should not be either.

> *Ritchie Calder (1906–1982)*, Science Profiles

He ever loved the Mathematics, because he said even God Almighty works by geometry.

> *S.R. Crockett (1859–1914)*, The Raiders

'How often have I said to you that when you have eliminated the impossible, whatever remains, however improbable, must be the truth?'

> *Sir Arthur Conan Doyle (1859–1930)*, The Sign of Four

'It is a capital mistake to theorise before one has data. Insensibly one begins to twist facts to suit theories, instead of theories to suit facts.'

> *Sir Arthur Conan Doyle*, A Scandal in Bohemia

Since Maxwell's time, Physical Reality has been thought of as represented by continuous fields, governed by partial differential equations, and not capable of any mechanical interpretation. This change in the concept of Reality is the most profound and the most fruitful that physics has experienced since the time of Newton.

> *Albert Einstein (1879–1955)*, *in* James Clerk Maxwell: A Commemorative Volume

It is the lone worker who makes the first advance in a subject: the details may be worked out by a team, but the prime idea is due to the enterprise, thought and perception of an individual.

> *Sir Alexander Fleming (1881–1955), Rectorial Address to Edinburgh University, 1951*

When the great English physicist Joule, who was one of Kelvin's staunch friends, was visiting his lordship's workshops, he came across a large coil of piano wire, and asked for what purpose it was to be used. When Kelvin replied it was for sounding, Joule asked, 'What note?' 'The deep C,' said Kelvin slyly, as it was for taking soundings in the ocean.

> *Charles Gibson*, Heroes of Science *(1913), on Lord Kelvin (1824–1907)*

The Creator, if he exists, has a specific preference for beetles.

> *J.B.S. Haldane (1892–1964), Lecture, April 1951*

No testimony is sufficient to establish a miracle, unless the testimony be of such a kind that its falsehood would be more miraculous than the fact which it endeavours to establish.

> *David Hume (1711–1776)*, An Enquiry Concerning Human Understanding

A bag of gravel is a history to me, and . . . will tell wondrous tales . . . mind, a bag of gravel is worth a bag of gold.

> *James Hutton (1726–1797)*

. . . when you can measure what you are speaking about, and express it in numbers, you know something about it.

> *Lord Kelvin (1824–1907), lecture to the Institution of Civil Engineers (1883)*

When I say a few million, I must say at the same time, that I consider a hundred millions as being a few.

> *Lord Kelvin*, On Geological Time

I was very anxious he should admire a beautiful picture of Glen Sannox, with mist resting among the mountains; but he remarked that it was an unfortunate time to choose, and the artist ought to have waited till the mist had cleared away, and all the outlines of the mountains were distinctly seen.

> *Agnes G. King*, Kelvin the Man *(1925)*

Like any other martyr of science, I must expect to be thought importunate, tedious, and a fellow of one idea, and that idea wrong. To resent this would show great want of humour, and a plentiful lack of knowledge of human nature.

Andrew Lang (1844–1912), Magic and Religion

He clings to statistics as a drunken man clings to a lamp-post; for support rather than illumination.

Attributed to Andrew Lang, perhaps in conversation

A million stars decide the place
Of any single star in space,
And though they draw it divers ways,
The star in steady orbit stays

Ronald Campbell Macfie (1867–1931), A Moral

Never refuse to see what you do not want to see or what might go against your own cherished hypothesis or against the view of authorities. Here are just the clues to follow up . . . The thing you cannot get a pigeon-hole for is the finger-post showing the way to discovery.

Sir Patrick Manson (1844–1922), quoted in Philip Manson-Bahr,
Patrick Manson *(1962)*

Gin a body meet a body
Flyin' through the air,
Gin a body hit a body,
Will it fly? and where?
Ilka impact has its measure,
Ne'er an ane hae I,
Yet a' the lads they measure me,
Or, at least, they try.

James Clerk Maxwell (1831–1879), In Memory of Edward Wilson:
Rigid Body (Sings)

In fact, whenever energy is transmitted from one body to another in time, there must be a medium or substance in which the energy exists after it leaves one body and before it reaches the other.

James Clerk Maxwell, Treatise of Electricity and Magnetism

No theory of evolution can be formed to account for the similarity of molecules, for evolution necessarily implies continuous change, and the molecule is incapable of growth or decay.

James Clerk Maxwell, Discourse on Molecules

Mathematicians may flatter themselves that they possess new ideas which mere human language is as yet unable to express.

James Clerk Maxwell

Dr Black dreaded nothing so much as error and Dr Hutton dreaded nothing so much as ignorance; the one was always afraid of going beyond the truth and the other of not reaching it

John Playfair (1748–1819), 'Life of Dr Hutton', in Transactions of the Royal Society of Edinburgh, *on Joseph Black and James Hutton*

I shall find out things, yes, yes!

Sir Ronald Ross (1857–1932), last words, quoted in John Carey, The Faber Book of Science *(1995)*

I had the chloroform for several days in the house before trying it . . . The first night we took it Dr Duncan, Dr Keith and I all tried it simultaneously, and were all 'under the table' in a minute or two.

Sir James Young Simpson (1811–1870), Letter to Mr Waldie, November 1847

However profoundly we may penetrate the depths of space, there still remain innumerable systems, compared to which those which seem so mighty to us must dwindle into insignificance or even become invisible; and . . . not only man, but the globe he inhabits, nay, the whole system of which it forms so small a part, might be annihilated, and its extinction unperceived in the immensity of creation.

Mary Somerville (1780–1872), The Mechanism of the Heavens

I could hardly believe that I possessed such a treasure when I looked back on the day thatI first saw the mysterious word 'Algebra', and the long course of years in which I had persevered almost without hope. It taught me never to despair.

Mary Somerville, Personal Recollections

Science is the great antidote to the poison of enthusiasms and superstition.

 Adam Smith (1723–1790), The Wealth of Nations

For the harmony of the world is made manifest in Form and Number, and the heart and soul and all the poetry of Natural Philosophy are embodied in the concept of mathematical beauty.

 Sir D'Arcy Wentworth Thompson (1860–1948), Growth and Form *(edition of 1942)*

The idea came into my mind, that as steam was an elastic body, it would rush into a vacuum, and if a communication was made between the cylinder and and an exhausted vessel, it would rush into it, and might there be condensed without cooling the cylinder.

 James Watt (1736–1819), quoted in H.W. Dickinson, James Watt, Craftsman and Engineer *(1935)*

The Sea and Seafaring

The waves have some mercy, but the rocks have no mercy at all
Gaelic Proverb

Into the pit-mirk nicht we northwart sail
Facin the bleffarts and the gurly seas
J.K. Annand (1908–1993), Arctic Convoy

In the bay the waves pursued their indifferent dances.
George Mackay Brown (1921–1996), A Winter Bride

The boats drove furrows homeward, like ploughmen
In blizzards of gulls.
George Mackay Brown, Hamnavoe

A wet sheet and a flowing sea,
A wind that follows fast,
And fills the white and rustling sail,
And bends the gallant mast.
Allan Cunningham (1791–1839), A Wet Sheet and a Flowing Sea

O weel may the boatie row,
That fills a heavy creel,
And cleads us a' frae head to feet,
And buys our parritch meal.
John Ewen (1741–1821), O Weel May the Boatie Row

I cast my line in Largo Bay,
And fishes I caught nine,
'Twas three to boil and three to fry,
And three to bait the line.
John Ewen, O Weel May the Boatie Row

They forgot all about the ship; they forgot everything, except the
herrings, the lithe silver fish, the swift flashing ones, hundreds and
thousands of them, the silver darlings.
Neil Gunn (1891–1973), The Silver Darlings

In and out of the bay hesitates the Atlantic
   Norman MacCaig (1910–1996), Neglected Graveyard, Luskentyre

The sea-shell wants to whisper to you.
   George Macdonald (1824–1905), Summer Song

The tide was dark and heavy with the burthen that it bore.
I heard it talkin', whisperin', upon the weedy shore.
   Fiona MacLeod (William Sharp, 1855–1905), The Burthen of the
   Tide

Sore sea-longing in my heart,
Blue deep Barra waves are calling;
Sore sea-longing in my heart.
   Kenneth MacLeod (1871–1955), Sea-Longing

Perhaps other seas have voices for other folk, but the western sea
alone can speak in the Gaelic tongue and reach the Gaelic heart.
   Kenneth MacLeod, Introduction to Marjory Kennedy-Fraser, Songs of
   the Hebrides

What care we though white the Minch is?
What care we for wind or weather?
Let her go, boys! Every inch is
Wearing home, home to Mingulay.
   Sir Hugh S. Roberton (1874–1952), The Mingulay Boat Song

No pipes or drum to cheer them on
When siccar work to do:
'Tis the music of the tempest's song
Leads on the lifeboat crew.
   R. Robertson, The Aith Hope Lifeboat Crew *(1899)*

Alang the shore
The greinan white sea-owsen ramp and roar.
   Tom Scott (1918–1995), Auld Sanct-Aundrians

It's no fish ye're buying: it's men's lives.
   Sir Walter Scott (1771–1832), The Antiquary

vague wishless seaweed floating on a tide
  Iain Crichton Smith (1928–1998), Old Woman

. . . my kinsmen and my countrymen,
Who early and late in the windy ocean toiled
To plant a star for seamen
  Robert Louis Stevenson (1850–1894), Skerryvore, *on the lighthouse-builders*

Seasons, Wind and Weather

'I will go tomorrow,' said the king.
'You will wait for me,' said the wind.
  Gaelic Proverb

Be it wind, be it weet, be it hail, be it sleet,
Our ship must sail the faem
  Anonymous, Sir Patrick Spens

The hadna sailed a league, a league,
A league but barely three,
When the lift grew dark, and the wind blew loud,
And gurly grew the sea.
  Anonymous, Sir Patrick Spens

West wind to the bairn
When ga'an for its name;
And rain to to the corpse
Carried to its lang hame.
A bonny blue sky
To welcome the bride
As she gangs to the kirk
Wi' the sun on her side.
  Traditional

Feetikin, feetikin,
when will ye gang?
When the nichts turn short
and the days turn lang,
I'll toddle and gang,
toddle and gang.
  Traditional nursery rhyme

Scottish weather is perfect for a romantic break. You won't go out
much.
  London agency's advertisement, 2001

It's dowie in the hint o' hairst,
At the wa-gang o' the swallow,
When the win' grows cauld, and the burns grow bauld,
And the wuds are hingin' yellow.
  Hew Ainslie (1792–1877), The Hint o' Hairst

Who is there who, at this season, does not feel his mind impressed
with a sentiment of melancholy? or who is able to resist that current
of thought, which, from such appearances of decay, so naturally
leads him to the solemn imagination of that inevitable fate which is
to bring on alike the decay of life, of empire, and of nature itself?
  Archibald Alison (1757–1839), Autumn

And saftly, saftly, ower the hill,
Comes the sma', sma' rain.
  Marion Angus (1866–1946), The Lilt

'Thu'll be shoors, lang-tailed shoors, an' rain a' 'tween, an' it'll ettle
tae plump; but thu'll no be a wacht o' weet.'
  Border farmer's weather forecast, quoted by J. Brown in W. Knight,
  Some Nineteenth-Century Scotsmen *(1903)*

In the north, on a showery day, you can see the rain, its lovely
behaviour over an island – while you stand a mile off in a patch of
sun
  George Mackay Brown (1921–1996), An Orkney Tapestry

Of a' the airts the wind can blaw,
I dearly like the west,
For there the bonie lassie lives,
The lassie I lo'e best.
  Robert Burns (1759–1796), Of A' the Airts the Wind Can Blaw

O wert thou in the cauld blast,
On yonder lea, on yonder lea,
My plaidie to the angry airt,
I'd shelter thee, I'd shelter thee.
  Robert Burns, O Wert Thou in the Cauld Blast

. . . yellow Autumn, wreath'd with nodding corn.
  Robert Burns, The Brigs of Ayr

And bleak December's winds ensuin',
Baith snell an' keen!
  Robert Burns, To a Mouse

And weary winter comin' fast
  Robert Burns, To a Mouse

Would ye partake of harvest's joys,
The corn must be sown in Spring.
  Thomas Carlyle (1795–1881), The Sower's Song

There are two seasons in Scotland: June and winter.
  Billy Connolly (1942–)

Is there any light quite like the June sun of the North and West? It
takes trouble out of the world.
  Sir Frank Fraser Darling (1903–1979), Island Days

A materialistic civilisation considers doing nothing a social crime.
On the contrary, it is an art which reaches its aesthetic zenith in the
sun and laziness of the northern June.
  Sir Frank Fraser Darling, Island Years

The licht begouth to quinkle out and fail,
The day to darken, decline and devaill . . .
Up goes the bat, with her pelit leathern flycht,
The lark descendis from the skyis hycht
Singand her complin song efter her guise.
  Gavin Douglas (1475–1522), Prologue to the Aeneid, *on a June
  Evening*

The rageand storm ourwelterand wally seas,
Riiveris ran reid on spate with water broun,
And burnis hurlis all their bankis doun
  Gavin Douglas, Prologue to the Aeneid, *on Winter*

In to thir dark and drublie dayis
Whone sabill all the Hevin arrayis,
With mystie vapouris, cluddis and skyis,
Nature all curage me denyis
  William Dunbar (c.1460–c.1520), Meditation in Winter

Now mirk December's dowie face
Glow'rs owre the rigs wi' sour grimace
 Robert Fergusson (1750–1774), The Daft Days

The rain falling Scotchly, Scotchly
 Ian Hamilton Finlay (1925–1996), Black Tomintoul

She was a dour bitch o' a back-end, yon.
 Flora Garry, 'Ae Mair Hairst', quoted in D.K. Cameron, Cornkister
 Days *(1984)*

My words go through the smoking air
Changing their tune on silence.
 W.S. Graham (1918–1986), Malcolm Mooney's Land

The showers of drizzly mist came down, all
voiceless; whispering and fragrant, soft and fresh, without
voice or melody
 George Campbell Hay (1915–1984), 'The Smirry Drizzle of Mist' (An
 Ciuran Ceoban Ceo)

I' the back end o' the year,
When the clouds hang laigh wi' the weicht o' their greetin'
 Violet Jacob (1863–1946), Craigo Woods

. . . the shilpit sun is thin
Like an auld man deein' slow
 Violet Jacob, The Rowan

. . . creeping over Rannoch, while the God of moorland
walks abroad with his entourage of freezing fog,
his bodyguard of snow.
 Kathleen Jamie (1962–), The Way We Live

Ah, pretty summer, e'en boast as you please;
Sweet are your gifts, but to Winter we owe
Snow on the Ochils and sun on the snow.
 Henry Johnstone (1844–1931), Winter

The world's a bear shrugged in his den.
It's snug and close in the snoring night.
And outside like chrysanthemums
The fog unfolds its bitter scent.
 Norman MacCaig (1910–1996), November Night, Edinburgh

I hear the little children of the wind
Crying solitary in lonely places.
   Fiona MacLeod (William Sharp, 1855–1905), Little Children of the
   Wind

Now skaills the skyis:
The night is neir gone.
   Alexander Montgomerie (c.1545–c.1611)

Silence is in the air:
The stars move to their places.
Silent and serene the stars move to their places.
   William Soutar (1898–1943), The Children

Autumnal frosts enchant the pool
And make the cart-ruts beautiful.
   Robert Louis Stevenson (1850–1894), The House Beautiful

Wee Davie Daylicht keeks owre the sea,
Early in the mornin', wi' a clear e'e;
Waukens all the birdies that are sleepin' soun':
Wee Davie Daylicht is nae lazy loon.
   Robert Tennant (1830–1879), Wee Davie Daylicht

Through the hushed air the whitening shower descends,
At first thin-wavering; till at last the flakes
Fall broad and wide and fast, dimming the day
With a continual flow.
   James Thomson (1700–1748), The Seasons

And one green spear
Stabbing a dead leaf from below
Kills winter at a blow.
   Andrew Young (1881–1975), Last Snow

Selves and Others

Individuals, real and imaginary

'I'll gie thee Rozie o' the Cleugh,
I'm sure she'll please thee weel eneuch.'
'Up wi' her on the bare bane dyke,
She'll be rotten or I'll be ripe.'
    Anonymous, Hey, Wully Wine

The doughty Douglas on a steed
Rode all his men beforn;
His armour glitter'd as did a glede,
Bolder bairn was never born.
    Anonymous, Chevy Chase

Up wi' the souters o' Selkirk,
And down wi' the Earl of Home
    Anonymous, Up Wi' the Souters o' Selkirk

If the Lord Chancellor knew only a little law, he would know a little
of everything.
    Anonymous, quoted in G.W.E. Russell, Collections and Recollections,
    on Lord Brougham (1778–1868)

There was a man lived in the moon,
Lived in the moon, lived in the moon;
There was a man lived in the moon,
And his name was Aiken Drum.
And he played upon a ladle, a ladle, a ladle;
He played upon a ladle, and his name was Aiken Drum.
    Traditional children's song

I am a very promising young man.
    Robert Adam (1728–1792), letter to his family, 1756

That other, round the flanks so slight of form,
Is Michael Scott, who verily knew well
The lightsome play of every magic fraud.
  Dante Alighieri (1265–1321), Inferno

Jeffrey, in conversation, was like a skilful swordsman flourishing his
weapon in the air; while Mackintosh, with a thin sharp rapier, in
the middle of his evolutions, ran him through the body.
  *Sir Archibald Alison (1792–1867), on Francis Jeffrey and Sir James
  Mackintosh*

Queens should be cold and wise,
And she loved little things
  Marion Angus (1866–1946), Alas! Poor Queen, *on Mary I*

There will be lots of arguments about who is the King of 19th-
century Science. But there is no doubt who is Queen. Her name is
Mary Somerville.
  *Australian Radio National programme on Mary Somerville (1780–
  1872) with Robyn Williams and Janet Wanless, 3 June 2001*

Fhairshon had a son
Who married Noah's daughter,
And nearly spoil'd ta Flood,
By trinking up ta water.
Which he would have done,
I at least pelieve it,
Had ta mixture peen
Only half Glenlivet.
  W.E. Aytoun (1818–1865), The Massacre of the MacPherson

. . . such was the wisdom and authoritie of that old, little, crooked
souldier, that all, with ane incredible sumission, from the beginning
to the end, gave over themselves to be guided by him, as if he had
been Great Solyman.
  Robert Baillie (1599–1662), Letters and Journals, *on Alexander Leslie,
  Earl of Leven*

My father had a strong dislike for marriages of necessity, common
enough at one time in Scotland. He was called to officiate at one
of these, and arrived with reluctance and disgust half an hour late.
'You are very late, Mr Baird,' said the bridegroom. 'Yes, about six
months too late,' replied Mr Baird.
  John Logie Baird (1888–1946), Sermons, Soap and Television

Everybody else is looking at me like I'm a bit of a mad fellow, but, hey, I'm used to that.

    Iain Banks (1954–), Raw Spirit

Oh the gladness of her gladness when she's glad,
And the sadness of her sadness when she's sad:
But the gladness of her gladness,
And the sadness of her sadness,
Are as nothing . . .
To the badness of her badness when she's bad.

    Sir J.M. Barrie (1860–1937), Rosalind

David Hume ate a swinging great dinner,
And grew every day fatter and fatter;
And yet the huge bulk of a sinner
Said there was neither spirit nor matter.

    James Beattie (1735–1803), On the Author of The Treatise of
Human Nature

With the publication of his Private Papers in 1952, he committed suicide twenty-five years after his death.

    Lord Beaverbrook (1879–1964), Men and Power, *on Earl Haig*

Dr Campbell, looking once into a pamphlet at a bookseller's shop, liked it so well as to purchase it; and it was not till he had read it halfway through that he discovered it to be of his own composition.

    Biographica Britannia, *on the author John Campbell (1708–1775)*

He appeared to take it for granted that all nature, animate and inanimate, was in a conspiracy to maim, injure and destroy him, John; and that he, John, was therefore justified in taking his revenge beforehand, whenever he got the chance.

    William Black (1841–1898), Highland Cousins

The wanderer, forgetting his assumed sex, that his clothes might not be wet, held them up a great deal too high. Kingsburgh mentioned this to him, observing it might make a discovery . . . He was very awkward in female dress. His size was so large, and his strides so great.

    James Boswell (1740–1795), Journal *(on Prince Charles Edward Stuart)*

I have some fixed principles; but my existence is chiefly conditioned by the powers of fancy and sensation.

James Boswell, Journal, *on himself*

I have heard the greatest understandings of the age giving forth their efforts in its most eloquent tongues, but I should, without hesitation, prefer, for mere intellectual gratification, to be once more allowed the privilege which I in those days enjoyed of being present while the first philosopher of his age was the historian of his own discoveries.

Lord Brougham (1778–1868), on Joseph Black

Untutor'd by science, a stranger to fear
And rude as the rocks where my infancy grew.

Lord Byron (1788–1824), As I Roved a Young Highlander

'He was a great fellow my friend Will,' he rang out in that deep voice of his. 'The thumb-mark of his Maker was wet in the clay of him.' Man, it made a quiver go down my spine.

George Douglas (George Douglas Brown, 1869–1902), The House With the Green Shutters

His behaviour under all that barbarous usage was as great and firm to the last, looking on all that was done to him with a noble scorn, as the fury of his enemies was black and universally detested.

Gilbert Burnet (1643–1715), History of His Own Time, *on the death of Montrose*

A little upright, pert, tart, tripping wight,
And still his precious self his dear delight.

Robert Burns (1759–1796), The Poet's Progress

To see her is to love her
And love her but for ever;
For nature made her what she is,
And never made anither!

Robert Burns, Bonnie Leslie

. . . a fine fat fodgel wight,
O' stature short, but genius bright

Robert Burns, On the Late Captain Grose's Peregrinations Through Scotland

Searching auld wives' barrels,
Ochon, the day!
That clarty barm should stain my laurels;
But – what'll ye say?
These movin' things ca'd wives and weans
Wad move the very hearts o' stanes!
    Robert Burns, On Being Appointed to an Excise Division

She's bow-hough'd, she's hen-shinned,
Ae limpin' leg a hand-breed shorter;
She's twisted right, she's twisted left,
To balance fair in ilka quarter.
    Robert Burns, Willie Wastle

It was very good of God to let Carlyle and Mrs Carlyle marry one
another and so make only two people miserable instead of four.
    Samuel Butler (1835–1902)

If you awakened him from his reverie, and made him attend to the
subject of the conversation, he immediately began a harangue, and
never stopped till he told you all he knew about it, and with the
utmost philosophical ingenuity.
    Alexander Carlyle (1722–1805), quoted in R.B. Haldane, Adam Smith,
    on Adam Smith (1723–1790)

Let me have my own way exactly in everything, and a sunnier and
pleasanter creature does not exist.
    ascribed to Thomas Carlyle (1795–1881), in conversation

I like to tell people when they ask 'Are you a native born?' 'No sir,
I am a Scotchman,' and I feel as proud as I am sure ever Roman did
when it was their boast to say 'I am a Roman citizen'.
    Andrew Carnegie (1835–1918), Autobiography

We know that he has, more than any other man, the gift of
compressing the largest amount of words into the smallest amount
of thought.
    Winston Churchill (1874–1965), speech in the House of Commons, 1933,
    on Ramsay Macdonald

Nobody could sit down like the Lady of Inverleith. She would sail like a ship from Tarshish gorgeous in velvet or rustling in silk, and done up in all the accompaniments of fan, ear-rings and finger-rings, falling sleeves, scent bottle, embroidered bag, hoop and train – all superb, yet all in the purest taste; and managing all this seemingly heavy rigging with as much ease as a full-blown swan does its plumage, she would take possession of the centre of a large sofa, and at the same moment, without the slightest visible exertion, would cover the whole of it with her bravery

> *Henry Thomas Cockburn (1779–1854)*, Memorials

Dr Joseph Black was a striking and beautiful person; tall, very thin, and cadaverously pale; his hair carefully powdered, though there was little of it except what was collected into a long thin queue; his eyes dark, clear and large, like deep pools of pure water.

> *Henry Thomas Cockburn*, Memorials

I never heard of him dining out, except at his relation's, Joseph Black's, where his son, Sir Adam (the friend of Scott) used to say 'It was delightful to see the two rioting over a boiled turnip'.

> *Henry Thomas Cockburn*, Memorials, *on Adam Ferguson*

Thinking of Helensburgh, J.G. Frazer
Revises flayings and human sacrifice;
Abo of the Celtic Twilight, St Andrew Lang
Posts him a ten-page note on totemism
And a coloured fairy book

> *Robert Crawford (1959–)*, Scotland in the 1890s

James Murray combs the dialect from his beard
And files slips for his massive Dictionary

> *Robert Crawford*, Scotland in the 1890s

He could start a party in an empty room, and he often did.

> *Donald Dewar (1937–2000), on John Smith, Labour Party leader (1938–1994)*

The Wardraipper of Venus boure,
To giff a doublett he is als doure,
As it war off ane futt syd frog:
Madame, ye hev a dangerouss Dog!

> *William Dunbar (c.1460–c.1520)*, Of James Dog, Kepar of the Quenis Wardrop

He is nae Dog; he is a Lam.
> *William Dunbar*, Of the Same James, When He Had Pleasit Him

It was Watt who told King George III that he dealt in an article of which kings were said to be fond – Power.
> *Ralph Waldo Emerson (1803–1882)*, Letters and Social Aims, *on James Watt*

Yonder's the tomb o' wise Mackenzie fam'd, Whase laws rebellious bigotry reclaim'd,
Freed the hail land frae covenanting fools,
Wha erst ha'e fash'd us wi' unnumbered dools.
> *Robert Fergusson (1750–1774)*, The Ghaists: A Kirkyard Eclogue, *on Sir George Mackenzie*

At the Council of Constance in 1414, a Dr Gray attended as Ambassador of Scotland, He had taken his degree at the Sorbonne, so was well qualified. As the offspring of a nun, he suffered a formidable handicap, but he was a man of such sterling character that four Popes granted him absolution, dispensation and rehabilitation.
> *Arnold Fleming*, The Medieval Scots Scholar in France

I am very strong and robust and not of the delicate sex nor of the fair but of the deficient in look. People who are deficient in looks can make up for it by virtue.
> *Marjory Fleming (1803–1811)*, Journals

I love in Isa's bed to lie
O such a joy and luxury
The botom of the bed I sleep
And with great care I myself keep
Oft I embrace her feet of lillys
But she has goton all the pillies
> *Marjory Fleming*, Journals

My mother . . . who had a genius for finding leaden linings.
> *Janice Galloway (1955–)*

He was a man of no smeddum in discourse
> *John Galt (1779–1839)*, The Provost

Sometimes even with the very beggars I found a jocose saying as well received as a bawbee, although naturally I dinna think I was ever what could be called a funny man, but only just as ye would say a thought ajee in that way.

John Galt, The Provost

He had sufficient conscience to bother him, but not sufficient to keep him straight.

David Lloyd George (1863–1945), recorded by A.J. Sylvester, 1938, on Ramsay Macdonald

And the funny thing about the creature was that she believed none spoke ill of her, for if she heard a bit hint of such, dropped sly-like, she'd redden up like a stalk of rhubarb in a dung patch.

Lewis Grassic Gibbon (James Leslie Mitchell, 1901–1935), Sunset Song

And because she just couldn't thole him at all, he made her want to go change her vest, Chris smiled at him and was extra polite.

Lewis Grassic Gibbon, Cloud Howe

Yet Knox himself was of truly heroic mould; had his followers, far less his allies, been of like mettle, the history of Scotland might have been strangely and splendidly different.

Lewis Grassic Gibbon, Scottish Scene

The 'heroic young queen' in question had the face, mind, manners and morals of a well-intentioned but hysterical poodle.

Lewis Grassic Gibbon, Scottish Scene, *on Queen Mary I*

She'd reddish hair, and high, skeugh nose, and a hand that skelped her way through life; and if ever a soul had seen her at rest when the dark was done and the day was come he'd died of the shock and never let on.

Lewis Grassic Gibbon, Smeddum

I am of that unfortunate class who never knew what it was to be a child in spirit. Even the memories of boyhood and young manhood are gloomy.

James Keir Hardie (1856–1915), quoted in K.O. Morgan, Keir Hardie

Nine quarteris large he was in lenth indeed,
Thrid part lenth in shouldris braid was he,
Richt seemly, strang and lusty for to see

'Blind Harry' (fl. 1490s), Wallace

Of riches he keepit no proper thing,
Gave as he wan, like Alexander the king.
In times of peace, meek as a monk was he,
Whan weir approachit, the richt Ector was he.
    'Blind Harry', Wallace

'Wallace, that has redeemit Scotland,
The best is callit this day beltit with brand.'
    'Blind Harry', Wallace

Auld Ramsay Mac kissed the magic duchess and turned into a
puddock.
    *Christopher Harvie (1944–), speech on the 75th anniversary of the
    Saltire Society, 16 June 2011*

. . . the most indolent of mortals and of poets. But he was also one of
the best both of mortals and of poets.
    William Hazlitt (1778–1830), Lectures on the English Poets, *on
    Thomas Campbell*

Bot in her face seemit great variance,
Whiles perfyt truth, and whiles inconstance.
    Robert Henryson (c.1425–c.1500), The Testament of Cresseid

Now hait, now cold, now blyth, now full of woe,
Now green as leaf, now witherit and ago.
    Robert Henryson, The Testament of Cresseid

'What a wonderful boy he is!' said my mother.
'I'm feared he turn out to be a conceited gowk,' said old Barnet, the
minister's man.
    James Hogg (1770–1835), The Private Memoirs and Confessions of
    a Justified Sinner

A sober, discreet, virtuous, regular, quiet, good-natured man of a
bad character.
    David Hume (1711–1776), letter to Dr Clephane, on himself

O Knox he was a bad man
he split the Scottish mind.
The one half he made cruel
and the other half unkind.
    Alan Jackson (1938–), Knox

. . . he was mainly impressed by what seemed to him the utter
futility of the world he surveyed.

> *E.O. James, in* Dictionary of National Biography, *on Sir James G.
> Frazer (1854–1941), author of* The Golden Bough

. . . for you know he lives among savages in Scotland, and among
rakes in London.

> *Samuel Johnson (1709–1784), to John Wilkes, on James Boswell, in
> Boswell's* Life of Johnson

Hardie was a collier, a journalist, an agitator who held fast to
his faiths in all the storms and tempests of an agitator's life; an
incorruptible if ever there was one.

> *Tom Johnston (1881–1965),* Memories, *on James Keir Hardie*

The classic instance of the man who lingered overlong in public
affairs is Ramsay Macdonald.

> *Tom Johnston,* Memories

I am a stranger, visiting myself occasionally.

> *Jackie Kay (1961–),* That Distance Apart

I've lived hereabouts all my life (more or less) largely waiting with
infinite impatience for fame to strike without warning . . . Ever the
apprentice Stoic.

> *Frank Kuppner (1951–),* PN Review *188, July-August 2009*

He doesnae juist drap a name
or set it up and say grace wi't,
he lays it oot on his haun
and hits ye richt in the face wi't.

> *T.S. Law (1916–1997),* Importance

Lord Kelvin – being Scotch, he didn't mind damnation, and he gave
the sun and the whole solar system only ninety million more years
to live.

> *Stephen Leacock (1869–1944)*

. . . that richt redoutit Roy,
That potent prince gentle King James the Ferde

> *Sir David Lindsay (c.1490–1555),* The Testament of the Papyngo, *on
> James IV*

He was the glory of princely governing
  Sir David Lindsay, The Testament of the Papyngo, on James IV

She looks like a million dollars, but she only knows a hundred and
twenty words and she's got only two ideas in her head.
  Eric Linklater (1899–1974), Juan in America

To sum all up, he was a learned, gallant, honest, and every other
way well-accomplished gentleman; and if ever a man proposes
to serve and merit well of his country, let him place his courage,
zeal and constancy as a pattern before him, and think himself
sufficiently applauded and rewarded by obtaining the character of
being like Andrew Fletcher of Saltoun.
  George Lockhart (1673–1731), The Lockhart Papers

When Hogg entered the drawing-room, Mrs Scott, being at
the time in a delicate state of health, was reclining on a sofa.
The Shepherd, after being presented, and making his best bow,
forthwith took possession of another sofa placed opposite to hers,
and stretched himself thereupon at all his length; for, as he said
afterwards, 'I thought I could never do wrong to copy the lady of
the house.'
  John Gibson Lockhart (1794–1854), Life of Scott, *on James Hogg,
  patronised as 'The Ettrick Shepherd'*

The government decreed that
on the anniversary of his birth
the people should observe
two minutes pandemonium
  Norman MacCaig (1910–1996), After His Death, *on Hugh
  MacDiarmid*

She was brown eggs, black skirts
and a keeper of threepenny bits
in a teapot.
  Norman MacCaig, Aunt Julia

There's a lesson here, I thought, climbing into the pulpit I keep in
my mind.
  Norman MacCaig, Country Dance

Mary was depressed,
She wanted real life, and here she was
acting in a play, with real blood in it.
And she thought of the years to come,
and of the frightful plays that would be written
about the play she was in.
Norman MacCaig, Queen of Scots

His socialism was skin-deep, his compassion as phoney as canned
laughter. Strip away the pious words and the practised facial
expressions and you were left with a zombie.
Alan McCombes on Tommy Sheridan, in The Downfall of Tommy
Sheridan, *2011*

No murder'd Beast within his bowels groans
Sir George Mackenzie (1636–1691), Caelia's Country House and
Closet, *on a vegetarian*

My heart is a lonely hunter, that hunts on a lonely hill.
Fiona MacLeod (William Sharp, 1855–1905), From the Hills of
Dream

an awkward, rusticated jungle wallah
Lachlan Macquarie (1762–1784), *Governor of New South Wales*,
describing how he felt on a visit to London

On returning to Buchanan's bedside, he meekly enquired of us,
'Have I told the truth?' My uncle replied, 'Yes, Sir, I think so.' All
that the patient could utter was, 'Pray to God for me, Melvyll, and
let him direct all.'
James Melville (1556–1614), Diaries, *on the death of George Buchanan*
(1517–1583)

Scot had answered unto Scot: an eccentric had elaborated a prodigy.
H. Miles, Introduction to the Life and Death of the Admirable
Crichton, *by Sir Thomas Urquhart (1611–1660)*

and washed his hands, and watched his hands, and washed
his hands, and watched his hands, and washed his hands.
Edwin Morgan (1920–2010), Pilate at Fortingall

James Hutton, that true son of fire
Edwin Morgan, Theory of the Earth

What Knox really did was to rob Scotland of all the benefits of the Renaissance.

Edwin Muir (1887–1959), John Knox

I knew he was one of the Macfarlanes. There were ten Macfarlanes, all men, except one, and he was a valet, but the family did their best to conceal the fact, and said he was away on the yachts

Neil Munro (1864–1930), The Vital Spark

'Hurricane Jeck was seldom very rife wi' money, but he came from Kinlochaline, and that iss ass good ass a Board of Tred certuficate.'

Neil Munro, In Highland Harbours with Para Handy

'He iss not a brat of a boy, I admit,' said the Captain, 'but he's in the prime o' life and cheneral agility.'

Neil Munro, In Highland Harbours with Para Handy

'I'm nae phenomena; I'm jist Nature; jist the Rale Oreeginal.'

Neil Munro, Erchie, My Droll Friend

'Fat does he dee? Ye micht as weel speir fat I dee mysel',
The things he hisna time to dee is easier to tell'

Charles Murray (1864–1941), Docken Afore His Peers

A penniless lass wi' a lang pedigree

Lady Nairne (1766–1845), The Laird o'Cockpen

The very worst play she wrote is better than the best o' any ither body's that hasna kickt the bucket.

Christopher North (John Wilson, 1785–1854), Noctes Ambrosianae, *on Joanna Baillie (1762–1851)*

I was a small, fat boy in a kilt with, as I saw it, limited career options . . . Half-human, half-traybake I may have been, but I was still keen to impress.

Don Paterson (1963–), *quoted in* The Observer, *20 December 2009*

With one hand he put a penny in the urn of Poverty, and with the other he took a shilling out.

Robert Pollok (1798–1827), The Course of Time, *on a landlord*

He scorned carriages on the ground of its being unmannerly to 'sit in a box drawn by brutes'.
> *Dean E.B. Ramsay (1793–1872)*, Reminiscences of Scottish Life and Character, *on Lord Monboddo*

His baptismal register spoke of him pessimistically as John Henry, but he left that behind with the other maladies of infancy.
> *Saki (H.H. Munro, 1870–1916)*, Adrian

And this is aa the life he kens there is.
> *Tom Scott (1918–1995)*, Auld Sanct-Aundrians

And dar'st thou then,
To beard the lion in his den,
The Douglas in his hall?
> *Sir Walter Scott (1771–1832)*, Marmion

In these far climes it was my lot
To meet the wondrous Michael Scott;
A Wizard, of such dreaded fame,
That when in Salamanca's pave,
Him listed his magic wand to wave,
The bells would ring in Notre Dame!
> *Sir Walter Scott*, The Lay of the Last Minstrel

His step is first in peaceful ha,
His sword in battle keen
> *Sir Walter Scott*, Jock o' Hazeldean *(additional verses)*

My foot is on my native heath, and my name is MacGregor.
> *Sir Walter Scott*, Rob Roy

O young Lochinvar is come out of the West,
Through all the wide Border his steed was the best
> *Sir Walter Scott*, Lochinvar

And there was Claverhouse, as beautiful as when he lived, with his long dark, curled locks streaming down over his laced buff-coat, and his left hand always on his right spule-blade, to hide the wound that the silver bullet had made.
> *Sir Walter Scott*, Redgauntlet

you have the Glasgow Bailie before you, with all his bustling conceit and importance, his real benevolence and his irritable habits.
Sir Walter Scott, letter to Lord Montagu, 1821

Up to her University days she carried the conviction that there was something about Scotland in the Bible.
Nan Shepherd (1893–1981), Quarry Wood

The Right Honourable Gentleman is indebted to his memory for his jests, and to his imagination for his facts.
Richard Brinsley Sheridan (1751–1816), speech in the House of Commons, on Henry Dundas (1742–1811)

He has less nonsense in his head than any man living.
Adam Smith (1723–1790), quoted in Lord Brougham, Lives of Men of Letters and Science in the Reign of George III, *on Joseph Black (1728–1799)*

Upon the whole, I have always considered him, both in his lifetime and since his death, as approximating as nearly to the idea of a perfectly wise and virtuous man, as perhaps the nature of human frailty will permit.
Adam Smith, letter to William Strachan, 1776, on David Hume (1711–1776)

I would rather be remembered by a song than by a victory.
Alexander Smith (1830–1867), Dreamthorp

Too coy to flatter, and too proud to serve,
Thine be the joyless dignity to starve.
Tobias Smollett (1721–1771), Advice

In bane he was sma'-boukit,
But had a muckle beard
And whan he gar'd it waggle
Baith men and beast were feared.
William Soutar (1898–1943), John Knox

My faither's deid, my mither's dottle,
My tittie's cowpit the creel;
My only brither is the bottle
And I've aye lo'ed him weel.
William Soutar, Cadger Jimmy

From my experience of life I believe my personal motto should be 'Beware of men bearing flowers'.

   Muriel Spark (1918–2006) Curriculum Vitae

... the nicest boy who ever committed the sin of whisky.

   Muriel Spark, A Sad Tale's Best for Winter

To this day his name smacks of the gallows.

   Robert Louis Stevenson (1850–1894), Some Portraits by Raeburn, *on Lord Braxfield*

Looking so cool,
his greed is hard to conceal,
he's fresh out of law school,
you've given him a licence to steal.

   Al Stewart (1945–) Scottish-born US lyricist and musician

... lanely I stray, in the calm simmer gloamin',
To muse on sweet Jessie, the flower o' Dunblane.

   Robert Tannahill (1774–1810), Jessie, the Flower o' Dunblane

An haena ye heard man, o' Barochan Jean,
How death an starvation cam' ower the haill nation:
She wrocht such mischief wi' her twa pawky e'en.

   Robert Tannahill, Barochan Jean

He has been known to have lectured for the hour before reaching the subject of the lecture.

   J.J. Thomson, Recollections and Reflections, *on Lord Kelvin (1824–1907)*

It is, therefore, as the typical Scotchman, intensely devoted to the truth, caring for nothing except truth, who has come to England to teach us half-Scots and no-Scots how the intellectual life is lived, that I bid you think of him.

   Professor Graham Wallas, 70th birthday tribute to John M. Robertson (1856–1933), sociologist and free-thinker

Five foot six, an unlucky thirteen stone . . . a sixth rate mathematician, a second-rate physicist, a second-rate engineer, a bit of a meteorologist, something of a journalist, a plausible salesman of ideas, liking to believe that there is some poetry in my physics and some physics in my poetry.

Sir Robert Watson-Watt (1892–1973), in a radio broadcast, about himself

We called Johnny 'Mother Superior' because ay the length ay time he'd hud his habit.

Irvine Welsh (1957–), Trainspotting

The Spirit of Scotland

My son, I tell thee truthfully,
No good is like to liberty.
Then never live in slavery
    Traditional, ascribed to William Wallace (c.1270–1305)

But after all, if the prince shall leave these principles he hath so
nobly pursued, and consent that we or our kingdom be subjected
to the king or people of England, we will immediately endeavour
to expel him as our enemy, and as the subverter both of his own
and our rights, and will make another king who will defend our
liberties. For as long as there shall but one hundred of us remain
alive, we will never consent to subject ourselves to the dominion of
the English. For it is not glory, it is not riches, neither is it honour,
but it is liberty alone that we fight and contend for, which no honest
man will lose but with his life.
    The Declaration of Arbroath, 1320, from Latin

From the lone sheiling on the misty island
Mountains divide us, and a waste of seas–
Yet still the blood is strong, the heart is Highland,
And we in dreams behold the Hebrides.
    Anonymous, Canadian Boat Song

For we have three great avantages;
The first is, we have the richt,
And for the richt ilk man suld ficht,
The tother is, they are comin here . . .
To seek us in our awn land . . .
The thrid is that we for our livis
And for our childer and our wifis
And for the fredome of our land
Are strenyeit in battle for to stand.
    John Barbour (c.1320–1395), The Brus

A! fredome is a noble thing!
Fredome maiss man to haif liking:
Fredome all solace to man giffis,
He levis at ease that freely levis!
A noble heart may haif nane ease,
Nae ellis nocht that may him please,
Gif fredome failye
    John Barbour, The Brus

My Lords, patricide is a greater crime than parricide, all the world
over
    *Lord Belhaven (1656–1708), Speech in Parliament, the Union Debates,
    1706*

None can destroy Scotland, save Scotland's self.
    Lord Belhaven, speech in Parliament, 1706

She's a puir auld wife wi' little to give,
And rather stint o' caressin';
But she's shown us how honest lives we may live,
And sent us out wi' her blessin'.
    William Black (1841–1898), Shouther to Shouther

. . . the smell of neeps after rain. Surely that exquisite aroma is
essential Scotland: it has the sharp tang of so many Scottish things;
of whisky, especially, and smoked fish, of pinewoods and of peat.
    Ivor Brown (1891–1974), A Word in Your Ear

And for my dear lov'd Land o' Cakes,
I pray with holy fire:
Lord, send a rough-shod troop o' Hell
O'er a' wad Scotland buy or sell,
To grind them in the mire!
    Robert Burns (1759–1796), Election Ballad

Auld Scotland has a raucle tongue;
She's just a devil wi' a rung;
An' if she promise auld or young
To tak their part,
Tho' by the neck she would be strung,
She'll no desert.
    Robert Burns, The Author's Earnest Cry and Prayer to the Right
    Honourable and the Honourable, the Scotch Representatives In
    the House of Commons

... the story of Wallace poured a Scottish prejudice in my veins
which will boil along there till the floodgates of life shut in eternal
rest.

> *Robert Burns, letter to Dr John Moore (August 1787)*

And though, as you remember, in a fit
Of wrath and rhyme, when juvenile and curly,
I rail'd at Scots to show my wrath and wit,
Which must be own'd was sensitive and surly,
Yet 'tis in vain such sallies to permit,
They cannot quench young feelings fresh and early:
I 'scotch'd not kill'd' the Scotchman in my blood,
And love the land of 'mountain and of flood'.

> *Lord Byron (1788–1824)*, Don Juan

Land of polluted river,
Bloodshot eyes and sodden liver
Land of my heart forever
Scotland the Brave.

> *Billy Connolly (1942–), quoted in Jonathan Margolis*, The Big Yin
> *(1994)*

So let us be known for our kind hospitality,
A hand that is open proper to friends;
A hard working people, proud and unbending,
Scotland will thrive and win out in the end.

> *The Corries*, Scotland will Flourish *(1985)*

I go wheresoever the shade of Montrose will direct me.

> *John Graham, Viscount Dundee (1648–1690), 18 March 1689*

In the garb of old Gaul, wi' the fire of old Rome,
From the heath-covered mountains of Scotia we come.

> *Henry Erskine (1720–1765)*, In the Garb of Old Gaul

The Scots deserve no pity, if they voluntarily surrender their united
and separate interests to the Mercy of an united Parliament, where
the English have so vast a Majority

> *Andrew Fletcher of Saltoun (1656–1716)*, State of the Controversy
> Betwixt United and Separate Parliaments *(1706)*

It is only fit for the slaves who sold it.

> *Andrew Fletcher of Saltoun, quoted in G.W.T. Ormond*, Fletcher of
> Saltoun *(1897), on Scotland after the Union*

It grows near the seashore, on banks, in clefts, but above all on the little green braes bordered with hazel-woods. It rarely reaches more than two feet in height, is neither white nor cream so much as old ivory; unassuming, modest, and known as the white rose of Scotland.

Neil Gunn (1891–1973), Highland Pack

Forty-eight Scottish kings buried in this tumbled graveyard – before the Norman conquest of England in 1066. And today should a man be bold enough to refer to the Scottish nation, he is looked upon as a bit of a crank.

Neil Gunn, Off in a Boat, *on Iona*

Towering in gallant fame,
Scotland, my mountain hame –
High may your proud banners gloriously wave!

Cliff Hanley (1922–1999), Scotland the Brave

All year long, each season through, each day and each fall of dusk for me,
it is Scotland, Lowland and Highland, that is laughter and warmth and life for me.

George Campbell Hay (1915–1984), 'The Four Winds of Scotland'
(Ceithir Gaothan na h-Albann)

The heather's in a blaze, Willie,
The White Rose is on the tree,
The Fiery Cross is on the braes,
And the King is on the sea!

Andrew Lang (1844–1912), Kenmure, 1715

From the damp shieling on the draggled island
Mountains divide you, and no end of seas.
But, though your heart is genuinely Highland,
Still, you're in luck to be away from these!

Andrew Lang, To Fiona

It is now the duty of the Scottish genius
Which has provided the economic freedom for it
To lead in the abandonment of creeds and moral compromises
Of every sort

Hugh MacDiarmid (C.M. Grieve, 1892–1978), Stony Limits and Other Poems

He canna Scotland see wha yet
Canna see the Infinite,
And Scotland in true scale to it.
  Hugh MacDiarmid, A Drunk Man Looks at the Thistle

Above all, it must be remembered that the Scottish spirit is in
general brilliantly improvisatory.
  Hugh MacDiarmid, Scottish Eccentrics

It has suffered in the past, and is suffering now, from too much
England.
  A.G. Macdonell (1895–1941), My Scotland

Scottishness isn't some pedigree lineage: it's a mongrel tradition.
  William McIlvanney (1936–), at a SNP rally, 1992

. . . the little band striving
When giving in would be good sense.
  Sorley Maclean (1911–1996), A Poem Made When the Gaelic
  Society of Inverness Was 100 Years Old

No other country has fallen so hard for its own image in the funfair
mirror. Tartan rock, and a Scottie dog for every pot.
  Candia MacWilliam (1957–), A Case of Knives

Fecht for Britain? Hoot, awa!
For Bonnie Scotland? Imph, man, na!
For Lochnagar? Wi' clook and claw!
  J.C. Milne, quoted in H. Brown, Poems of the Scottish Hills *(1982)*

Must we be thirled to the past,
To the mist and the unused shieling?
Over love and home and the Forty-Five,
Sham tunes and a sham feeling?
  Naomi Mitchison (1897–1999), The Cleansing of the Knife

The Thistle, Scotland's badge,
Up from Freedom's soil it grew,
Her foes aye found it hedged round
With rosemarie and rue.
  David Macbeth Moir (1798–1851), The Blue Bell of Scotland

Of Scotland's king I haud my hoose,
He pays me meat and fee;
And I will keep my gude auld hoose,
While my hoose will keep me.

> *'Black' Agnes Randolph, Countess of March (fl. 14th century), to the*
> *besiegers of Dunbar Castle*

The solitudes of land and sea assuage
My quenchless thirst for freedom unconfined;
With independent heart and mind
Hold I my heritage.

> *Robert Rendall (1898–1967)*, Orkney Crofter

There is a storm coming that shall try your foundations. Scotland
must be rid of Scotland before the delivery come.

> *James Renwick (1662–1688), Cameronian leader, at his execution*

If we don't have some self-respect we
Might as well be in the ground
If we've got nothin' else at least
We've got our pride.

> *Tony Roper (1941–), 'Pride', from* The Steamie *(1987)*

Hou sall aa the folk I've been ere meet
And bide in yae wee house?
Knox wi' Burns and Mary, Wishart and Beaton
Aa be snod and crouse?
Campbell and MacDonald be guid feirs,
The Bruis sup wi Comyn?
By God, I dout afore sic love appears,
Nae man sall kiss a woman!

> *Tom Scott (1918–1995)*, Fergus

Front, flank and rear, the squadrons sweep
To break the Scottish circle deep
That fought around their king . . .
The stubborn spearmen still made good
Their dark impenetrable wood,
Each stepping where his comrade stood,
The instant that he fell.

> *Sir Walter Scott (1771–1832)*, Marmion

Breathes there the man with soul so dead
Who never to himself hath said,
This is my own, my native land!
    Sir Walter Scott, The Lay of the Last Minstrel

O Caledonia! stern and wild,
Meet nurse for a poetic child!
Land of brown heath and shaggy wood;
Land of the mountain and the flood!
    Sir Walter Scott, The Lay of the Last Minstrel

There are too many 90-minute patriots whose nationalist
outpourings are expressed only at major sporting events.
    Jim Sillars (1937–)

Resentment of my country's fate
Within my filial breast shall beat;
And, spite of the insulting foe,
My sympathising verse shall flow,
'Mourn, hapless Caledonia, mourn
Thy banish'd peace, thy laurels torn.'
    Tobias Smollett (1721–1771), The Tears of Scotland

. . . my young nephew Patrick, the taciturn Scot of all the Scots; he
who, at the age of three, held up before a mirror by his grandmother
and asked by her, 'Wha's that?' had lived up to the highest tradition
of the Scots by his riposte, 'Wha wad it be?'
    Sir Robert Watson-Watt (1892–1973), Three Steps to Victory

O Flower of Scotland
When will we see your like again
That fought and died for
Your wee bit hill and glen . . .
These days are past now
And in the past they must remain,
But we can still rise now,
And be a nation again.
    Roy Williamson (1936–1990), Flower of Scotland *(1969)*

Sports and Pastimes

'At a big fitba' match . . . when the crowd wave their hankies for
the ambulance men to come, and then the man's taken along the
touchline to the pavilion – on a stretcher, ken – well, if he's carried
heid foremost he's a' right, but if he's feet foremost, he's deid!'

    Anonymous football lore, quoted in James Ritchie, The Singing Street
    (1964)

Everywhere we go-o!
People want to know-ow
Who the hell we a-are
And where we come from.
We're the Tartan Army,
We're mental and we're barmy.

    Anonymous, 'Everywhere We Go', Quoted in Ian Black, Tales of the
    Tartan Army *(1997)*

The grouse shooters were often rather pathetic people, going
through a ritual imposed on them because they could afford it . . .
They were stung, by everything and everybody.

    John R. Allan (1906–1986), Farmer's Boy

Th' athletic fool to whom what Heav'n denied
Of soul is well compensated in limbs . . .
The men of better clay and finer mould
Know nature, feel the human dignity,
And scorn to vie with oxen or with apes.

    John Armstrong (c.1709–1779), The Art of Preserving Health

The charm of fishing is that it is the pursuit of what is elusive but
attainable: a perpetual series of occasions for hope.

    John Buchan (1875–1940)

Tully produced a complimentary admission ticket from the waistband of his playing shorts during a game in which he was getting the better of his immediate opponent, the fearsome full-back Don Emery. He handed it to Emery, with the observation, 'Here, would you not be better watching from the stand?'

> *Peter Burns and Pat Woods*, Oh, Hampden in the Sun *(1997), on Charlie Tully, Celtic star of the late 1940s*

Make it pay or give it up.

> *Advice from his father to Byron 'Jim' Clark (1936–1968), later world motor racing champion*

My son was born to play for Scotland. He has all the qualities, a massive ego, a criminal record, an appalling drink problem, and he's not very good at football.

> *'Mrs Alice Cosgrove', quoted on the back cover of Stuart Cosgrove,* Hampden Babylon *(1991)*

Football management these days is like a nuclear war. No winners, only survivors.

> *Tommy Docherty (1928–), quoted in Peter Ball and Phil Shaw,* The Umbro Book of Football Quotations *(1993)*

To the Scot, football's lovely incurable disease.

> *Tommy Docherty, 'It's Only a Game', BBC TV, 1985*

I talk a lot. On any subject. Which is always football.

> *Tommy Docherty*

The only game in which you can put on weight while playing it.

> *Tommy Docherty, on cricket*

He says, 'Who are you?' I says, 'Albion Rovers.' He says, 'Never heard of them.' I said, 'You ignorant bugger.' But it was a natural thing, I mean, it wisnae him alone – there were other people who'd never heard of Albion Rovers.'

> *Tom Fagan of Albion Rovers, on a FIFA meeting, 1985, quoted in K. Macdonald,* Scottish Football Quotations, *1994*

If Johnson had deliberately intended an attack on the referee, his right foot would not have missed the target.

> *F.A. Disciplinary Report on Willie 'Wee Bud' Johnson (1976), quoted in S. Cosgrove,* Hampden Babylon *(1991)*

You can't applaud a referee.
  Sir Alex Ferguson (1941–)

There are goals here. I can smell them.
  Sir Alex Ferguson

The doctor said, 'This child's very ill. Have to get him to hospital.'
'I canny take him,' the man says. 'Celtic are playing Leeds United
tonight.'
  Hugh Ferrie, Celtic supporter, quoted in S. Walsh, Voices of the Old
  Firm *(1995)*

''Twas the short fourteenth,' the Duke was saying. 'Need I tell thee
what 'tis like? A hint of slice and you're dead. I laid my pitch pin-
high, and damme if Paterson didn't miss the putt.'
'Codso!' exclaimed King Charles.
  George Macdonald Fraser (1925–2008), The Pyrates

Play Up, Play Up, And Get Tore In
  George Macdonald Fraser, title of short story

Would you also be good enough to bring your ball with you in case
of any breake down, and thus prevent interruptsion. Hoping the
weather will favour the Thistle and Queen.
  *Robert Gardner, Letter to the Secretary of Thistle FC, Glasgow, June
  1867, arranging the first known inter-club football game in Scotland*

Bi' ma knees is skint and bluddan,
an ma breeks they want the seat,
jings! ye get mair nir ye're eftir,
pleyan fi'baw in the street.
  Robert Garioch (Robert Garioch Sutherland, 1909–1981), Fi'baw in
  the Street

. . . an intensely Presbyterian activity. In golf, you do not play
against an opponent. You may play alongside him, but he can't
touch your ball or interfere with your swing. You are on your
own, one man matching his effort and his conscience against the
enigma of life. You may lie about the number of strokes you took
to kill a snake in the heather; but you know, and so does the Big
Handicapper in the Sky from Whom nothing is hidden.
  Cliff Hanley (1922–1999), The Scots

Referees are following rules made by men who don't pay to watch football. These rules are ruining the game for those who do.
David Hay, of St Mirren, August 1991, quoted in K. Macdonald, Scottish Football Quotations *(1994)*

There was a woman there with the blue eye-shadow and the red lipstick and I was walking off and she called me a big dirty Fenian bastard. I turned and said, 'Oh, come on,' and she said, 'Nothing personal, I know your Auntie Annie.'
Tony Higgins, Hibernian striker, in 'It's Only a Game', BBC TV, 1985

Even in the Foreign Office I could set my watch by the evening flight of the ducks from St James's Park – over the Horse Guards Parade to the Thames estuary – and select a right and a left with my imaginary gun.
Lord Home (1903–1995), Border Reflections

. . . English football players have been quoted as saying that the Hampden Roar is the equivalent of two goals for Scotland. Unfortunately this has not always proved true.
Jack House (1906–1991), The Third Statistical Account of Scotland: Glasgow *(1958)*

Why is it that I play at all?
Let memory remind me
How once I smote upon my ball,
And bunkered it *– behind me.*
Andrew Lang (1844–1912), Off My Game

The secret of my success over the four hundred metres is that I run the first two hundred metres as hard as I can. Then, for the second two hundred metres, with God's help, I run faster.
Eric H. Liddell (1902–1945), on winning the Olympic gold medal (1924)

The wee bit pat, nae mair nor that,
The canny touch, scarcely sae much.
The stroke that sends the ballie in,
O that's the stroke to gar you win!
Wallace Martin Lindsay (1858–1937), A Song of Putting

All I've got against it is that it takes you so far from the clubhouse.
Eric Linklater (1899–1974)

Five grand a week? That's my kind of pressure.
> *Lou Macari, quoted in K. Macdonald,* Scottish Football Quotations, *1994*

The thunderbolt struck him in the midriff like a red-hot cannonball upon a Spanish galleon, and with the sound of a drumstick on an insufficiently stretched drum. With a fearful oath, Boone clapped his hands to his outraged stomach, and found the ball was in the way. He looked at it for a moment in astonishment and then threw it down angrily and started to massage the injured spot while the field rang with applause at the brilliance of the catch.
> *A.G. Macdonell (1895–1941),* England, Their England

The game's a bogey!
> *Children's cry, also used as a play title by John McGrath, 1974*

Oh, he's football crazy, he's football mad
And the football it has robbed him of the wee bit sense he had.
And it would take a dozen skivvies, his clothes to wash and scrub,
Since our Jock became a member of that terrible football club.
> *Jimmy MacGregor (1932–),* Football Crazy

Right, let's hospitalise these bastards!
> *Alastair McHarg, rugby international, in a match against England, 1971, quoted by Quintin Dunlop,* Scotsman, *5 March 2011*

. . . the game is hopelessly ill-equipped to carry the burden of emotional expression the Scots seek to load upon it. What is hurting so many now is the realisation that something they believed to be a metaphor for their pride has all along been a metaphor for their desperation.
> *Hugh McIlvanney (1934–),* McIlvanney on Football

Eck: . . . This is where I come to do what the Scots are best at.
Willie: Shinty?
Eck: Moping.
> *John McKay,* Dead Dad Dog *(1988)*

He's like a demented ferret up a wee drainpipe.
> *Bill McLaren (1923–2010), rugby commentator*

It's high enough, it's long enough, and it's straight enough.
> *Bill McLaren, on a rugby conversion*

If I ask the players for less than perfection they'll definitely give me less.

> *Jim McLean, football manager, quoted in K. Macdonald*, Scottish
> Football Quotations *(1994)*

One would throw two pennies up in the air, and all the other members of the group would bet they would come down as tails . . . It reminds me of the visitor who came to a mining village and said the miners had a queer kind of religion; a group of miners stood in a ring every Sunday morning and they all looked up at the sky and looked down on the ground and together they would say, 'Jesus, tails again.'

> *Abe Moffat, 'My Life With the Miners', quoted in T. C. Smout*, A
> Century of the Scottish People, 1830–1950 *(1986)*

Among the Scots, licking of wounds is second only to football as a national sport, ecstasy occurring when the two activities merge (as they often do) into one.

> *Tom Nairn (1932–1963)*, The Guardian, *May 1986*

Golf is not a relaxation, golf is everything, golf is a philosophy, it's a religion, absolutely, I mean really absolutely.

> *Sir Bob Reid, quoted in the* Sunday Times *(November 1989)*

Some people think football is a matter of life and death . . . I can assure them it is much more serious than that.

> *Bill Shankly (1914–1981), quoted in* The Guardian, *1973*

I don't drop players. I make changes.

> *Bill Shankly, quoted in* The Guardian, *1973*

If you're in the penalty area and don't know what to do with the ball, put it in the net and we'll discuss the options later.

> *Bill Shankly, quoted by Alastair Mackay in* The Scotsman *(July 1998)*

The trouble with you, son, is that your brains are all in your head.

> *Bill Shankly to a Liverpool player, 1967*

I've been basically honest in a game in which it's sometimes difficult to be honest. Sometimes you've got to tell a little white lie to get over a little troublesome period of time.

> *Bill Shankly*

The ultimate Scottish international team would be: Knox, Wallace, Bruce, Burns, Montrose, Dunbar, Adam, Napier, Smith, Telford and Stewart. Absolute certainty of salvation in goal; tigerish tackling and devilish cunning at full back; a centre back of legendary courage . . . the left winger can be Charles Edward, Lachie, or Jackie, they could all shift a bit when the going was good or bad.

>   *W. Gordon Smith (1928–1996),* This is My Country *(1976)*

Shankly, who once played for a very minor Scottish team called Glenbuck Cherrypickers, is also alleged to have put his head round the door of the visitors' dressing-room after a goalless game and announced: 'The better team drew.'

>   *W. Gordon Smith,* This Is My Country

We all end up yesterday's men in this business.

>   *Jock Stein (1922–1985), quoted in Archie Macpherson,* The Great Derbies

I would have been a much more popular World Champion if I had always said what people wanted to hear. I might have been dead, but definitely more popular.

>   *Sir Jackie Stewart (1939–), motor racer and campaigner for better safety provision in the sport*

Glaswegian definition of an atheist – a man who goes to a Celtic-Rangers match to watch the football.

>   *Sandy Strang, quoted in S. Walsh,* Voices of the Old Firm *(1995)*

Thoughts, Wishes and Reflections

I heard the cuckoo, with no food in my stomach,
I heard the stock dove on the top of the tree . . .
I saw the wheatear on a dike of holes,
I saw the snipe while sitting bent.
And I foresaw that the year
Would not go well with me.

    Omens, *from Gaelic*

What is hotter than fire? The face of an hospitable man, when
strangers come, and there is nought to offer.

    Anonymous, from 'Fionn's Questions', quoted by Amy Murray in Father
Allan's Island *(1936)*

Sa lang as I may get gear to steal, I never will wirk.

    Anonymous, How the First Hielandman was Made

Steal ane cow, twa cow, tat be common tief. Steal hundred cow, tat
be shentleman drover.

    Anonymous Highlander, 18th century

O that the peats would cut themselves,
The fish jump on the shore,
And that I in my bed could lie
And sleep for ever more.

    Anonymous, The Crofter's Prayer

There's many a horse has snappit and fa'n,
And risen an' gane fu' rarely;
There's many a lass has lost her lad,
An' gotten anither richt early.

    Traditional, Mormond Braes

Even to be happy is a dangerous thing.

    Sir William Alexander (c.1567–1640), Darius

Its all one thing, both tends unto one Scope
To live upon Tabacco and on hope,
The one's but smoake, the other is but wind.
   Sir Robert Ayton (1570–1638), Upone Tabacco

Endurance is not just the ability to bear a hard thing, but to turn it
into glory.
   William Barclay (1907–1978), in The British Weekly

As soon as you can say what you think, and not what some
other person has thought for you, you are on the way to being a
remarkable man.
   Sir J.M. Barrie (1860–1937), Tommy and Grizel

I said it was not true that the world is grown old and no good men
now to be found as in former times, for new men of worth are
always appearing. He answered . . . 'Yes, yes, the pot is continually
boiling, and there's always fresh broth.' I love such metaphorical
sallies.
   James Boswell (1740–1795), Journal

The Big House of the bairn, so enormous, majestic, what is it? Just
decently earning its keep as a farm. Oh, never revisit!
   Ivor Brown (1891–1974), Never Go Back

I'll be merry and free,
I'll be sad for naebody;
Naebody cares for me,
I care for naebody.
   Robert Burns (1759–1796), I Hae a Wife

O wad some Power the giftie gie us
To see oursels as ithers see us!
It wad frae monie a blunder free us,
And foolish notion.
   Robert Burns, To a Louse

Contented wi' little, and cantie wi' mair,
Whene'er I forgather wi' Sorrow and Care,
I gie them a skelp as they're creepin alang,
Wi' a cog o' gude swats and an auld Scottish sang.
   Robert Burns, Contented Wi' Little and Cantie Wi' Mair

The honest heart that's free frae a'
Intended fraud or guile,
However Fortune kick the ba'
Has ay some cause to smile.
    Robert Burns, Epistle to Davie

Everything's intentional. It's just filling in the dots.
    David Byrne (1952–), Scottish-born US musician

'Tis distance lends enchantment to the view
    Thomas Campbell (1777–1844), The Pleasures of Hope

Like pensive beauty, smiling in her tears
    Thomas Campbell, The Pleasures of Hope

Like angel visits, few and far between.
    Thomas Campbell, The Pleasures of Hope

All, all forsook the friendless guilty mind,
But Hope, the charmer, still remain'd behind.
    Thomas Campbell, The Pleasures of Hope

Silence is the element in which great things fashion themselves
together.
    Thomas Carlyle (1795–1881), Sartor Resartus

The person who comes up to you and makes the most noise and is
the most intrusive is invariably the person in the room who has no
respect for you at all, and it's really all about them.
    Robbie Coltrane (1950–)

Me, made after the image o' God?
Jings, but it's laughable, tae.
    Joe Corrie (1894–1968), Miners' Wives

Secure your birthright; set the world at naught;
Confront your fate; regard the naked deed;
Enlarge your Hell; preserve it in repair;
Only a splendid Hell keeps Heaven fair.
    John Davidson (1857–1909), The Testament of an Empire-Builder

FEEL LIKE A BOY AGAIN
    Norman Douglas (1868–1952), double-entendre *telegram to a friend.*

And all the gay deceased of old,
The wise, the generous, the good,
The poet sage, the warrior bold,
The man of brain, the man of blood
Their songs I grant, were wild and free,
To match their deeds I would not strive,
But put your money, boys, on me,
For they are dead and I'm alive.
    T.L. Douglas, 'A Living Dog', from Glasgow University Poems, *1910*

What sweet delight a quiet life affords
And what it is from bondage to be free,
Far from the madding worldlings' hoarse discords
    William Drummond (1585–1649), The Cypresse Grove

The stars are filming us for no-one.
    Carol Ann Duffy (1955–)

Flattery weiris ane furrit goun,
And Falsett with the Lordis dois roun;
And Trewth standis barrit at the dure,
And Honour exul is of the toun:
In to this warld may none assure.
    William Dunbar (c.1460–c.1520), None May Assure in This Warld

Excess of thocht does me mischeif.
    William Dunbar, To the King

The sea, I think, is lazy,
It just obeys the moon
    Ian Hamilton Finlay (1925–1996), Mansie Considers the Sea, in the
    Manner of Hugh MacDiarmid

Conflict is one of the givens of the universe. The only way it can
ever be tamed or managed or civilised is within culture. You cannot
pretend that it does not exist.
    Ian Hamilton Finlay, quoted in Alec Finlay, Wood Notes Wild: Essays
    on the Poetry and Art of Ian Hamilton Finlay *(1995)*

To every man the hardest form of slavery is to serve as a slave in
one's own native country, there where one was wont to be free lord.
    John Fordun (d.1385), Scotichronicon, *translated from Latin*

I thought people understood what humour was, that it was invented
by the human race to cope with the dark areas of life, problems and
terrors.

    Bill Forsyth (1946–)

. . . good triumphs and the villain bites the dust. If anyone
believes that, the story of the Border Reivers should convince him
otherwise. Its moral is clear: there is little justice to be had. The
good man survives, if he is lucky, but the villain becomes the first
Lord Roxburgh.

    George Macdonald Fraser (1925–2008), The Steel Bonnets *(1971)*

The posters show my country blonde and green,
Like some sweet siren, but the travellers know
How dull the shale sky is, the airs how keen

    G.S. Fraser (1915–1980), Meditation of a Patriot

Poverty, many can endure with dignity. Success, few can carry off,
even with decency and without baring their innermost infirmities
before the public gaze.

    R.B. Cunninghame Graham (1852–1936), Success and Other
    Sketches

Now up in the mornin's no for me,
Up in the mornin' early;
When snaw blaws into the chimley cheek,
Wha'd rise in the mornin' early?

    John Hamilton (1761–1814), Up in the Morning Early

Tiresome 'tis to be a dreamer.
When will it be time to dine?

    James Hedderwick (1814–?), The Villa by the Sea

I carena muckle for folk that bairns and dogs dinna like.

    James Hogg (1770–1835), quoted in Margaret Garden, Memorials of
    James Hogg

From my heart I can say I like no such titles & if you value your
own comfort & my peace of mind you will at once, if offered to you,
refuse it.

    Margaret Hogg (1790–1870), Letter to her husband James in London,
    who had been speculating on whether he would be offered a knighthood
    (March 1832)

An' what'll I get when my mither kens
   Violet Jacob (1863–1946), The End O't

O besy goste! ay flickering to and fro,
That never art in quiet nor in rest,
Til thou cum to that place thou cam fro
   King James I (1394–1437), Animula, Vagula, Blandula

Pass the sick-bag, Alice.
   John Junor (1919–1997), The Sunday Express, *his catch-phrase*

The party's almost over. Though at times a trifle odd, I've
thoroughly enjoyed it. Thank you for having me, God.
   Maurice Lindsay (1918–2009), To Catch the Last Post

What more lovely than to be alone
With a Teasmade, a radio and a telephone?
   Liz Lochhead (1947–), Heartbreak Hotel

Nae man or movement's worth a damn unless
The movement 'ud gang on withoot him if
He de'ed the morn.
   Hugh MacDiarmid (C.M. Grieve, 1892–1978), Depth and the
   Chthonian Image

I'll ha'e nae hauf-way hoose, but aye be whaur
Extremes meet – it's the only way I ken
To dodge the curst conceit o' bein' richt
That damns the vast majority o' men
   Hugh MacDiarmid, A Drunk Man Looks at the Thistle

They sang that never was sadness
But it melted and passed away;
They sang that never was darkness
But in came the conquering day.
   George Macdonald (1824–1905), The Old Garden

To be trusted is a greater compliment than to be loved.
   George Macdonald, The Marquis of Lossie

I mauna cuddle in the wyme o' yesterdays.
   Alastair Mackie (1925–1995), Aiberdeen Street

It's only when at home that I forgo
The luxury of knowing who I am.
    Alasdair Maclean (1926–1994), Home Thoughts from Home

Therefore put quite away
All heaviness of thocht:
Thoch we murne nicht and day
It will avail us nocht.
    Sir Richard Maitland (1496–1586), Advice to Leesome Merriness

O grant me, Heaven, a middle state,
Neither too humble nor too great;
More than enough for nature's ends,
With something left to treat my friends.
    David Mallett (c.1705–1765), Imitation of Horace

. . . no-one need expect to be original simply by being absurd.
There is a cycle in nonsense . . . which ever and anon brings back
the delusions and error of an earlier time.
    Hugh Miller (1820–1856), The Testimony of the Rocks

We let the day grow old among the grass.
    Edwin Morgan (1920–2010), From a City Balcony

The thochts o' bygane years
Still fling their shadows ower my path,
And blind my een wi' tears.
    William Motherwell (1797–1835), Jeanie Morrison

We bear the lot of nations,
Of times and races,
Because we watched the wrong
Last too long
With non-commital faces.
    Edwin Muir (1887–1959), The Refugees

And without fear the lawless roads
Run wrong through all the land
    Edwin Muir, Hölderlin's Journey

God has to nearly kill us sometimes, to teach us lessons.
    John Muir (1838–1914), *quoted in* National Parks Magazine *(US)*,
2007

On one occasion he declared that he was richer than magnate E. H. Harriman: 'I have all the money I want and he hasn't.'

John Muir, quoted in C. Fadiman, The Little Brown Book of Anecdotes *(1985)*

Concerning all acts of initiative (and creation), there is one elementary truth the ignorance of which kills countless ideas and splendid plans: that the moment one definitely commits oneself, then providence moves too. A whole stream of events issues from the decision, raising in one's favour all manner of unforeseen incidents, meetings and material assistance, which no man could have dreamt would have come his way. I learned a deep respect for one of Goethe's couplets:
Whatever you can do or dream you can, begin it.
Boldness has genius, power and magic in it!

W.H. Murray (1913–1996), The Scottish Himalayan Expedition *(1951)*

There can be no peace in the world so long as a large proportion of the population lack the necessities of life and believe that a change of the political and economic system will make them available. World peace must be based on world plenty.

John Boyd Orr (1880–1971)

There's meikle good done in the dark.

Allan Ramsay (1686–1758), The Marrow Ballad

The future is not what it used to be.

Sir Malcolm Rifkind (1946–), Tory politician

Sometimes, if you want things to stay the same, things have to change.

Sir Malcolm Rifkind, BBC News Channel, May 2005

A prophet, as you have him in ancient history, and more recently in Carlyle, may be defined as a person whose language is strong and whose theory is wrong.

John M. Robertson (1856–1933), Modern Humanists

Whit trasherie will I turn up the day?

Christopher Rush (1944–), Monday Morning

There's a gude time coming

Sir Walter Scott (1771–1832), Rob Roy

It isna what we hae done for oursels, but what we hae done for ithers, that we think on maist pleasantly.
Sir Walter Scott, The Heart of Midlothian

But THOU hast said, The blood of goat,
The flash of rams I will not prize;
A contrite heart, a humble thought,
Are mine accepted sacrifice.
Sir Walter Scott, 'Rebecca's Hymn', *from* Ivanhoe

Still if the question was eternal company without the power of retiring within yourself or Solitary confinement for life I should say, 'Turnkey, lock the cell.'
Sir Walter Scott, Journal, *December 1825*

Sorrow remembers us when day is done
Iain Crichton Smith (1928–1998), When Day is Done

We ever new, we ever young,
We happy creatures of a day!
C.H. Sorley (1895–1915), Untitled Poem

Darkness is your only door;
Gang doun wi' a sang, gang doun.
William Soutar (1898–1943), Song

Ah! forgive me, fellow-creatures,
If I mock when you are gone;
And if sometimes at life's concert
I would rather sit alone
William Soutar, Impromptu in an Eremitic Mood

How easily a small inconvenience can cover the sun and make us forget the misery of a universe; and the tragic element in self-pity is this, that at last the power of maintaining proportion between the world and the self is lost, and is not known to have been lost.
William Soutar, Diary of a Dying Man

But oh! what a cruel thing is a farce to those engaged in it!
Robert Louis Stevenson (1850–1894), Travels With a Donkey

Truth in spirit, not truth to letter, is the true veracity.
Robert Louis Stevenson, Truth of Intercourse

The world is so full of a number of things
I'm sure we should all be as happy as kings.
    Robert Louis Stevenson, Happy Thought

The faculty of imagination is the great spring of human activity
. . . Destroy this faculty, and the condition of man will become as
stationary as that of the brutes.
    Dugald Stewart (1753–1828), Elements of the Philosophy of the
    Human Mind

At the First Supper
The guests were but one:
A maiden was the hostess,
The guest her son.
    Jan Struther (J. Anstruther, 1901–1953), The First Supper

This warl's a tap-room owre and owre,
Whaur ilk ane tak's his caper,
Some taste the sweet, some drink the sour,
As waiter Fate sees proper.
    Robert Tannahill (1774–1810), The Tap-Room

What the future may have in store, no-one can tell; we are bound to
say ignoramus, but not ignorabimus.
    Sir J. Arthur Thomson (1861–1933), The Wonder of Life *(we do not
    know; we shall not know)*

. . . a cold rage seizes one at whiles
To show the bitter old and wrinkled truth
Stripped naked of all vesture that beguiles
False dreams, false hopes, false masks and modes of youth.
    James Thomson (1834–1882), The City of Dreadful Night

The world rolls round for ever like a mill;
It grinds out death and life and good and ill;
It has no purpose, heart or mind or will.
    James Thomson, The City of Dreadful Night

Noo slings aboot an' stars a' oot, an' auld moon chowin' sin,
Here ye wonner really at the din,
As fit aboot of ebbs salute, and fetters all the score,
Hyfon pland often really soar.
    Thomas Thomson (1837–1924), Hyfons, Hyfons

Aye, it's on the highways
The feck o' life maun gang:
But aye it's frae the byways
Comes hame the happy sang.

    Walter Wingate (1865–1918), Highways and Byways

Toasts and Greetings

May the best ye've ever seen
Be the worst ye ever see.
Traditional

May the mouse never leave our meal pock wi' the tear in its eye.
Traditional

Would it not be the beautiful thing now
If you were coming instead of going?
Traditional island farewell, from Gaelic

Here's to the king, sir,
Ye ken wha I mean, sir.
Jacobite toast

The King ower the Water.
Jacobite toast

The little gentleman in black velvet.
*Jacobite toast, to the mole on whose hill King William III's horse
stumbled, causing his death*

Here's to the horse wi' the four white feet,
The chestnut tail and mane –
A star on his face and a spot on his breast,
An' his master's name was Cain.
Traditional horsemen's toast

Grace be here, and grace be there,
And grace be on the table;
Ilka one tak' up their speen,
An' sup a' that they're able.
Anonymous bothy grace, from D.K. Cameron, The Cornkister Days
(1984)

For auld lang syne, my dear,
For auld lang syne,
We'll tak' a cup o' kindness yet,
For auld lang syne.
    Robert Burns (1759–1796), Auld Lang Syne

Fair fa' your honest, sonsie face,
Great chieftain o' the pudding-race!
    Robert Burns, Address to a Haggis

Napoleon is a tyrant, a monster, the sworn foe of our nation. But
gentlemen – he once shot a publisher.
    *Thomas Campbell (1777–1844), proposing a toast to Bonaparte at a
    writers' dinner*

Every glass during dinner had to be dedicated to someone. It was
thought sottish and rude to take wine without this, as if forsooth
there was nobody present worth drinking with.
    Henry Thomas Cockburn (1779–1854), Memorials

Good night, and joy be wi' you a';
We'll maybe meet again the morn.
    James Hogg (1770–1835), Good Night, and Joy Be Wi' You

May the hills lie low,
May the sloughs fill up
In the way.
    Kenneth MacLeod (1871–1955), Blessing of the Road

Highland honours are one foot on the chair and the other on the
table, with the exclamation of 'Neish, neish, shouterish, shouterish,
hurrah!' which is translated 'Now, now, again, again, hurrah!'
the company brandishing and emptying their glasses, and then
throwing each glass into the fire. The latter part of the ceremony
was omitted in this case, but I have seen it done. Being inconvenient
and expensive, it is not generally adopted, particularly if there is a
lady in the house.
    Joseph Mitchell (1803–1883), Reminiscences of My Life in the
    Highlands

The traditional Orkney invitation to a visitor was, 'Put in thee
hand.'
    Edwin Muir (1887–1959), Autobiography

I'll drink a cup to Scotland yet,
Wi' a' the honours three!
> *Henry Scott Riddell (1798–1870)*, The Three Honours of Scotland

Plenty herring, plenty meal,
Plenty peat to fill her creel –
Plenty bonny bairns as weel,
That's the toast for Mairi.
> *Sir Hugh S. Roberton (1874–1952)*, The Lewis Bridal Song

Transport and Travel

The king sits in Dunfermline town,
Drinking the blood-red wine;
'O where will I get a skeely skipper,
To sail this new ship o' mine?'
 Anonymous, Sir Patrick Spens

Had you seen these roads before they were made,
You would lift up your hands and bless General Wade.
 Anonymous, lines on the military roads constructed under General George Wade during 1726–37

The earth belongs unto the Lord,
And all that it contains;
Except the Western Isles alone,
And they are all MacBrayne's.
 Anonymous rhyme on the MacBrayne Steamship Company, 20th century

The bonnie wee Sultana,
The bully of the Clyde –
She's gone and took the Jeanie Deans,
And laid her on her side.
 Boys' rhyme on rival Clyde steamers, quoted in George Blake, Down to the Sea: The Romance of the Clyde

Anyone can go. It's just a question of looking at the horizon and deciding whether you really want to go.
 Sir Chay Blyth (1940–), on single-handed sailing round the world, interview with Herb McCormick in Cruising World, *March 1997*

I am travelling with a general desire to improve myself.
 James Boswell (1740–1795), Letter to Jean-Jacques Rousseau, December 1764

In the event of a cabin failure, oxygen masks will drop from the ceiling, and untangling them will annoy you before you die.
 Frankie Boyle (1972–)

A grand old boat is the Waverley,
She'll tak ye doon tae Rothesay and be back for tea,
The way she did when ye were wee.

> *Jim Brown, 'The Waverley Polka', in Ewan MacVicar,* One Singer,
> One Song *(1990)*

I'm now arriv'd – thanks to the gods!
Thro' pathways rough and muddy:
A certain sign that makin' roads
Is no this people's study.
Altho' I'm not wi' Scripture cram'd,
I'm sure the Bible says
That heedless sinners shall be damn'd,
Unless they mend their ways.

> *Robert Burns (1759–1796),* Epigram on Rough Roads

If any man wants to be happy, I advise him to get a public allowance
for travelling.

> *Henry Thomas Cockburn (1779–1854),* Circuit Journeys

Oh, ye should hear his manly voice when cryin' ilka day,
'The ither side for Wilsontown, Carnwath and Auchengray!'
An' then he's aye sae cheery, aye the foremost i' the ploy:
My bonnie porter laddie wi' the green corduroy.

> *T.S. Denholm, 'The Green Corduroy', in Caledonian Railway*
> Christmas Annual, *1909*

Jokes were made about the Highland Railway . . . You heard, until
you were sick of it, about the Highland mail train from Inverness
which reached Helmsdale twelve hours late and, when it finally
arrived at Wick, was mistaken for the next day's train running to
time.

> *C. Hamilton Ellis,* The Trains We Loved *(1947)*

The minister of Dolphinton, being eager to have a railway through
his parish, set himself to ascertain the number of cattle that passed
along the road daily in front of his manse. He was said to have
counted the same cow many times in the same day.

> *Sir Archibald Geikie (1835–1924),* Scottish Reminiscences

A worthy countryman who had come from the north-east side of
the kingdom by train to Cowlairs, was told that the next stoppage
would be Glasgow. He at once began to get all his little packages
ready, and remarked to a fellow-passenger, 'I'm sailin' for China this
week, but I'm thinkin' I'm by the warst o' the journey noo.'
   Sir Archibald Geikie, Scottish Reminiscences

I remember a crofter on the island of Eigg, who, when asked when
the steamer would arrive, replied at once, 'Weel, she'll be comin'
sometimes sooner, and whiles earlier, and sometimes before that
again.'
   Sir Archibald Geikie, Scottish Reminiscences

But I need the rides most, hurling warm through all weathers and
seasons, with a paperback thriller on my lap, and always Scotland
outside the window in more changes of scenery in ten miles than
England in fifteen or Europe in twenty, or India, America or Russia
in a hundred.
   Alasdair Gray (1934–), 1982 Janine

. . . there was at least one class of criminals from which Scotland
was exempt, and that was of highwaymen. That fraternity, so large
and prosperous beyond the border, was here unknown; they would
have grown weary of waiting for passengers to waylay, and died of
poverty from finding so little to plunder from their persons.
   H. Grey Graham, The Social Life of Scotland in the Eighteenth
   Century *(1899)*

To the rail, to the rail, now the pent-up desires
Of the pale toiling million find gracious reply.
On the pinions of steam they shall fly, they shall fly.
   Janet Hamilton (1795–1873), The Sunday Rail, *on the first running of
   Sunday trains on the North British Railway*

There was a naughty boy,
And a naughty boy was he –
He ran away to Scotland,
The people for to see.
But he found,
That the ground was as hard,
That a yard was as long,
That a song

Was as merry,
That a cherry
Was as red . . .
And a door was as wooden, as in England
    John Keats (1795–1821), There Was a Naughty Boy

But the whole notion of standing at bus stops! Awful. The whole
notion of a bus even! Because he required the exact sum of money
for the fare. If he didni have this exact sum the driver would refuse
to give him change, he would just take the entire £1 or £5 or
whatever it was and keep it on behalf of the transport company that
employed him.
    A situation fraught with awkwardidity.
    James Kelman (1946–), A Disaffection

Hammered like a bolt
diagonally through Scotland (my
small dark country) this
train's a
swaying caveful of half–
seas over oil-men (fuck
this fuck that fuck
everything) bound for Aberdeen and North Sea Crude
    Liz Lochhead (1947–), Inter-City

No doubt he'd come home by instinct, the poor man's taxi.
    Brian McCabe (1951–), The Other McCoy

I don't like this, being carried sideways through the night. I feel
wrong and helpless – like a timber broadside in a fast stream.
    Norman MacCaig (1910–1996), Sleeping Compartment

My feeling is that we probably didn't have the right skill mix.
    *Edinburgh Councillor Gordon Mackenzie, a member of the board of the
    wound-up Transport Initiative Edinburgh company, 2010*

I wasn't aware he had qualifications in theology, but I don't myself
believe that the One who made the heavens and the earth would
be stumped by a pair of 6-cylinders, 4-stroke, 3266kW 600rpm
Mirrlees Blackstone K6 Major engines.
    *Mr John Macleod, Lewis, on a CalMac spokesman who said the Sunday
    ferry's failure was engine trouble and not divine intervention (July
    2009)*

I'll tak ye on the road again,
When yellow's on the broom.
>   *Adam McNaughtan*, When Yellow's On the Broom *(2001)*

. . . we were graciously received by Lady Seafield, to whom we
explained the purport of our visit. She very decidedly told us she
'hated railways,' – they brought together such an objectionable
variety of people. Posting, in her opinion, with four horses, was the
perfection of travelling.
>   *Joseph Mitchell (1803–1883)*, Reminiscences of My Life in the
>   Highlands

The Vital Spark, I confessed, was well known to me as the most
uncertain puffer that ever kept the Old New Year in Upper
Lochfyne.
>   *Neil Munro (1864–1930)*, The Vital Spark

May God bless the bark of Clan-Ranald
The first day she floats on the brine:
Himself and his strong men to man her –
The heroes whom none can outshine.
>   *Alexander Nicolson (1827–1893)*, The Galley of Clanranald, *from the*
>   *Gaelic of Alastair Macdonald*

The end of the world is near when the MacBrayne's ship will be on
time.
>   *Iain Crichton Smith (1928–1998)*, Thoughts of Murdo

the silent ferryman standing in the stern
clutching his coat about him like old iron.
>   *Iain Crichton Smith*, By Ferry to the Island

Faster than fairies, faster than witches,
Bridges and houses, hedges and ditches;
And charging along like troops in a battle,
All through the meadows the horses and cattle,
All the sights of the hill and the plain
Fly as thick as driving rain.
>   *Robert Louis Stevenson (1850–1894)*, From a Railway Carriage

I travel not to go anywhere, but to go. I travel for travel's sake. The
great affair is to move.
>   *Robert Louis Stevenson*, Travels with a Donkey

To travel hopefully is a better thing than to arrive.
  Robert Louis Stevenson, Virginibus Puerisque

All I ask, the heavens above,
And the road below me.
  Robert Louis Stevenson, The Vagabond

No 224. This was the engine that had gone down with the Tay
Bridge on 27th December 1879, had been recovered, and had spent
part of 1880 at Cowlairs being refurbished. Someone christened her
The Diver, and she was known by that name until the end of her
long career.
  John Thomas (1914–1982), The Springburn Story

Will someone ever rise to write the saga of the 'Flying Scotsman'?
There would be sardonic stories in that book, like that of the two
enterprising ladies who, during the war years, drove a thriving trade
catering for the amorous needs of men going on and returning from
leave, and who must have been the most consistent passengers the
London and North-Eastern Railway ever had.
  George Malcolm Thomson (1899–1996), The Rediscovery
  of Scotland

As we rush, as we rush in the train,
The trees and the houses go wheeling back,
But the starry heavens above the plain
Come flying in on our track.
  James Thomson (1834–1882), The Train

The bus station concourse is like a Social Security office turned
inside out and doused with oil.
  Irvine Welsh (1957–), Trainspotting

Highways for eident feet,
That hae their mile to gae.
  Walter Wingate (1865–1918), Highways and Byways

War and Warriors

'Thou shalt not yield to lord nor loun,
Nor yet shalt thou to me;
But yield thee to the bracken bush
Grows on yon lily-lee.'
Anonymous, The Battle of Otterburn

This fray was fought at Otterbourne,
Between the night and the day;
Earl Douglas was buried at the bracken bush,
And the Percy led captive away.
Anonymous, The Battle of Otterburn

In doubtsome victory they dealt;
The bludy battle lasted long;
Ilk man his neighbour's force there felt
The weakest oft-times got the wrong.
Anonymous, The Battle of Harlaw

'Fight on, my men,' says Sir Andrew Barton,
'I am hurt, but I am not slain;
I'le lay me down and bleed awhile,
And then I'le rise and fight again.'
Anonymous, Sir Andrew Barton

Fair maiden Lylliard lies under this stane
Little was her stature but great was her fame
Upon the English louns she laid many thumps,
And when her legs were cuttit off she fought upon the stumps.
Inscription recorded from 'Lilliard's Stone', Midlothian

Teribus ye teri odin,
Sons of heroes slain at Flodden,
Imitating Border bowmen,
Aye defend your rights and common.
Traditional Hawick rhyme, quoted in Charles Mackay, Poetry and
Humour of the Scottish Language *(1882)*

'O are ye come to drink the wine,
As ye hae doon before, O?
Or are ye come to wield the brand,
On the dowie houms o' Yarrow?

> *Anonymous*, The Dowie Houms o' Yarrow

Of this sort the said galliasse in schort tyme cam on windwart of
the tothir schip. Than eftir that thay had hailit utheris, thay maid
them reddie for batail. Than quhair I sat I herd the cannonis and
gunnis maik monie hideous crak, duf duf duf duf duf duf. The
bersis and falconis cryit tirdif, tirdif, tirdif, tirdif, tirdif, tirdif. Then
the small artailzie cryit tik tak, tik tak, tik tak, tik tak, tik tak. The
reik, smuik, and the stink of the gun pulder fylit all the air

> *Anonymous*, The Complaynt of Scotland *(1549), account of a sea battle*

It fell on a day, and a bonnie simmer day,
When green grew aits and barley,
That there fell out a great dispute
Between Argyll and Airlie.

> *Anonymous*, The Bonny House o' Airlie

I faught at land, I faught at sea,
At hame I faught my aunty, O;
But I met the devil and Dundee,
On the braes o' Killiecrankie, O

> *Anonymous, on the battle of Killiecrankie (26 July 1689)*

Everybody else took the road he liked best

> *Contemporary comment on the end of the 1715 Rising, following the*
> *secret departure of the 'Old Pretender' and the Earl of Mar, quoted in*
> *C. Stewart Black*, Scottish Battles *(1936)*

A Gordon for me, a Gordon for me:
If you're no' a Gordon you're nae use to me.
The Black Watch are braw, the Seaforths and a',
But the cocky wee Gordon's the pride o' them a'.

> *Anonymous*, A Gordon for Me

The wind may blaw, the cock may craw,
The rain may rain, and the snaw may snaw;
But ye winna frichten Jock McGraw,
The stoutest man in the Forty-Twa.

> *Anonymous*, The Stoutest Man in the Forty-Twa

'They're a' out o' step but oor Jock!'
>   *Apocryphal mother looking through the railings of a Glasgow barracks*

Had I been there with sword in hand,
And fifty Camerons by,
That day through high Dunedin's streets
Had pealed the slogan-cry.
>   *W.E. Aytoun (1818–1865)*, The Execution of Montrose

For the king had said him rudely
That ane rose of his chaplet
Was fallen
>   *John Barbour (c.1320–1395)*, The Brus: *Bruce's rebuke to the Earl of*
>   *Moray on the field of Bannockburn, 1314*

'Beis not abasit for their schor,
Bot settis speris you before
And back to back set all your rout
And all the speris pointis out'
>   *John Barbour*, The Brus

Henry V . . . ordered the plunder of the shrine of Saint Fiacre,
the holy son of an ancient Scottish king. For this sacrilege he was
smitten by the saint with a kind of leprosy, and shortly died of it,
cursing the Scots, and lamenting that 'I can go nowhere without the
finding the Scots at my beard, dead or alive'.
>   *C. Stewart Black*, Scottish Battles *(1936)*

'Fight on!' he cried to them. 'Fight on! Stand ye fast by the Cross of
Saint Andrew!'
>   *C. Stewart Black*, Scottish Battles, *quoting the last words of Sir*
>   *Andrew Barton (d.1511)*

There is no such thing as an inevitable war. If war comes it will be
from failure of human wisdom.
>   *Andrew Bonar Law (1858–1923), speech*

Scots, wha hae wi' Wallace bled,
Scots, wham Bruce has aften led,
Welcome to your gory bed,
Or to victory.
>   *Robert Burns (1759–1796)*, Bruce's Address to His Army Before
>   Bannockburn

Now's the day and now's the hour,
See the front o' battle lour . . .
Wha for Scotland's king and law
Freedom's sword would strongly draw,
Freeman stand, and freeman fa'–
Let him on wi' me!
  Robert Burns, Bruce's Address to His Army Before Bannockburn

I am a son of Mars who have been in many wars,
And show my cuts and scars wherever I come:
This here was for a wench, and that other in a trench,
When welcoming the French at the sound of the drum.
  Robert Burns, The Jolly Beggars

I once was a maid, tho' I cannot tell when,
And still my delight is in proper young men;
Some one of a troop of dragoons was my daddie,
No wonder I'm fond of a sodger laddie.
  Robert Burns, The Jolly Beggars

Cock up your beaver, and cock it fu' sprush,
We'll over the Border and gie them a brush
  Robert Burns, Cock Up Your Beaver

O Kenmure's lads are men, Willie,
O Kenmure's lads are men;
Their hearts and swords are metal true,
And that their foes shall ken.
  Robert Burns, Kenmure's On and Awa', Willie

Ye hypocrites! are these your pranks?
To murder men, and gie God thanks!
For shame! Gie o'er – proceed no farther –
God won't accept your thanks for murther.
  Robert Burns, Verses Written on a Pane of Glass on the the
  Occasion of a National Thanksgiving for a Naval Victory

And wild and high the 'Cameron's gathering' rose!
The war-note of Lochiel, which Albyn's hills
Have heard, and heard, too, have her Saxon foes:–
How in the noon of night that pibroch thrills,

Savage and shrill! But with the breath that fills
Their mountain-pipe, so fill the mountaineers
With the fierce native daring which instils
The stirring memory of a thousand years,
And Evan's, Donald's fame rings in each clansman's ears!
> *Lord Byron (1788–1824)*, Childe Harold's Pilgrimage, *on the Battle of Waterloo*

'Ninety-third! Ninety-third! Damn all that eagerness.'
> *Sir Colin Campbell to the 'Thin Red Line' at Balaclava, 1854; quoted in C. Woodham-Smith*, The Reason Why *(1953)*

When was a war not a war? When it was carried on by means of barbarism.
> *Sir Henry Campbell-Bannerman (1836–1908), Speech to the National Reform Union Dinner, June 1901, on the Boer War*

It was during this time that Billy joined the Parachute Regiment of the Territorial Army, seeking adventure, and trying to make himself windswept and interesting. Billy claims that at the medical exam, the doctor said, 'You're not very big downstairs, are you?' to which Billy quipped, 'I thought we were only going to fight them.'
> *Billy Connolly (1942–), quoted by James McGowan*, The Billy Connolly Website, *1998*

I cannot reproach myself; the manner in which the enemy came on was quicker than could be described, and . . . possibly was the cause of our men taking a most destructive panic.
> *Sir John Cope (c. 1690–1760), reporting to Lord Tweeddale after the battle of Prestonpans (September 20, 1745)*

On fut sould be all Scottis weir,
By hill and moss thaimself to steir,
Lat woodis for wallis be bow and speir,
That enemyis do thaim na deir.
In strait placis keip all store,
And burn the planeland thaim befoir . . .
This is the counsail and intent
Of Guid King Robert's Testament
> *John Fordun (d.1385)*, Scotichronicon, *translation written in Latin on the margin of a copy belonging to Hector Boece (c. 1465–1536)*

. . . when the Scots saw the Englishmen recoil and yield themselves, then the Scots were courteous and set them their ransoms and every man said to his prisoner, Sir, go and unarm you and take your ease: I am your master, and so made their prisoners as good cheer as if they had been brothers, without doing them any damage.

> *Jean Froissart (c. 1333–c.1404)*, Chroniques, *on the Battle of Otterburn, 1388, translated from French*

Victory belongs to those who hold out the longest.

> *Field Marshal Earl Haig (1861–1928), Order to the British Expeditionary Force, April 1918*

Never volunteer for nothing

> *Hamish Henderson (1919–2002)*, Fort Capuzzo

In the battle of Inverkeithing, between the Royalists and Oliver Cromwell, five hundred of the followers of the Laird of Maclean were left dead on the field. In the heat of the conflict, seven brothers of the clan sacrificed their lives in defence of their leader, Sir Hector Maclean. Being hard pressed by the enemy, he was supported and covered from their attacks by these intrepid men; and as one brother fell, another came up in succession to cover him, crying, 'Another for Hector!'

> *David Stewart of Garth (1772–1829)*, Sketches of the Highlanders of Scotland

Like Douglas conquer, or like Douglas die

> *John Home (1724–1808)*, Douglas

The main force used in the evolving world of humanity has hitherto been applied in the form of war.

> *Sir Arthur Keith (1866–1955)* Evolution and Ethics

I canna see the sergeant,
I canna see the sergeant,
I – canna – see the – sergeant:
He's owre far awa'.

> *Joseph Lee (1878–1949)*, Ballads of Battle

Every bullet has its billet;
Many bullets more than one.
God! Perhaps I killed a mother,
When I killed a mother's son.

> *Joseph Lee*, The Bullet

Then the King broke out publicly, in these words, saying, 'O you who were wont to say that my Scotsmen were useless to the King and the kingdom, worth naught save as eaters of mutton and guzzlers of wine, see now who have earned the honour, victory, and glory, of this battle.

> Liber Pluscardensis, *quoting King Charles VII of France, on the Scots who fought at the Battle of Beaugé (1421), translated from Latin*

The Captain whispered, 'Come on!' Merriman, lurching forward on his belly, thrust his bayonet stiffly in front of him and heard a muffled cry of pain.
'What's the matter?' he asked.
Another muted whimper answered him, and a moment later one of the patrol, in the broad, untroubled accents of Buchan, said hoarsely, 'Michty God, ye've fair ruined the Captain. You've stuck your bayonet clean up his airse!'

> *Eric Linklater (1899–1974)*, Magnus Merriman

They are a song in the blood of all true men.

> *Hugh MacDiarmid (C.M. Grieve, 1892–1978)*, The International Brigades

You remember the place called the Tawny Field?
It got a fine dose of manure;
Not the dung of sheep and goats,
But Campbell blood, well congealed.

> *Iain Lòm Macdonald (c.1620–c.1707)*, Las Inbhir Lochaidh *(The Battle of Inverlochy)*

'I will follow you to death, were there no other to draw a sword in your cause.'

> *Ronald MacDonald (fl. mid 18th century), quoted in Dugald Mitchell,* History of the Highlands and Gaelic Scotland *(1900), to Prince Charles Edward Stewart, on the* Doutelle, *July 1745*

'We had an English subaltern once in our battery who used to run and extinguish fires in ammunition dumps . . . He said that shells cost five pounds each and it was everyone's duty to save government money.'
'Where is he buried?' asked Cameron.

> *A.G. Macdonell (1895–1941)*, England, Their England

Duncan gave orders that if it came to fighting, every one of the
ships must fight until she sank, and added that he had carefully
noted the soundings, and the flags could still fly though the ships
were at the bottom . . . in fact he stopped the Dutch without losing
a man.

> *Agnes Mure Mackenzie*, Scottish Pageant, *1707–1802, on Admiral*
> *Lord Duncan in 1797*

Fat civilians wishing they
'Could go and fight the Hun.'
Can't you see them thanking God
That they're over forty-one?

> *E.A. Mackintosh (1893–1916)*, Recruiting

Lads, you're wanted. Come and die.

> *E.A. Mackintosh*, Recruiting

Lest we see a worse thing than it is to die,
Live ourselves and see our friends cold beneath the sky,
God grant that we too be lying there in wind and mud and rain
Before the broken regiments come stumbling back again.

> *E.A. Mackintosh*, Before the Summer

The only war that is worth waging is the Class War

> *John Maclean (1879–1923)*, The Vanguard

There's some say that we wan,
Some say that they wan,
Some say that nane wan at a', man;
But o' ae thing I'm sure,
That at Sheriffmuir,
A battle there was that I saw, man.
And we ran, and they ran,
And they ran, and we ran,
And they ran and we ran awa', man.

> *Murdoch MacLennan (fl. early 18th century)*, Sheriffmuir *(1715)*

O children of Conn, remember
Hardihood in time of battle:
Be watchful, daring,
Be dextrous, winning renown,
Be vigorous, pre-eminent,
Be strong, nursing your wrath,
Be stout, brave,
Be valiant, triumphant . . .

> *MacMhuirich, 'Incitement to Clan Donald before the Battle of Harlaw'*
> *(1411), from Gaelic, quoted in Hugh Cheape and I. F. Grant,* Periods in
> Highland History *(1987)*

Tonight's the night – if the lads are the lads!

> *The Macnab's rallying cry to his twelve sons, quoted in Augustus Muir,*
> Heather Track and High Road *(1944)*

Cathmor feels the joy of warriors, on his mossy hill: their joy in
secret when dangers rise equal to their souls.

> *James Macpherson (1736–1796),* Temora

Greybeards plotted. They were sad.
Death was in their wrinkled eyes.
At their table – with their maps,
Plans and calculations – wise
They all seemed; for well they knew
How ungrudgingly Youth dies.

> *Harold Monro (1879–1932),* Youth in Arms

There's nothing noo in the heids o' the gyurls but sodgers. But ye
canna blame the craturs! There's something smert aboot the kilt
and the cockit bonnet.

> *Neil Munro (1864–1930),* Hurricane Jack of the Vital Spark

Gin danger's there, we'll thole our share,
Gi'es but the weapons, we've the will
Ayont the main to prove again,
Auld Scotland counts for something still.

> *Charles Murray (1864–1941),* A Sough of War

. . . some said the hair shirt rather than arms was their protection

> *Guillaume de Nangis,* Chronicon *(c.1315), quoted in Agnes Mure*
> *Mackenzie,* Scottish Pageant *(1946), on the Scots at Bannockburn,*
> *from Latin*

There are more than birds on the hill tonight,
And more than winds on the plain!
The threat of the Scotts has filled the moss,
'There will be moonlight again.'
   Will H. Ogilvie (1869–1963), The Blades of Harden

It was perhaps one of the most innocent and orderly hosts ever seen,
considering they had no discipline and not much pay.
   John Ramsay of Ochtertyre (1736–1814), Letter to Elizabeth Dundas,
   February 1810, on Prince Charles Edward Stewart's army

In winter 1779, after Scotland had been exhausted by raising new
levies, Sir William Augustus Cunningham boasted in the House of
Commons that 20,000 men might yet be raised in that country and
never be missed . . . The Hon. Henry Erskine said he believed it was
true. But they must be raised from the churchyards.
   Charles Rodger, Boswelliana *(1874)*

Hail to the Chief who in triumph advances!
   Sir Walter Scott (1771–1832), The Lady of the Lake

On right, on left, above, below,
Sprung up at once the lurking foe.
   Sir Walter Scott, The Lady of the Lake

Come one, come all! This rock shall fly
From its firm base as soon as I.
   Sir Walter Scott, The Lady of the Lake

. . . the stern joy which warriors feel
In foemen worthy of their steel.
   Sir Walter Scott, The Lady of the Lake

I hae swaggered wi' a' thae arms, and muskets, and pistols, buff-
coats and bandoliers, lang eneugh, and I like the pleugh-paidle a
hantle better.
   Sir Walter Scott, Old Mortality

'Aye, if ye had fower legs ye wouldnae stand there lang.'
   Wat Scott of Harden (fl. late 16th century), quoted in G.M. Fraser, The
   Steel Bonnets *(1971), remark made on passing an English haystack on*
   the way home from a raid

If that you will France win
Then with Scotland first begin.
    William Shakespeare (c.1530–1601), Henry V

Now Johnnie, troth, ye are na blate
To come wi' the news o' your ain defeat,
And leave your men in sic a state,
Sae early in the morning.
    Adam Skirving (1719–1803), Johnnie Cope

The security of every society must always depend, more or less,
upon the martial spirit of the great body of the people.
    Adam Smith (1723–1790), The Wealth of Nations

Doutless he deed for Scotland's life;
Doutless the statesmen dinna lee;
But och tis sair begrutten pride,
And wersh the wine o' victorie!
    Sydney Goodsir Smith (1915–1975), The Mither's Lament

The captain's all right, really. A touch of the toasted tea-breid. You
know the type.
    W. Gordon Smith (1928–1996), Mr Jock *(1987)*

As a nation we've fallen in and marched behind some damned funny
folk.
    W. Gordon Smith, Mr Jock

Earth that blossom'd and was glad
'Neath the cross that Christ had,
Shall rejoice and blossom too
When the bullet reaches you.
    C.H. Sorley (1895–1915), Untitled Poem

Machines of death from east to west
Drone through the darkened sky;
Machines of death from west to east
Through the same darkness fly . . .
They leave a ruin; and they meet
A ruin on return
    William Soutar (1898–1943), Revelation

You can understand, from the look of him, that sense, not so much of humour, as of what is grimmest and driest in pleasantry, which inspired his address before the fight at Camperdown. He had just overtaken the Dutch fleet under Admiral de Winter. 'Gentlemen,' says he, 'you see a severe Winter approaching; I have only to advise you to keep up a good fire.'

> *Robert Louis Stevenson (1850–1894),* Some Portraits by Raeburn, *on Admiral Lord Duncan (1731–1804)*

'. . . it may come to a fecht for it yet, Davie; and then, I'll confess I would be blythe to have you at my oxter, and I think you would be none the worse of having me at yours.'

> *Robert Louis Stevenson,* Catriona

'A warrior', said he, 'should not care for wine or luxury, for fine turbans or embroidered shulwars; his talwar should be bright, and never mind whether his papooshes are shining.'

> *W.M. Thackeray (1811–1863), of Sir Charles James Napier (1782–1853)*

'Men, remember there is no retreat from here. You must die where you stand.'
To the Russian cavalry as they came on, the hillock appeared unoccupied, when suddenly, as if out of the earth, there sprang up a line two deep of Highlanders in red coats – the line immortalised in British history as 'the thin red line'.

> *Cecil Woodham-Smith,* The Reason Why *(1953), on Sir Colin Campbell (1792–1863), and the Argylls at Balaclava (October 1854)*

Words, Language and Speech

Baith in one.

> *Traditional. An esoteric phrase used as the 'Horseman's word', given to young farmhands on their initiation.*

Words of affection, howsoe'er express'd,
The latest spoken still are deemed the best.

> *Joanna Baillie (1762–1851)*, Address to Miss Agnes Baillie on Her Birthday

Let us treat children and fairies in a more summary manner . . .
Nowadays if in reading a book I come across a word beginning with
'c' or 'f' I toss it aside.

> *Sir J.M. Barrie (1860–1937)*, Speech to the Royal Literary Fund, *1930*

A word, he says, is short and quick, but works
A long result

> *John Stuart Blackie (1809–1895)*, The Wise Men of Greece

Our school was in Scotland, in almost every respect a Scottish
public school, and yet a strong Scottish accent was a real stigma . . .
When people spoke with a strong Scottish accent we would make
harsh retching sounds in the base of our throats or emit loose-jawed
idiot burblings.

> *William Boyd (1952–)*, Old School Ties, *on Gordonstoun School in the 1960s*

The tinkers have curious voices – angular outcast flashing accents
like the cries of seagulls.

> *George Mackay Brown (1921–1996)*, Five Green Waves

It is a word, blossoming as legend, poem, story, secret, that holds
a community together and gives a meaning to its life . . . Decay of
language is always the symptom of a more serious sickness.

> *George Mackay Brown*, An Orkney Tapestry

Most words descend in value.

> *Ivor Brown (1891–1974)*, A Word in Your Ear

Glamour . . . this beautiful word has been bludgeoned to death by modern showmanship . . . an English importation from Scotland where it had long signified magic with magical effect.

Ivor Brown, A Word in Your Ear

I can perceive without regret the gradual extinction of the ancient Scottish language, and cheerfully allow its harsh sounds to die away, and give place to the softer and more harmonious tones of the Latin.

George Buchanan (c.1506–1582), quoted in A. L. Williamson, Scottish National Consciousness in the Age of James VI *(1979)*

The mair they talk I'm kend the better;
E'en let them clash!

Robert Burns (1759–1796), The Poet's Welcome to His Bastart Wean

I realised that Gaelic was a missing part of my world, since with the modern Gael I share a history but not a language . . . his history remains mine; written into my conscience in invisible ink, in a language I have forgotten how to understand.

James Campbell, Invisible Country *(1984)*

The coldest word was once a glowing new metaphor

Thomas Carlyle (1795–1881), Past and Present

Sarcasm I now see to be, in general, the language of the devil.

Thomas Carlyle, Sartor Resartus

Great the blindness and the sinful darkness and ignorance and evil will of those who teach, write and foster the Gaelic speech; for to win for themselves the empty rewards of the world, they both choose and use more and more to make vain and misleading tales, lying and worldly, of the Tuath de Danann, of fighting men and champions, of Fionn MacCumhal and his heroes, and many more whom now I will not number.

John Carswell, Kirk Superintendent of Argyll (fl mid 16th century), translated from Gaelic, in the Introduction to a Gaelic translation of the Liturgy of the English Congregation at Geneva, quoted in Agnes Mure Mackenzie, Scottish Pageant 1513–1625 *(1948)*

In Scotland we live between and across languages.

Robert Crawford (1959–), Identifying Poets

... the Society's design was ... not to continue the Irish language, but to wear it out, and learn the people the English tongue

> *Committee of the Society for the Propagation of Christian Knowledge (1720), quoted in Agnes Mure Mackenzie*, Scottish Pageant 1707–1802 *(1950)*

Edinburgh, one of the few European capitals with no anti-semitism in its history, accepted them with characteristic cool interest. In its semi-slums they learned such English as they knew, which meant in fact that they grafted the debased Scots of the Edinburgh streets onto their native Yiddish to produce one of the most remarkable dialects ever spoken by man.

> *David Daiches (1912–2005)*, Two Worlds

Doric has a secret world of its own, an atmosphere I am unable to define.

> *A.M. Davidson (1897–1979)*, The Tinker's Whussel

Traist weill, to follow ane fixt sentence or matter
Is mair practic, difficil, and mair straiter,
Though thine ingyne be elevate and hie,
Than for to write all ways at libertie.

> *Gavin Douglas (1475–1522)*, Prologue to the Aeneid, *on translation*

The beauty of his ornate eloquence
May nocht all time be keepit with the sentence ...
Wha haldis, quod he, of wordis the properteis
Full oft the verity of the sentence fleeis.

> *Gavin Douglas*, Prologue to the Aeneid

Telling the secret, telling, clucking and tutting,
Sighing, or saying it served her right,
the bitch! – the words and weather both are cutting
In Causewayend, on this November night.

> *G.S. Fraser (1915–1980)*, Lean Street

I got my mother a phone, and she only ever spoke on the phone in a Yorkshire accent. Because a Scottish accent was plain. A Yorkshire accent – what's going on here?

> *Janice Galloway (1955–), interviewed in* The List.

A fouth o' flours may yet be fund
Wi' pains, on Caledonian grund.
Dig for their roots, or they be dead,
Fra Gretna Green to Peterhead;
And plant them quick, as soon as got,
In ae lexicographic pot;
I trou they'll soon baith live and thrive
And gie you flours eneuch belyve.

> *Alexander Geddes (1737–1802),* Transactions of the Society of
> Antiquaries *(1792)*

Chris would say they needn't fash, if she said it in Scots the woman
would think, Isn't that a common-like bitch at the Manse? If she
said it in English the speak would spread round the minister's wife
was putting on airs.

> *Lewis Grassic Gibbon (James Leslie Mitchell, 1901–1935),* Cloud Howe

What is the language
Using us for?
For the prevailing weather or words
Each object hides in a metaphor.

> *W.S. Graham (1918–1986),* What Is the Language Using Us For?

The fishermen have always had taboos on certain words while at
sea . . . The forbidden words in the north were priest or minister,
salmon, pig, hare, rats and rabbits (exactly like the east coast).
Rabbits were alluded to as 'little feeties'.

> *I.F. Grant,* Highland Folk Ways *(1961)*

You can hear from my voice I don't sound particularly Scottish, so
despite the fact that, as far as I know, that's what I am, I'm quite
used to being asked how long I'm here for.

> *David Greig (1969–),* BBC 'Belief' interview

A 'Gadgie' when he is a 'Chor',
A 'Jugal' always fears,
For 'Jugals' as a rule are kept
By 'Gadgies' with big 'keirs';
This means a man who goes to steal
A watchdog may expect;
'Tis mystifying all the same,
This Berwick dialect.

> *Thomas Grey, Tweedmouth, in* The Berwick Advertiser *(1910), quoted
> in J. Grant, Introduction to* The Scottish National Dictionary *(1934)*

Words are well adapted for description and arousing of emotions, but for many kinds of precise thought, other symbols are much better.

> *J.B.S. Haldane (1892–1964)*

The gude auld honest mither tongue!
They kent nae ither, auld or young;
The cottar spak' it in his yaird,
An' on his rigs the gawcie laird.

> *Hugh Haliburton (J. Logie Robertson, 1864–1922)*, On the Decadence of the Scots Language, Manners and Customs

the tung has the poo'er . . . whit other tung could pit glory and grimness gleich afore us?

> *Christopher Harvie (1944–)*, speech on the 75th anniversary of the Saltire Society, 16 June 2011

Would you repeat that again, sir, for it sounds sae sonorous that the words droon the ideas?

> *James Hogg (1770–1835), quoted in Christopher North (John Wilson, 1785–1854), 'Noctes Ambrosianae'*

Since word is thrall, and thought is free,
Keep well thy tongue, I counsel thee.

> *King James VI (1566–1625)*, Ballad of Good Counsel

It is harder to take words back than it is to get a refund.

> *Jackie Kay (1961–)*, Why Don't You Stop Talking?

what's your favourite word dearie
is it wee
I hope it's wee
wee's such a nice wee word

> *Tom Leonard (1944–)*, The Voyeur

awright fur
funny stuff
ur
Stanley Bax–
ter ur but
luv n science
n thaht naw

> *Tom Leonard*, Unrelated Incidents

'Learn English!' he exclaimed, 'no, never; it was my trying to learn that language that spoilt my Scots; and as to being silent, I will promise to hold my tongue if you will make fools hold theirs.'

> *Dr John Leyden (1775–1811), quoted in John Reith,* The Life of Dr John Leyden *(1909), when asked, on his arival in Bombay, not to discuss literature and to speak 'English'*

Douglas Young, anxious to demonstrate the living quality of Scots, held up his empty beer glass and called to the barman, 'Some mair.' To everyone's astonishment, the barman presently came across carrying a long pole and pulled open an upper window.

> *Maurice Lindsay (1918–2009),* Thank You for Having Me

It's soon', no' sense, that faddoms the herts o' men,
And by my sangs the rouch auld Scots I ken
E'en herts that hae nae Scots'll dirl richt thro'
As nocht else could – for here's a language rings
Wi' datchie sesames, and names for nameless things.

> *Hugh MacDiarmid (C.M. Grieve, 1892–1978),* Gairmscoile

'Tis the speech used in the Garden–
Adam left it to mankind.

> *Duncan Bàn MacIntyre (1724–1812),* Rann Do 'N Ghaidhlig 'S Do 'N Phiob-Mhoir *(Ode to Gaelic and the Great Pipe)*

The Scotch is as spangled with vowels as a meadow with daisies in the month of May.

> *Charles Mackay (1814–1889),* The Poetry and Humour of the Scottish Language

To me it appears undeniable that the Scotish Idiom of the British Tongue is more fit for Pleading than either the English Idiom or the French Tongue; for certainly a Pleader must use a brisk, smart and quick way of speaking . . . Our Pronunciation is like ourselves, fiery, abrupt, sprightly and bold.

> *Sir George Mackenzie (1636–1691),* What Eloquence is Fit for the Bar

Lord Kelly, a determined punster, and his brother Andrew were
drinking tea with James Boswell. Boswell put his cup to his head,
'Here's t'ye, my Lord.' – At that moment, Lord Kelly coughed.
– 'You have a coughie,' said his brother. – 'Yes,' said Lord Kelly, 'I
have been like to choak o' late.'

> *Henry Mackenzie (1745–1831), recorded in H.W. Thomson,* The
> Anecdotes and Egotisms of Henry Mackenzie

It is natural for a poet to love his own language if it is the language
of his ancestors and dying, even if it were a poor defective thing.
Gaelic is not a poor language, in art at any rate.

> *Sorley Maclean (1911–1996)*

You could drive a train across the Firth of Forth on her vowels.

> *Bruce Marshall (1899–1987),* Teacup Terrace

The accent of the lowest state of Glaswegians is the ugliest one can
encounter, it is associated with the unwashed and the violent.

> *Anonymous university lecturer, quoted in Janet Menzies,* Investigation
> of Attitudes to Scots and Glaswegian Dialect Among Secondary
> School Pupils *(1975)*

Language is mobile and liable to change. It is a free country, and
man may call a 'vase' a 'vawse', a 'vahse', a 'vaze', or a 'vase', as he
pleases. And why should he not? We do not all think alike, walk
alike, dress alike, write alike, or dine alike; why should not we use
our liberty in speech also, so long as the purpose of speech, to be
intelligible, and its grace, are not interfered with?

> *Sir James Murray (1837–1915), founder of the* Oxford English
> Dictionary

Greitand doun in Gallowa
mar bu dual don gallow breid (the habit of yon gallows breed)
a' dranndail is ag cainntearachd (muttering and deedling, piper-like)
le my trechour tung, gun teagamh (with my traitor tongue,
doubtless) that hes tane ane hyland strynd. (that has taken a
Highland twist)

> *William Neill (1922–2010),* De A Thug Ort Sgriobhadh Ghaidhlig?
> *(What Made You Write in Gaelic?)*

I speak just the fine English now,
My own ways left behind;
The good schoolmaster taught me how;
they purified my mind
from the errors of any kind.

> *William Neill*, Dh' fhalbh sin is tha 'inig seo *(That's Gone and This Has Come)*

Anywhere in the world where there's dying language, the neighbours say the people are lazy and prone to drink.

> *Sir Iain Noble (1935–), quoted in Kenneth Roy*, Conversations in a Small Country *(1989)*

. . . none can more sincerely wish a total extinction of the Scotish colloquial dialect than I do, for there are few modern Scoticisms which are not barbarisms

> *John Pinkerton (1758–1826)*, Preface to Ancient Scotish Poems *(1786)*

A conscientious Chinaman who contemplated a thesis on the literary history of Scotland would have no doubt as to his procedure: 'I will learn a little Gaelic, and read all I can find about Gaelic literature . . .' He would be rather mystified when he found that historians of Scotland and its literature had known and cared as much about Gaelic as about Chinese.

> *William Power (1873–1953)*, Literature and Oatmeal

. . . the story was told of . . . Henry Dundas, applying to Mr Pitt for the loan of a horse 'the length of Highgate' – a very common expression in Scotland, at that time, to signify the distance to which the ride was to extend. Mr Pitt good-humouredly wrote back to say that he was afraid he had not a horse in his possession quite so long as Mr Dundas had mentioned, but he had sent the longest he had.

> *Dean E.B. Ramsay (1793–1872)*, Reminiscences of Scottish Life and Character

There is no greater impediment to the advancement of knowledge than the ambiguity of words.

> *Thomas Reid (1710–1796)*, Essays on the Intellectual Powers of Man

We've words afouth, that we can ca' our ain,
Tho' frae them now my childer sair refrain.

> *Alexander Ross (1699–1784)*, Helenore

Ae day laest ouk, whin I was gaen t' da sola, I met wir skülmaister.
I gees him da time o da day, an' speaks back an' fore, dan he says
to me, 'Fat's yer wee bit loonie deein', that he's nae been at skool
syne Monday week?' Noo sir, haed I been askin' dis question I wid
hae said, 'What's your peerie boy düin' 'at he's no been at skül frae
last Moninday?' . . . we pay dem fur laernin' bairns English, no fur
unlearnin' wir Shetlan' speech.'
  Shetland Times, *'Recollections of the Past' (November 1880)*

He who loses his language loses his world.
  Iain Crichton Smith (1928–1998), Shall Gaelic Die?

Transposing Greek to Gaelic is no toil.
They had their clans, their sea terms. And the style
Of the great Odyssey is what Gaelic knows.
  Iain Crichton Smith, Oban, 1955–82

. . . wi' sic clash
Gang up the slogans an' gab-gash
O' what-for-noes, fornents, forbyes,
Tae-hell-wi'-yous an' here-am-Is
That only glegest lugs are able
Frae oot the blethers oo' oor Babel
Tae wale a modicum o' wit.
  William Soutar (1898–1943), Vision

Man is a creature who lives not by bread alone, but principally by
catchwords.
  Robert Louis Stevenson (1850–1894)

'Lallans' – a synthesised Burnsian esperanto; 'Plastic Scots' its
enemies called it.
  John Sutherland, The Times Literary Supplement *(August 1998)*

Many people think that Scots possesses a rich vocabulary, but this is
a view not wholly borne out by a close examination . . . It is as if the
Doric had been invented by a cabal of scandal-mongering beldams,
aided by a council of observant gamekeepers.
  George Malcolm Thomson (1899–1996), The Rediscovery of Scotland

I am fascinated and frightened by the power and danger of words,
which are so often grave obstacles to full honesty of thought.
  Sir Robert Watson-Watt (1892–1973), Three Steps to Victory

Work and Leisure

O can ye sew cushions?
Or can ye sew sheets?
An' can ye sing ba-la-loo
When the bairnie greets?
> *Anonymous*

If it wasna for the weavers, whit wad we do?
We wadna hae claes made o' oor woo',
We wadna hae a cloot, neither black nor blue,
If it wasna for the wark o' the weavers.
> *Traditional*, The Wark o' the Weavers

O' a' the trades that I do ken,
The beggin' is the best,
For when a beggar's weary,
He can aye sit doon an' rest.
> *Traditional*, Tae the Beggin' I Will Go

Nothing is really work unless you would rather be doing something else.
> *Sir J.M. Barrie (1860–1937)*

Oh dear me, the mill's gaen fest,
The puir wee shifters canna get a rest:
Shiftin' bobbins, coorse and fine,
They fairly mak' ye work for your ten and nine.
> *Mary Brooksbank (1897–1980)*, The Jute Mill Song

I never was cannie for hoarding o' money,
Or claughtin' together at a', man;
I've little to spend, and naething to lend,
But deevil a shilling I awe, man.
> *Robert Burns (1759–1796)*, The Ronalds of the Bennals

It is the first of all problems for a man to find out what kind of work
he is to do in this Universe.

> *Thomas Carlyle (1795–1881), Rectorial Address, Edinburgh University,*
> *2nd April 1866*

Work is a grand cure for all the maladies and miseries that ever
beset mankind – honest work, which you intend getting done.

> *Thomas Carlyle, Rectorial Address, Edinburgh University*

A man willing to work, and unable to find work, is perhaps the
saddest sight that fortune's inequality exhibits under this sun.

> *Thomas Carlyle*, Chartism

What worship, for example, is there not in mere washing!

> *Thomas Carlyle*, Past and Present

Rest is for the dead.

> *Thomas Carlyle, quoted by J. A. Froude*, Life of Carlyle: The First
> Forty Years

It's just the power of some to be a boss,
And the bally power of others to be bossed.

> *John Davidson (1857–1909)*, Thirty Bob a Week

Work and play! Work and play!
The order of the universe.

> *John Davidson*, Piper, Play

. . . with thy neichbours gladly lend and borrow;
His chance tonight, it may be thine tomorrow.

> *William Dunbar (c.1460–c.1520)*, No Treasure without Gladness

I'm far owre weill to wark the day.

> *Robert Garioch (Robert Garioch Sutherland, 1908–1981)*, Owre Weill

Custom, then, is the great guide of human life.

> *David Hume (1711–1776)*, Essay on Human Understanding

Oh, it's nice to get up in the mornin'
And nicer to stay in bed.

> *Sir Harry Lauder (1870–1950)*

You would not think any duty small
If you yourself were great.
    George Macdonald (1824–1905), Willie's Question

Work, eh. What a stupid way to earn a living.
    Ian Pattison (1950–), 'At the Job Centre', from Rab C. Nesbitt: The
Scripts *(1990)*

'No-one has ever said it,' observed Lady Caroline, 'but how
painfully true it is that the poor have us always with them!'
    Saki (H.H. Munro, 1870–1916)

I consider the capacity to labour as part of the happiness I have
enjoyed.
    Sir Walter Scott (1771–1832) quoted in Lockhart's Life of Scott

I was not long, however, in making the grand discovery, that
in order to enjoy leisure, it is absolutely necessary it should be
preceded by occupation.
    Sir Walter Scott, Introductory Epistle to The Monastery

'If your honour disna ken when ye hae a gude servant, I ken when I
hae a gude master.'
    Sir Walter Scott, Rob Roy

Practical wisdom is only to be learned in the school of experience.
    Samuel Smiles (1812–1904), Self-Help

It will generally be found that men who are constantly lamenting
their ill-luck are only reaping the consequences of their own
neglect, mismanagement, and improvidence; or lack of application.
    Samuel Smiles, Self-Help

Our business in this world is not to succeed, but to continue to fail,
in good spirits.
    Robert Louis Stevenson (1850–1894)

There is no duty we so much under-rate as the duty of being happy.
    Robert Louis Stevenson, An Apology for Idlers

Extreme busyness, whether at school or college, kirk or market, is
a symptom of deficient vitality; and a faculty for idleness implies a
catholic appetite and a strong sense of personal identity.
    Robert Louis Stevenson, An Apology for Idlers

It is not by any means certain that a man's business is the most important thing he has to do.

Robert Louis Stevenson

'Ye'll need tae gie us a bung though Gav. Ah'm fuckin brassic until this rent cheque hits the mat the morn.'

Irvine Welsh (1957–), Trainspotting

Writers and Readers

Walter Scott has no business to write novels, especially good ones.
– It is not fair – He has fame and fortune enough as a poet, and
should not be taking the bread out of other people's mouths.
Jane Austen (1775–1817), letter to Anna Austen, 1814

There is no mood to which a man may not administer the
appropriate medicine at the cost of reaching down a volume from
his bookshelf.
A.J. Balfour (1848–1930), Essays and Addresses

Biography should be written by an acute enemy.
A.J. Balfour, quoted in The Observer, *1927*

The worst books make the best films.
Iain Banks (1954–)

Still am I besy bokes assemblynge
For to have plenty it is a pleasant thynge
In my conceyt and to have them ay in honde
But what they mene do I nat understonde
Alexander Barclay (c.1475–1552), The Shyp of Folys of the Worlde

The life of every man is a diary in which he means to write one
story, and writes another, and his humblest hour is when he
compares the volume as it is with what he vowed to make it.
Sir J.M. Barrie (1860–1937), The Golden Book

It is all very well to be able to write books, but can you waggle your
ears?
Sir J.M. Barrie, letter to H.G. Wells

I remember being asked by two maiden ladies about the time I left
the university, what I was to be, and when I replied brazenly, 'An
Author,' they flung up their hands, and one exclaimed reproachfully,
'And you an MA!'
Sir J.M. Barrie, Margaret Ogilvy

For several days after my first book was published, I carried it about
in my pocket, and took surreptitious peeps at it to make sure that
the ink had not faded.

  Sir J.M. Barrie, speech to the Critics' Circle, 1920

... copulation is a sweet and necessary act ... it is like defecation,
an exceedingly interesting process; but it is much better described
in physiological textbooks than in all the works of all the novelists
ancient and modern who have ever existed.

  *James Bridie (Osborne Henry Mavor, 1888–1951), letter to Neil Gunn,
  January 1932*

Critics! appall'd I venture on the name,
Those cut-throat bandits on the path of fame.

  Robert Burns (1759–1796), On Critics

Through and through th'inspired leaves,
Ye maggots, make your windings;
But O, respect his lordship's taste,
And spare the golden bindings!

  Robert Burns, The Book Worms

Quelle vie! Let no woman who values peace of soul ever dream of
marrying an author!

  Jane Welsh Carlyle (1801–1866), letter to John Sterling, 1837

If a book come from the heart, it will contrive to reach other hearts;
all art and authorcraft are of small amount to that.

  Thomas Carlyle (1795–1881), On Heroes, Hero-Worship, and the
  Heroic in History

In the true Literary Man there is thus ever, acknowledged of not
by the world, a sacredness: he is the light of the world; the world's
Priest, – guiding it, like a sacred Pillar of Fire, in its dark pilgrimage
through the waste of Time.

  Thomas Carlyle, On Heroes, Hero-Worship, and the Heroic in
  History

No good Book, or good thing of any sort, shows its best face at first.

  Thomas Carlyle, Novalis

... a well-written life is almost as rare as a well-spent one
  Thomas Carlyle, Essays, *on Jean Paul Richter*

A man should keep his little brain attic stocked with all the
furniture that he is likely to use, and the rest he can put away in the
lumber room of his library, where he can get it if he wants it.
  Sir Arthur Conan Doyle (1859–1930), The Adventures of Sherlock
  Holmes

I cannot endure that man's writing – his vulgarity beats print.
  *Susan Ferrier (1782–1854), quoted by James Irvine in his Introduction
  to* The Inheritance *(1984), on John Galt*

Nobody told me Shakespeare would be a thrill.
  Janice Galloway (1955–), All Made Up

the pleasure of creating something where nothing had been.
  Janice Galloway, All Made Up

The only apology which this work perhaps requires is with regard
to the title, for otherwise it belongs to a class of publications, of
which the value is so obvious as to admit of no question.
  John Galt (1779–1839), The Bachelor's Wife

He also was a poet and painter – the author of Poems of a Painter
– which Carlyle, misreading, took to be Poems of a Printer and
severely criticised, recommending to the supposed printer the habit
of doing instead of saying.
  William Gaunt, The Pre-Raphaelite Tragedy *(1942), on William Bell
  Scott (1811–1890)*

For Mora
At long last, a book by her brother which will not make her blush.
  Alasdair Gray (1934–), Dedication of The Fall of Kelvin Walker

I can't write a play unless I have a question I can't answer.
  David Greig (1969–), BBC 'Belief' interview

we're very lucky – we don't have Shakespeare – you know we don't
have ... anybody hanging over us, who we have to do.
  David Greig, BBC 'Belief' interview

I mend the fire, and beikit me about,
Then took ane drink my spreitis to comfort,
And armit me weill fra the cauld thereout;
To cut the winter nicht and mak it short,
I look ane quair, and left all other sport
    Robert Henryson (c.1425–c.1500), The Testament of Cresseid

Never literary attempt was more unfortunate than my Treatise of
Human Nature. It fell dead-born from the press.
    David Hume (1711–1776), My Own Life

She read the manuscript of her first novel, Marriage, to her father,
behind the cover of a screen that he could not see what she was
reading. He told her 'It was the best book you have ever brought
me.' He considered her assertion that it was written by a woman as
'nonsense', and then she confessed that it was her own work.
    James Irvine, Introduction to The Inheritance *by Susan Ferrier*
    (1782–1854)

Often the least important parts of a book are the ones you
remember, which means that its meaning often lies in the bits you
forget.
    Robin Jenkins (1912–1992), quoted by Brian Morton in Scottish
    Review of Books, *vol 1, no. 3, 2005*

I told him that William Sharp had confided to a friend of mine that
whenever he was preparing to write as Fiona Macleod he dressed
himself entirely in woman's clothes. 'Did he?' said W. P. – 'the
bitch!'
    Recorded of W.P. Ker (1855–1923) in E.V. Lucas, Reading, Writing
    and Remembering *(1932)*

With a yell of triumph he finishes the great work;
He slumps back in his seat, exhausted but happy;
Idly, he fingers through it, and reads the very first lines;
Little by little the smile disappears from his face.
    Frank Kuppner (1951–), A Bad Day for the Sung Dynasty

Few books today are forgivable.
    R.D. Laing (1927–1989), The Politics of Experience

Authors and uncaptured criminals are the only people free from
routine.
    Eric Linklater (1899–1974), Poet's Pub

Our principal writers have nearly all been fortunate in escaping regular education.
> *Hugh MacDiarmid (C.M. Grieve, 1892–1978) quoted in* The Observer

It seems fatal to write a Scottish novel of promise!
> *Hugh Macdiarmid,* The Raucle Tongue, *vol 2*

I do think the whole climate for writers these days is so vulgar. It's all so money-led. I hate going into book shops and seeing, you know, the Top Ten Bestsellers, a sort of self-fulfilling prophecy. I just find the whole thing so vulgar.
> *Shena Mackay (1944–), quoted in* The Guardian, *10 September 1999*

The Kailyard School mortgaged Scottish literature to indignity.
> *Compton Mackenzie (1883–1972),* Literature in My Time

With the birth of each child you lose two novels.
> *Candia MacWilliam (1957–), quoted in* The Guardian, *1993*

Men of sorrow, and acquainted with Grieve
> *Edwin Muir (1887–1959), quoted in Karl Miller,* Memoirs of a Modern Scotland *(1970), on Scottish writers of the 1930s*

I knew the game was up for me the day
I stood before my father's corpse and thought
If I can't get a poem out of this . . .
> *Don Paterson (1963–)*

Writers can redeeem a wasted day in two minutes; alas this knowledge leads them to waste their day like no-one else.
> *Don Paterson*

And better had they ne'er been born,
Who read to doubt, or read to scorn.
> *Sir Walter Scott (1771–1832),* The Monastery

I have seen his pen gang as fast ower the paper, as ever it did ower the water when it was in the grey goose's wing.
> *Sir Walter Scott,* The Heart of Midlothian

To live the life of a mere author for bread is perhaps the most dreadful fate that can be encountered.
> *Sir Walter Scott, Letter to James Bailey, 1817*

Please return this book: I find that though many of my friends are poor arithmeticians, they are nearly all good book-keepers.
Bookmark alleged to belong to Sir Walter Scott

The great and good do not die even in this world. Embalmed in books, their spirits walk abroad.
Samuel Smiles (1812–1904), Character

Style, after all, rather than thought, is the immortal thing in literature.
Alexander Smith (1830–1867), Dreamthorp

The skin of a man of letters is peculiarly sensitive to the bite of the critical mosquito, and he lives in a climate in which such mosquitoes swarm. He is seldom stabbed to the heart – he is often killed by pinpricks.
Alexander Smith, Dreamthorp

Every person of importance ought to write his own memoirs, provided he has honesty enough to tell the truth.
Tobias Smollett (1721–1771)

Books are good enough in their own way, but they are a mighty bloodless substitute for life . . . There are not many works extant, if you look the alternative all over, which are worth the price of a pound of tobacco to a man of limited means.
Robert Louis Stevenson (1850–1894), Virginibus Puerisque

There is no quite good book without a good morality; but the world is wide, and so are morals.
Robert Louis Stevenson, A Gossip on a Novel of Dumas's

Fiction is to the grown man what play is to the child; it is there that he changes the atmosphere and tenor of his life.
Robert Louis Stevenson, A Gossip on Romance

There is but one art – to omit! O if I knew how to omit, I would ask no other knowledge.
Robert Louis Stevenson, Letter to R.A.M. Stevenson (1883)

Nothing, in truth, has such a tendency to weaken not only the powers of invention, but the intellectual powers in general, as a habit of extensive and various reading without reflection. The activity and force of mind are gradually impaired in consequence of disuse; and, not infrequently, all our principles and opinions come to be lost in the infinite multiplicity and discordancy of our acquired ideas.

Dugald Stewart (1753–1828)

The Scots are incapable of considering their literary geniuses purely as writers or artists. They must be either an excuse for a glass or a text for the next sermon.

George Malcolm Thomson, (1899–1996), Caledonia

Give a man a pipe he can smoke,
Give a man a book he can read:
And his home is bright with a calm delight,
Though the room be poor indeed.

James Thomson (1834–1882), Sunday Up the River

Write and write
And read these stupid, worn-out books!
That's all he does, read, write and read.

James Thomson, In the Room

I enjoy the freedom of the blank page.

Irvine Welsh (1957–)

Youth and Age

Welcome eild, for youth is gone.
Anonymous, Welcome Eild

I'm not young enough to know everything.
Sir J.M. Barrie (1860–1937), The Admirable Crichton

An' O for ane an' twenty, Tam!
And hey, sweet ane an' twenty, Tam!
I'll learn my kin a rattlin sang,
An' I saw ane an' twenty, Tam
Robert Burns (1759–1796), O For Ane An' Twenty, Tam

The canty auld folk crackin' crouse,
The young ones rantin' through the house
Robert Burns, The Twa Dogs

The dreams of age are deeper than the dreams of youth, because the
dreams of youth are sharp and thin like new wine, and the dreams
of age are rich and fragrant, and tinged with tragic knowledge.
H. J. Cameron (1873–1932), Under the Diamond

Heaven gives our years of fading strength
Indemnifying fleetness;
And those of Youth, a seeming length,
Proportioned to their sweetness.
Thomas Campbell (1777–1844), A Thought Suggested by the New
Year

The auld wife sat ayont her man,
But nae auld carle saw she;
And, gin he keekit owre at her,
An auld wife saw na he.
Wi tousy head a cottar lad
Sat in the auld man's place,
And glowered, tongue-tackit, at the stars
That lauched in Jeanie's face.
A.M. Davidson (1897–1979), Auld Fowk

I wes in yowth on nureis knee
Dandely, Bischop, dandely;
And quhen that ege now dois me greif,
Ane simple vicar I can nocht be.
> *William Dunbar (c.1460–c.1520)*, To the King

Worldly prudence is very suitable at seventy, but at seventeen it is
absolutely disgusting.
> *Susan Ferrier (1782–1854), Letter to Walter Ferrier, in J. A. Doyle,*
> Memoir and Correspondence of Susan Ferrier *(1898)*

Eild comes owre me like a yoke on my craig
> *George Campbell Hay (1915–1984)*, The Auld Hunter, *translated from*
> *Gaelic by Hugh MacDiarmid*

The moir of ege the nerrer hevynis bliss.
> *Robert Henryson (c.1425–1500)*, The Praise of Age

It's frightening to get old anyway, but if your looks were the
cornerstone of your life, well, it would be very difficult.
> *Lulu (Lulu Kennedy-Cairns, 1948–)*

If you think you're old, you'll feel old.
> *Lulu*

Our hearts are young 'neath wrinkled rind:
Life's more amusing than we thought.
> *Andrew Lang (1844–1912)*, Ballade of Middle Age

Youth having passed, there is nothing to lose but memory.
> *George Macdonald (1824–1905)*, Fifty Years of Freethought

Age is not all decay; it is the ripening, the swelling, of the fresh life
within, that withers and bursts the husk.
> *George Macdonald*, The Marquis of Lossie

Young people grow up today in a society of deep-set gloom and
despondency. They live in a glitz, glam and celeb culture where
superficiality and owning more things seems the order of the day,
unsustainable materialism, and where greed, lack of responsibility
and respect are constant reminders of a hopeless decline in our
values and vision.
> *Henry McLeish (1948–)*, Holyrood *magazine, October 2011*

After a certain age all of us, good and bad, are guilt-stricken because of powers within us which have never been realised; because, in other words, we are not what we should be.

Edwin Muir (1887–1959), Autobiography

My heart's still light, albeit my locks be grey.

Allan Ramsay (1686–1758), The Gentle Shepherd

My Peggy is a young thing,
And I'm nae very auld

Allan Ramsay, The Waukin' o' the Fauld

Be sure ye dinna quit the grip
Of ilka joy, when ye are young,
Before auld age your vitals nip,
And lay ye twa-fold o'er a rung.

Allan Ramsay, Miscellany

On his bold visage middle age
Had slightly press'd its signet sage,
Yet had not quench'd the open truth
And fiery vehemence of youth.

Sir Walter Scott (1771–1832), The Lady of the Lake

All sorts of allowances are made for the illusions of youth; and none, or almost none, for the disenchantments of age.

Robert Louis Stevenson (1850–1894), Virginibus Puerisque

Old and young, we are all on our last cruise.

Robert Louis Stevenson, Virginibus Puerisque

After a certain distance, every step we take in life we find the ice growing thinner below our feet, and all around us and behind us we see our contemporaries going through.

Robert Louis Stevenson, Virginibus Puerisque

For God's sake give me the young man who has brains enough to make a fool of himself.

Robert Louis Stevenson, Virginibus Puerisque

Index of Persons Quoted

Index of Subjects and Names